Driven by concern, Campbell stepped outside to a sky opening to a torrential rain. A barrage of icy droplets pricked her face and clear vision was impossible, but she knew the approaching car was a compact, and that it was traveling fast. And it was almost upon her.

Her memory was working better than her vision, and she reached a hand out into the driveway. Yet no sooner did she step out onto the walkway than she realized the driver didn't intend to slow down. Worse yet, she heard the car accelerate.

It was going too fast to miss her and far too fast to make the necessary ninety-degree left turn out onto the drive.

Campbell flung herself backward. Although she struck hard against the booth's rough stone exterior, she kept her eyes open and focused her attention to try to catch a closer look at the maniac speeding by.

The car was a Grand Am. The driver was—

"Maida?" Campbell gasped. "Maida, stop!"

Ignoring the pain in her back, Campbell launched herself after the car. Brakes squealed and the rear end swung wildly through that first impossible turn. She got close enough to slam her hand on the trunk, but either Maida Livingstone didn't hear her, or the sound had the opposite effect and frightened her.

After several stumbling strides, Campbell gave up and stared in horror as the car accelerated again. The elderly widow was racing toward the next hairpin turn.

HELEN R. MYERS

WHILE OTHERS SLEEP

MIRA

ISBN 0-7783-2041-3

WHILE OTHERS SLEEP

Visit us at www.mirabooks.com

Printed in U.S.A.

ACKNOWLEDGMENTS

A special salute to Texas Bluegrass singer Terri Hendrix, who inspired many of the characters in this book with her song about *night wolves*, those individuals who either suffer from insomnia, work, or otherwise maneuver through life while others sleep. Also thanks to the Longview Police Department and Longview Board of Education for their strong public access commitment.

To the Hide-Away-Lake Book Club and residents who asked that I feature a character who has experienced my own too-close encounters with lightning—I hope this adds insight. Your lovely development was, indeed, the inspiration for Maple Trails, even though I had to relocate it. But I will always cherish your graciousness and hospitality.

Finally, ongoing appreciation to my editor Valerie Gray and always to my agent Ethan Ellenberg. Couldn't have done this without your wisdom, support and humor.

Violence can only be concealed by a lie,
and the lie can only be maintained by violence.
—Alexander Solzhenitsyn
Nobel Prize lecture, 1973

1

Maple Trails, a gated retirement community
Longview, Texas
11:30 p.m.

A lightning-fractured sky, followed by the quick crack of thunder, gave clear warning that the approaching storms weren't only accelerating across Texas, but intensifying. Precipitation would be welcome in this section of the piney woods where residents continued to miss out on replenishing rains due to another El Niño in the Pacific. To the most grateful, the storm would serve as a lullaby.

To Campbell Cody, it felt like a combination of mockery and curse. Standing with her hands on her hips as the overly warm February wind tugged at her hair and khaki uniform, she had to wonder—would tonight be the night she got deep-fried? Like the answer of answers, the next bolt shot into the earth with the precise and deadly trajectory of a smart bomb achieving a direct hit on her nerves, elevating her tension to a level she had experienced all too often in the last fourteen months. She turned her back on the

intimidating scene, but the damage was done. Dark
memories, rife with immutable images flashed before
her—scenes from another night filled with fury: a domestic disturbance turned Code 30, followed by a tor-
ment-filled wait in Emergency and, days later, a funeral. She could almost hear the condemning voices
of the bitter and the bereaved within the gusting wind.

Another crack of thunder snapped her back to the
present. It came as fast as it took Internal Affairs to
convince her that her career with the Longview Police
Department was over.

Uneasy as she was with what was about to befall
the area, Campbell had anticipated trouble hours ago.
Company policy required all staff to review the latest
weather report and the local news, and to make notes
on significant alerts coming over the police radio
scanner before reporting to their posts. These proce-
dures were twice as strict for the daughter of Yancy
Cody, owner of Cody Security, Inc. The company
might only be a regional name in the expanding and
increasingly complicated world of corporate and private protection, but they were a growing one thanks
to a solid reputation—another reason why she could
not succumb to old vulnerabilities tonight. But neither
could she rid herself of concern over what could become a worst-case scenario.

Two air masses were colliding over the Lone Star
State tonight, resulting in a system that was powerful
enough to evolve into one of those freak, heart-of-
winter storms that sent eighteen-wheelers flipping,
splintered houses, and ripped apart lives. It was no

time for man or beast to be outdoors, and while, technically, she could avoid that, the stone-and-glass gatehouse marking the entrance to the private and exclusive retirement community of Maple Trails could be just as dangerous. Come what may, it was Campbell's post until her twelve-hour shift ended at six the next morning, and there was no use wishing she could have avoided working tonight.

Her father had always been as selective in scheduling staff as he was in hiring new employees, and that practice was all the more evident at this exclusive community just outside the eastern perimeter of Longview's city limits. Maple Trails had been the firm's first sizable client, and personnel were not arbitrarily switched from one location to another. In addition, no one worked at a Cody-protected site who didn't know it as well as their own home. Unfortunately, that could catch them in a bind. Morton "Munch" Robbins, who should have had Campbell's shift tonight, had split open his thigh earlier in the day while testing his newly repaired chain saw, and Doug Sutton, their backup, had developed pneumonia. She would not be relieved until tomorrow, even though this was her fourth twelve-hour shift without a break. Company guidelines prohibited staff working without adequate rest, but Campbell refused to complain. Her father had just come through his own health scare and needed support, not whining.

"Another week, ten days tops, and we'll be back to normal," Yancy had assured her six hours ago as she'd prepared for work. "The background checks on the new applicants are coming in as clean as I expected, and we should be ready to start training by Friday.''

She wasn't the only staff member who hoped he was right. These were challenging times for security firms, and investigating the people who were issued badges, carried guns and had access to private homes and the most privileged areas in corporations needed to be screened with increased care.

The next sky-to-ground flash had Campbell ducking deeper into her fluorescent-yellow rain gear, but there was no escaping the high-pitched crack that left the earth shuddering. Pushed by the wind, she stumbled to the gatehouse and reached for the hand radio.

"Gate to Patrol One, over." She released the speaker key.

"Patrol One" came the static-filled reply. "Seen any flying cattle yet? Over."

Campbell appreciated Ike Crenshaw's attempt at humor. The widower and grandfather of five was often her partner on these shifts, and since the movie *Twister,* he'd been referring to that cow scene whenever this region came under a storm alert.

"Not yet, and the likelihood of having a shot of tequila anytime soon is nil, so I guess spotting Day-Glo pink pigs with wings is out, too. Listen, Ike, you'd better go ahead and pull into the recreation center to get some solid shelter. The lightning has become downright ugly. Over."

"You're the one out on the ledge. Over."

Built on a slight bluff, the entrance to the Trails,

as it was sometimes called, did seem precarious, especially as the driveway cut a serpentine path through the terraced ground, which, after four hairpin turns, spilled onto Highway 259. Highway 259—or 59 as it was known farther south—was frequently used as a reliable alternate route for drug traffickers using Houston as a hub.

The gatehouse was built of the same stone as the semicircular walls that flanked it. On each side, the walls bore the distinct three-foot-high brass nameplates of the beautifully designed community.

When weather conditions grew treacherous, those on duty were instructed to dive into the deepest corner of the booth, tuck under the built-in desks and cover up with a blanket from the first aid closet for protection from breaking glass and other flying debris. However, Campbell was one of the few people in Tornado Alley who didn't live in fear of them. She had her own particular dread.

"I'm about to retreat into my hole," she told him. "But I'll sit this out better if I know you aren't parked under some ancient old tree or playing Good Samaritan by chasing hyper pets at the risk of your own safety. Over."

"No way I can do that—not with the arthritis this storm is aggravating. You know where to find me, then. I'll holler as soon as the worst is past." The radio cracked as another flash streaked across the sky. "Now, get off this thing. Over'n out."

Reassured about her partner, Campbell headed for the first aid closet to get a blanket, but paused again at the sound of an engine. It was coming from inside the development. They didn't monitor exiting traffic—guests could leave at will. Should it be a resident with a medical emergency, they were to call here for assistance. But with so many senior citizens in residence there were always extenuating circumstances.

Driven by concern, Campbell stepped outside to a sky opening to a torrential rain. A barrage of icy droplets pricked her face, and clear vision was impossible, but she knew the approaching car was a compact and that it was traveling fast. It was almost upon her.

Her memory was working better than her vision, and she reached a hand out into the driveway. She knew of several elderly residents who drove this type of vehicle and it concerned her to think of one in particular venturing out in these conditions. Yet, no sooner did she step down onto the asphalt than she realized the driver didn't intend to slow down; worse yet, she heard the car accelerate.

It was going too fast to miss her. Far too fast to make the necessary ninety-degree left turn onto the road.

Campbell flung herself backward. Although she struck hard against the booth's rough stone exterior, she kept her eyes open and focused her attention to try to catch a closer look at the maniac speeding by.

The car was a Grand Am. The driver was—

"Maida?" Campbell gasped. "Maida, stop!"

Ignoring the pain in her back, Campbell launched herself after the car. Brakes squealed and the rear end swung wildly through that first impossible turn. She got close enough to slam her hand on the trunk, but either Maida Livingstone didn't hear that or the sound had the opposite effect and frightened her.

After several stumbling strides, she gave up and stared in horror as the car accelerated again. The elderly widow was racing toward the next hairpin turn.

"No!" she yelled. Convinced her friend had gone mad, she ran after her, frantically waving her arms. "Mai—"

A deafening crack and a flash of blue-white light to her left locked the cry in her throat. Simultaneously, some instinct ordered, "Drop!" But with a demon's speed, lightening shot through a pine.

Determined and merciless, the skeletal finger gripped her hand. Robbed of her remaining strength and control, of her very breath, Campbell collapsed onto the flooding road.

The devilish light vanished, leaving punishing rain...and the depressing image of the Grand Am reaching the main highway.

2

While driving north on Highway 259, lightning struck close, close enough for Jackson Blade to turn his head away. If he hadn't, he might have missed the white car parked to his right at the back of the darkened restaurant.

Even though the deadly bolt went to ground as close as a block away, he instantly lost interest in the storm. He squinted through the rain-splattered passenger window of his El Camino for a better view of the compact car, with its front end almost kissing the Dumpster, but he saw something that had him braking fully and lowering the passenger window.

The vehicle was a Grand Am and it was blocked from behind by two patrol cars. Driving rain and activity made it impossible to see whoever was in the front seat, but his experience told him this wasn't a routine license check or a Lovers' Lane scare.

He turned the vintage Chevy into the next driveway. The sloped ingress led him up to a house-turned-office where he quickly inspected the privacy fence running between the properties. There would be no easy view from this vantage point, but there were several breaks in the fence. If he was willing to risk getting struck by lightning, and ruining his signature leather jacket, he might be able to answer some nagging questions without being spotted.

Pushing aside his disgust at having lost the vehicle he'd been following through the city, Blade parked and made his way to the closest set of broken slats. What he saw chilled him as much as the rain sluicing under the neckline of his clothes.

Whether the car below was the one belonging to the person he'd been keeping an eye on these last weeks or not, there was serious trouble below, serious enough for the EMTs to have arrived at the scene. One medic hurried up front to the driver. In the break between moving bodies, Blade saw blond hair, enough of it to determine the victim was female. His concern deepened.

Right model car…the hair matched, too.

Accepting that he needed to get down there if he was to get answers, he eased through a wider section of broken fence and leaped off the slick grass and red clay to the asphalt. He lingered in that crouched position in the deeper shadows provided by the storage shed, hoping to recognize one of the cops. It would be less problematic—not to mention dangerous—to have a semifriendly present. Then a third patrol car pulled in behind the others.

Damn, Jackson thought. His identity was about to

be compromised beyond what he was willing to risk. Whatever he could learn here wouldn't offset the dangers of being seen by someone he didn't know—or didn't trust. But as he started to retreat, one of the officers spotted him.

Blade almost swore out loud. She would have to be one of the rookies.

"You—freeze! Up slowly. Show me your hands."

Tight-lipped, he did as directed. The pounding rain had him shrinking deeper into his jacket and muted the intentional heel-dragging of his well-worn Tony Lama boots. He knew what he looked like under normal conditions, and the weather and harsh light only made that worse, especially to an inexperienced cop. If he couldn't get away, he wanted to attract the attention of her partner. In the meantime, he hoped the rookie didn't panic.

"Hands!"

To his relief the female officer's second warning caught the attention of someone else. Though Blade's primary focus stayed on her and the .9 mm she gripped between her hands, he risked a glance toward the middle-aged man, who'd been slipping on his rain gear.

"You going to just stand there with your mouth open and let her shoot me, Parsons?" he drawled to the squinting cop.

As he peered at him, Phil Parson's expression turned into a sneer. "I should," he finally replied. "Might get a citation for enforcing the mayor's 'clean up the city' program."

"Your daughter seems to like what she sees." Blade allowed a benign smile. Inside, however, he seethed. The asshole knew dressing like an assistant D.A. or rookie FBI agent could get him killed. Maybe his reply was a low blow and an outright lie—he only knew Parson's daughter from the photo he'd seen on Phil's locker door—but if the cop wanted to trade insults, Blade would have the last word. His work, his survival depended on it.

Not surprisingly, veins protruded at each side of the older cop's eyes, spittle formed at the corners of his mouth. "Fuck you, Blade. My girl hasn't been within miles of you. As soon as we got her out of that—that joint and into rehab, she became her old self again. She's off of everything and I'll kick any SOB who says otherwise."

"Relax. I heard she's one of the lucky ones."

The cop's cheeks puffed as he collected himself. He cast his confused partner a quick look as though wishing he could somehow retract his outburst from her memory. "Damn fool," he grumbled at Blade. "What did you say that for, then?"

"Wanted your attention. I'm in a hurry."

"You got it."

Blade nodded at the car behind the two officers. "What's wrong with her?" At this point he could definitely tell the driver was female and that she was lying back against the headrest.

Ignoring his partner's continued stare, the broad-faced man shook his head. "Belly shot. And I suspect you know she's small."

"If she's who I think she is," Blade replied.

"Doesn't look good. The EMTs just said they can't risk waiting to stabilize her here."

The technicians were, in fact, already removing her from the vehicle and making quick work of loading her into the ambulance. Although he'd seen scenes like this many times—too many—Blade kept his face blank, his tone flat. "Has she said anything?"

"Nah. Nothing sensible, anyway."

"Come on, Phil, before I have to worry about a bullet in the back as well as the front."

"Just what is going on here?" the female officer demanded.

Another close flash of lightning, followed by a loud peal of thunder, had Sergeant Parsons cringing. In the next moment, he snapped, "Put that thing away before somebody gets hurt." To Blade he said, "It sounded like she mumbled something, but it could have been a moan. So what's up with her? She something to you? We haven't spotted a purse yet. Our check on the plates identifies the owner as Raymond Holms. Car could be stolen for all we know."

Blade nodded, though he didn't offer what he knew about the matter. He simply replied, "I've just seen her here and there."

"And?"

New sirens were sounding in the north. He couldn't tell if they were heading this way, but it was a good bet. "Who called this in?"

The female officer stepped forward. "I did. We were at the traffic light and I saw a dog sniffing around the car. The dog was on its hind legs and leaning into the window. I guess he smelled the blood. I'm Cathy Miles. I just started this week.'' She took a step forward as though about to extend her hand.

"Give him your phone number while you're at it,'' Parsons muttered.

The rookie's tentative smile vanished. "I—I'll go see if they need—" Swallowing hard, she beat a fast retreat.

"Smooth,'' Blade murmured.

Parsons waved away the criticism. "Hey. I'm sick of being given all the females to train. I feel like some kind of one-man feminist nursery school.''

"Ever think it's because somebody thinks you're a good teacher, or are you determined to be pissed because she's cute and you can't do anything about it?'' Having seen and heard enough, Blade was ready to retreat himself. "Who're they sending to take the case?''

"Snow.''

Always tenacious, Detective Gordon Snow took his time. Everyone else's, too, but Blade would vote for the Snowman's brand of caution any day. "I'm going to the hospital.''

"I'll let him know that's where he can find you.''

"Uh-uh. You forget I was here.'' Blade pointed a finger over his shoulder. "Make that clear to your partner, too—and that if our paths cross again she never uses my name if anyone else is around. If there's something Snow needs to hear, I'll make sure he gets the information. You know how I operate, Phil.''

Despite the initial tension between them, he suspected Phil Parsons would oblige. The guy was a good cop, even if he was an old-school redneck when it came to women. Parsons would remember that Blade's role in the world of night wolves required extreme caution.

The storm was moving east and Blade made it to Good Shepherd Medical Center in five minutes. Parking his two-tone gray 1982 El Camino between two larger trucks, as far away from the tall security lights as possible, he sprinted to catch up with the ambulance. He could see the EMTs wheeling the victim through the automatic glass doors of Emergency.

Only an arm's reach from the entry himself, he collided with another person. He heard a surprised, pained gasp, and then a woman fell hard onto the concrete, immediately curling into a tight fetal position. Blade's religious workouts kept him extremely fit, but she wasn't exactly Tinkerbell. When they'd collided they'd been shoulder to shoulder, and while she was slim, his impression of her was of toned muscle, too.

A split second later it registered with him that she wore a uniform. He squinted in the harsh light to read the patch on her sleeve. *Cody Security.* His lips twisted. Just what he needed—appeasing a wannabe.

Impatient to get inside, Blade extended his hand. ''Come on, I'll help you up.'' Meanwhile, his attention had returned to the EMTs. He wanted to make sure he knew where they were going.

"Back off."

The harsh warning, accompanied by a sting as his hand was slapped away, jerked his attention back to the security guard. She might be a mess—as soaked as he was and blue from the cold—but she had a great head of hair. No amount of rain could diminish the toffee-gold in that long plait. His gaze lingered for a second too long.

"Are you deaf?" she demanded.

Once again Blade found it necessary to raise his hands. "I only want to know if you need some help from inside?"

Instead of answering, she rolled to her knees and struggled to her feet. It was as clear as a traffic signal for him.

"Good girl. So watch it in the future, okay?" Leaving her to her injured pride or whatever, he resumed his race inside.

The waiting room and hallways of Emergency were flooded with people tonight, and it was only Tuesday. Most of the dazed souls he passed appeared to have been dragged out of bed. The rest looked in dire need of one.

Blade didn't have to worry about getting by the reception desk. The clerk had all the work she could handle dealing with people looking for information about loved ones. He passed through another set of glass doors and strode by the nurses' station, relying on what always worked for him—confidence. But his step faltered moments later.

The EMTs were already leaving the second triage unit. He didn't like the look of it. When he saw their expressions, his first question was "Did she ever say anything?"

The older of the haggard-faced men glanced his way, but appeared intent on continuing past him. Blade took no offense. It had been a grueling forty-eight hours, and his usual five o'clock shadow was beyond disreputable. There wasn't much he could do about genetics—in his work his swarthy coloring usually proved an asset—nor could he help his bad timing. He needed answers. Determined to get them, he quickly blocked the men's path and stuck his ID in their faces.

The technician closest to him blinked a few times. "Ah. Okay…no. She never said a word. She was already flat-lining in transit. They were never able to bring her back."

Blade made the badge disappear as quickly as he'd flashed it. "Thanks."

"That it?" The technician looked unsure that the questions were over.

"Unless you know who killed her?"

"Somebody as lost as she was."

He had that right. Blade wasn't surprised at the guy's reaction—people in emergency care tended to see the same view of the world that he did.

"If only we'd been able to get to her a few minutes sooner," the man continued.

Blade frowned. "I thought the wound was such that she wouldn't have pulled through?"

"But I think we might have briefly revived her. Maybe long enough to get some kind of statement. It's not in the job description, but we know it's part of what's asked of us. Somebody took a helluva risk leaving her in that condition."

The two men moved on, leaving Blade to consider that bit of speculation. It took the reproachful stares of passing hospital personnel to remind him that this was nowhere to do his thinking, and he followed the men out.

Beyond the Emergency doors, he was held up by a group who had just received similar news to his. He shut his mind to the sobs, his eyes to the anguish, and stepped around them. Directly ahead was Ms. Cody Security in intense dialogue with a nurse.

"Sorry, ma'am," the harried nurse said. "Maybe they did just bring her in, but I don't have paperwork on any shooting victim."

The EMT who'd spoken to Blade paused on his way out and backtracked. "You know the kid who was shot?" he asked the security guard.

Bewilderment had her smoke-gray eyes appearing all the larger. Under different circumstances Blade would have been tempted, wanting to linger and find out her name. It was her fierce grip on her upper left arm that snapped him back to attention. Could he be responsible for that? Her jacket was flight-style like his, only canvas. It would have offered no protection whatsoever when she fell down.

"Kid...?" She shook her head in slow motion as though caught up in some dream. "No. The woman in the white Pontiac. A Grand Am. She's seventy-nine. Five-two...though she insists it's still five-three. She wears a platinum blond wig."

"Right car, close hair, wrong driver," the EMT said. "Our passenger was an eighteen-year-old girl." He glanced at his partner. "What was the name Phil gave us?"

"Holms. Well...maybe."

Blade watched the woman frown in confusion and barely heard her murmur, "I guess I made a mistake."

The EMT shrugged. "Good luck." He and his partner moved on.

The nurse looked ready to escape, too. Blade stepped closer and said to her, "Maybe you'd better get the lady some help. I think her arm—"

"It's nothing," the guard interjected, staring at something light years beyond his left shoulder. But when she did focus on him she physically recoiled, as though backing from the deepest of black holes, bringing her up hard against the admittance desk. "Son of a—" While she checked the curse in time, she directed all of her pain at Blade. "Will you please get lost? It was just a little lightning, okay?"

3

Maple Trails
5:45 a.m.

But nothing was okay, and as dawn approached, Campbell had new symptoms to apply to her definition of sick-of-mind and sick-at-heart. Being on the phone again with her father wasn't doing much to help that.

"No, there's still no word on Maida," she told Yancy. "I'm ready to notify the sheriff." Since they were located just beyond the city limits, the property fell under the jurisdiction of the Gregg County Sheriff's Department rather than the Longview Police.

"Give her another hour," Yancy replied. "I know you two have grown particularly close in the last year, but she still has a right to her privacy."

Campbell switched from rubbing her arm to massaging the intensified throbbing building in the middle of her forehead. "I know, I know. You warned me of this very possibility, of not keeping some professional distance, and whether you believe it or not, I have. But you weren't the one to witness what happened.''

''I wish it had been me there last night. Then you wouldn't be hurting now.'' Yancy sighed. ''Look, you've been to the hospital and we've both listened to the police scanner throughout the night. There's been nothing to indicate she's had an accident, so why not give her family time to wake calmly. I'm still betting she's over at their place, but even if she's not, it's not fair to upset them before we can say with certainty there's a legitimate problem.''

He was as resistant to what she'd told him about Maida's deteriorating relationship with her only son and his family as he was to the reason for the woman's strange departure. Earlier, he'd suggested the sirens going off around town warning of a tornado in the area was what had scared Maida out of her home. That could be, but Campbell wasn't convinced—and he'd pushed her close to the end of her patience. She wanted answers.

''If you knew a twister was headed here, wouldn't you call me to make sure I was secure?'' Yancy asked. ''And wouldn't you check with me directly afterward to see if I needed anything?''

''Stop with the fairy tales—we aren't a good example for any of this. What's more, Maida thinks her daughter-in-law Patsy is more attracted to Dwayne's pension fund than she is to Dwayne and she's disgusted that he can't see that. This is a dysfunctional iceberg, Dad.'' Campbell paused as she saw a familiar bronze compact pull in. "Kelsey is here. Have you updated her about this?"

"No. I thought you'd prefer to do that. I didn't want to risk getting any facts wrong or anything."

Campbell couldn't completely repress her annoyance. It wasn't facts he was concerned about. After all, she'd been careful to be explicit as she detailed information to him. He was, she suspected, continuing to believe she was overreacting. Now she had to update Kels without putting Yancy in a bad light, because a junior partner didn't challenge the senior one in front of staff, no matter how badly he had stumbled.

"Fine," she replied. "Just FYI... I'm leaving a set of the notes I made, so all staff will have firsthand data to work from."

"I'd like to see them first."

"You've heard me over the phone. There are no surprises. Everyone needs to be on the same page—and fast," she added.

"You'll bring the original for me to review?" he asked, the command clear.

"After I go over and recheck Dogwood Lane."

"You said Ike's been there twice since the storm. Both times he's reported the same thing—the garage is empty. Besides, you'd have been the first person to see her if she came back," Yancy said.

"That doesn't mean there isn't something of value to note, something that might give us a clue as to what sent her charging out of here. It was dark the last time he checked around the house."

"It still will be for a while yet. Dyle or Travis should be driving up at any second. Have one of them inspect the house as soon as they check in."

"They'll have plenty to do closing off areas around the marina that suffered wind damage, and then checking the vacant homes on the east rim of the lake, which Ike says appears to have taken the brunt of the storm. Besides, one of Maida's neighbors might be outside inspecting their property. You know they're more likely to talk to me about her than anyone else."

"Yeah, but you're hurting," her father said again. "Kelsey may not hear it in your voice, but I do. Let Ike go as soon as the others relieve him. You can tell him particular places to check."

What was draining her faster was convincing her father that she knew how to do her job. "The guys are already on the clock and Ike left the premises five minutes ago. He's beat, too, Yancy. In any case, I have to stick around. No one has arrived at the administration office yet, and you know they aren't likely to before 7:30."

"You can't sit there half the morning waiting on them. Besides, you and I need to talk first."

"Administration deserves to know something could be wrong."

"Damn, Belle, what are you trying to do, send me back to the hospital? Slow down. Maida Livingstone is downright obdurate about people invading her privacy."

"I've had nothing but time to sit here contemplating worse-case scenarios. We don't want Bryce Tyndell undermining us with the Residents' Committee and suggesting that we kept things secret due to misconduct or neglect.''

"That tight-collared prick would do it, too,'' Yancy muttered. "How he's managed to keep his job as operations manager for this long, I don't know.''

Campbell could visualize Yancy's sun-bronzed face hardening into a craggy mask. Bryce remained a chink in Cody's well-oiled machine and she saw no sense in rehashing what wasn't going to change, at least not today.

With her characteristic burst of energy, Kelsey McGraw swept into the small building swinging her knapsack routinely full of bottled water and assorted veggie-or fruit munchies. During her last physical, the ex-lifeguard, former Miss Galveston had learned she was borderline diabetic and had announced she wasn't succumbing to pills or injections.

This morning her focus was all on Campbell. One look at Campbell's coloring and overall condition and she demanded, "What's wrong?''

"Hear that?'' Campbell said into the phone. "Kels just walked in. I'll see you as soon as I'm through.''

"All right. But under no circumstances do you use your key over at the house, understood? I don't care what understanding you have with Maida. You don't have it in writing, you protect your—*our* asses.''

She rolled her eyes as she caught Kelsey's questioning glance. "I know the drill. Unless we spot Maida through a window bleeding or otherwise in distress, we need authorized personnel—namely

Bryce Tyndell or a member of the Gregg County Sheriff's Department—to give us permission to enter her residence.''

As soon as Campbell hung up, Kelsey stopped putting away her supplies and faced her. ''What's up with Maida that has you and Boss One all tied in knots?''

Campbell took a moment to get her breathing back under control. One of the problems she was experiencing as a result of the lightning strike was muscle and nerve pain. The more agitated she became, the worse the throbbing became down her left side.

''She went off in a crazed rush during the storm last night.''

''Madam Livingstone on Dogwood, who's been warned how many times about speeding on the grounds?''

''The very one. The same person who happens to hate driving in the rain so much so that she'll cancel an appointment. It's her cataracts.''

''Apparently they weren't bothering her last night.'' Blue eyes that usually twinkled with goodwill darkened with concern. ''This is for real? It didn't start raining until almost midnight.''

''And she has yet to return,'' Campbell added.

''Huh.'' Kelsey stashed her satchel and purse in the file cabinet she used as a locker. ''Was she alone?''

''Yes.''

''Maybe not for long,'' the model-thin blonde said. ''What do you mean?''

"Maybe she decided to ride out the storm with a gentleman friend."

Even miserable, Campbell appreciated the idea. "No one would be happier than me if she was rushing to meet some pill-invigorated dish."

Another wave of gnawing pain struck Campbell, all but stealing her breath. She quickly reached for three more Tylenol, downing them with what was left of her bottled water. One more dose remained in the container and she doubted it would help any more than the others had. Her next choice would be Scotch—at Yancy's where she could crash in the spare bedroom. This would be her smartest move if she wanted to avoid being targeted by cops with long memories and deeper prejudice. She spent far too much time keeping the past from crushing her, and now those memories compounded her physical condition and sent her into another spasm of pain.

She doubled over at the waist. It didn't fool Kelsey, who dropped to her knees to peer at her.

"Campbell? Hey, what's wrong?"

"I told you. It was a rough night."

"Got it, Ms. Understatement. Tell me the rest…did Maida clip you with a fender or something as she left? What?"

Campbell thought of what the internist told her. "It would have been better long-term, if she had."

Those intelligent blue eyes under the curtain of shaggy, genuine blond bangs exhibited some fast calculations. "Long term…oh, hell. You were struck again, weren't you? Why aren't you at the hospital? You need X rays, an MRI.''

Aside from being a health nut, twenty-seven-year-old Kels was a quick study. These days, Campbell rated her memory better than her own. Kelsey had also been present during Campbell's last close encounter with lightning.

"I've seen a doctor," she told her. "Don't give me that look."

"Why not? You leaving your post?"

"So I went to Good Shepherd for more than one reason."

Kelsey narrowed her eyes. "There was a shooting. I was listening on my radio. The victim was just a kid. Wait…you thought it could have been Maida?"

"All I heard was that a white Grand Am was involved. There was no question in my mind but to rush to the hospital to find out more."

"Stacie," Kelsey said, thinking out loud. "Stacie…"

"Holms."

"It drives me nuts to think of kids driving around in that kind of weather, never mind at such an hour." It was then that Kelsey focused on the tear in Campbell's slacks. "That bolt really flattened you. It didn't happen in here on the linoleum, did it?"

"No, and not outside. Well, not here. Some creepy biker dude knocked me over outside Emergency."

Kelsey looked practically starstruck. "You were run over by a Harley after being struck by lightning?"

"*No.*" Campbell rocked until she didn't feel the

need to scream. "He just looked the part— I didn't see any bike. I don't know who he was other than someone in a hurry."

Looking somewhat disappointed, Kelsey inspected her from head to foot. "Tell me straight, how bad was the jolt this time?"

How bad…? She thought of the movie *Six Degrees of Separation,* of astronauts at NASA struggling against Gs…all the comparative situations Campbell's tired mind could rattle to the surface. "You might say I shook hands with the devil," she said, massaging the worst area.

Kelsey rose. "This is nuts. Can we shift someone around and I'll do your running for you so you can rest? I know you're off tonight, but—"

Catching on, Campbell put a quick stop to the idea. "If we fiddle with that schedule one more time, none of us will know who's on deck when or where. Not to worry. I'd as soon stay busy. Lying there trying to sleep would turn me into an AA candidate."

Looking as if she wanted to press the issue, Kelsey refocused on the clipboard containing the list of those who had entered the park in the last twenty-four hours, and any notes about unusual conduct. She opened her mouth to speak.

"Maida's odd departure isn't listed there because I just didn't have time last night to include it. My priority was to make the most accurate notes I could in case we need to call in reinforcements," Campbell said, to get the jump on Kelsey's next question. The idea of needing the next level of law enforcement made her stomach roll; nevertheless, she calmly indicated the other pad on the desk. "Do me a favor. After you go through the list, add an abbreviated version in the log." A copy of it would be forwarded to Administration and the other copy would be filed at Cody Security.

"Will do." Kelsey studied the detailed notes. "How strange…maybe she had a bad reaction to medication."

"The way she was driving, I could believe it. But then why hasn't anyone found her?" Campbell collected her things, including her two-way radio that would be dropped off at the office for recharging. "Don't hesitated to holler if you hear or see anything while I'm up the road."

"Do you want me to feel out her buddies if they happen to pass by?"

The residents of Maple Trails were guaranteed their privacy, and it was a rule that kept echoing in Campbell's mind. "Only if they pause while exiting and bring her up first. We don't want to start a panic, especially when we don't know what we're dealing with."

"True. Okay."

Kelsey's gaze dropped momentarily to the gun on Campbell's hip. Kels was about to take her second-grade qualifications and wouldn't be eligible to carry a weapon for a while yet. She had recently voiced doubts about wanting to go that far in this field, and the mystery behind Maida's whereabouts brought the reality of the job into a clearer perspective than ever.

''Be careful.''

With a nod, Campbell headed for Maida's residence. It didn't offend her that Kelsey had exposed a hint of reserve or doubt about her as much as the job. They'd only known each other for a year, and she knew true trust took far longer. Besides, rumors remained fluid throughout the grapevine about her much-publicized resignation from the Longview Police Department.

The Jeep's heater had just begun to thaw her aching body by the time Campbell made it up Dogwood Lane. Parking in front of the ranch-style dwelling, she thought again how much it resembled a smaller version of Cody headquarters, Yancy's own home. This creamy white-brick rendition was more elegant though, comparable to anything in Dallas's Highland Park or Houston's River Oaks. Most of the credit had to go to Maida. Despite her age and the number of trees on the lot, she kept the lawn meticulous, the flower beds free of weeds and debris. She loved puttering in the yard, even through the cold snaps during winter. But this morning a large branch from her favorite pink dogwood dangled like a broken arm. On the lawn lay the culprit—a heftier limb from a towering black oak. It would break Maida's heart to see such loss.

Strolling up the curved sidewalk, Campbell picked up the newspaper, setting it on the iron-and-redwood bench at the front door. If the Jeremys or the Smarts were watching from their living-room windows across the street, they would observe typical behavior, since she often stopped by Maida's for a cup of coffee at the end of a shift. But once she glanced around, she concluded that she was the only person up and about this morning, for every house she could see had plastic-wrapped newspapers lying untouched in the yards.

Relieved, she made her way to the back of the house, testing locks and peering into the windows of the garage door to make sure she was also correct about the Pontiac being gone. The rear patio doors had sheers covering them, but the heavier drapes were wide open. That struck her as unusual.

Typical of many in her generation, Maida was always concerned with discretion and safety. "Be paranoid and live another day," she'd declare in her musical voice, a finger wagging at whomever she felt needed a warning. Why hadn't Maida closed the drapes last night? Had she been watching the storm from here before rushing from the house? Not likely. The storm had approached from the northwest, which was her front yard.

Glancing down, Campbell saw the shortened broomstick that was lodged in the aluminum track of the sliding glass door—Maida's economical version of a dead bolt. The woman could spend thousands on a couch no one would ever sit on, but if a piece of wood could offset the expense of a computerized alarm system, she would rush to the discount store and buy out their stock of cheap brooms.

Cupping her hands beside her eyes, Campbell peered inside. No lights had been left on, and overcast skies were slowing dawn. For once, she wished Maida had a dog or cat: a curious, devoted pet that would move the damn sheers so she could get a better view.

With a sigh, she cast a frustrated glance up and down the alley. In keeping with the neighbors' landscaping decisions, Maida had opted not to close in her yard. That was all right, since she didn't have to worry about a pet disturbing the neighbors. Also, the Trails's privacy fence on the far side of the alley blocked intrusion and noise from the farm-to-market road beyond. But it did feel rather bare and lonely this winter day. More leaves and branches littered the alley, but there was no real damage…

Her gaze fell on Liz Junior.

Maida had won the life-size black ceramic cat with violet eyes—à la namesake Elizabeth Taylor—in a bingo game at the recreation center along with its purple ceramic ottoman. It sat at the corner of the patio…or it had. The wind must have knocked the gaudy, but amusing, figurine onto the concrete.

"Now who's going to help her do the newspaper crossword puzzles?" she murmured to the beheaded figurine.

Wondering what else was going to go wrong today, Campbell reached for her radio and returned to her vehicle.

4

6:27 a.m.

Finding that the Maple Trials administration office
was still locked, Campbell continued on to Cody
headquarters. This time she beat receptionist-
dispatcher Beth Greer, and punched the entry code on
the keyboard lock to gain access inside. She found
Yancy in the kitchen pouring himself a mug of coffee.

"You want one of these or something stronger?"
he asked.

He didn't so much as glance over his shoulder, but
Campbell refused to be impressed, guessing he'd
spotted her arrival on one of the outside cameras. Or
maybe he'd called Kelsey after she'd left the Trails.
What she cared about was whether he'd taken his
medicine—and the vitamins she'd bought for him.

She went straight to the refrigerator and helped herself to a Diet Pepsi.

"Poison."

As he muttered, Yancy lifted and dropped her braid
as though it was a door knocker and continued by. It
was the only gesture of physical affection she would

get from him for a while, a sign of how concerned and upset he'd been over her experiences last night.

"Be glad it's not chardonnay," she replied with equal crustiness. But Campbell's lips twitched as she followed him. For all his insight into what made people tick, he was a big, clumsy lug when it came to personal relationships.

At six-three, and with his steel-gray hair cut in the renowned marine burr, he continued to resemble the toughie she'd always called him, although he was a good twenty-five pounds lighter since the prostate surgery he'd recently undergone. The white shirt and jeans that had become his uniform since establishing Cody Security were still too loose, but he never stopped trying to fool people that he'd gotten back all of his robust energy and gung-ho personality.

Following him into his office, she watched him ease himself into the black leather chair behind the desk. Behind him, on the wall, were credentials and citations. Campbell knew if he'd had his way, Yancy would have boxed them away years ago. She'd been the one to insist that clients would be impressed and reassured by them—proof of his training and skills. She suspected they meant more to him now than ever as he struggled to regain his stride.

Taking a sip of his coffee, he set it on the coaster. "I haven't seen you looking this wiped out since—"

"I know." Campbell hoped to cut short any lecture he'd been planning.

"Hurts worse than you'll admit."

Yancy's conversational approach was to state con-

clusions like a twenty-dollar fortune-teller. It used to
drive Campbell nuts, until she realized he took no
pleasure in anyone's pain or defeat, he simply believed in shorthand and shortcuts whenever possible.

"When you start fessing up, I will too."

His grunt could have been a chuckle and he indicated his pen and pencil holder. "Well, your mother
said you got your stubbornness from me. Feel free to
bite down on one of my freshly sharpened No.2s if it
gets so bad your teeth start to itch. In the meantime,
tell me more about what you think is going on."

"I'm done guessing. I'm going to dig up more answers." Too weary to simply stand and in too much
pain to sit without rocking, she wandered around his
office.

"Maida has to be at her son's house, that's all there
is to it. Her family would have screamed bloody murder until they had squad cars lined up at the gatehouse
if she hadn't arrived."

"If they knew she was coming."

That possibility had Campbell's mouth going dry
again, and she took a deep drink of her soda. "The
only way we can determine whether they did or
didn't—or if she even spoke to them—is to go inside
the house and check her answering machine."

"Forget it. If we get to where that becomes our
only choice, we call the sheriff and hand things over
to his department. I mean it, Belle. You know Tyndell
won't let us into the house under these vague conditions—and he's our only option if we don't contact
the sheriff."

His expression reflected her feelings about having to call in the local authorities. "Fine, then I'm ready," Campbell said. "But let me pay the family a courtesy call. Regardless of his neglect, and Patsy's resentment of her mother-in-law, Dwayne eventually does what needs to be done."

"Because his mother is going to leave him more comfortable than he probably is."

Far more than he deserves to be, Campbell thought, rubbing her thumb over the condensation on the soda can. "We need him working with us not against us, especially since the procedure for filing missing persons reports has been upgraded. With the National Crime Information Center program at officers' fingertips, it takes nothing for police departments to research a subject on their computers. The only people who will get criticized now are those who delay reporting a missing person in the first place." This was basically the same technology that was allowing the Amber Alert to go national.

"One big problem," Yancy said. "Maida wouldn't qualify for priority listing. She might be over seventy, but she's fully cognizant and no real threat to herself or anyone else."

Campbell signaled for his patience. "I have to confide something she hasn't told anyone yet. There's a health wrinkle aside from the cataracts."

Yancy didn't hesitate. "Alzheimer's?"

"Osteoporosis. Advancing fast."

"How would that influence a situation like this?"

"She wants to live in her own home as long as

possible.'' Campbell knew she had to confide more. It didn't matter that this was her father, the head of a company that held privacy and confidences as sacred. She saw it as breaking her word to a friend. ''She's had two episodes of allergic reactions to medication. The first time she simply developed hives around her neck and her eyes swelled shut. The next time she had some trouble breathing.''

''She called you and you didn't get her to the hospital?''

''She told me afterward. She took Benadryl and used cool packs. They worked.'' Campbell stopped pacing to face her father. ''I was as upset as you are when she confided this. That's the point. Maybe she's had another reaction, a worse one, but was determined not to involve or inconvenience me and tried to get to Emergency on her own. You know how proud some of these people are.''

''You said yourself, she's not at the hospital.''

''Dad, a favorite figurine is lying broken on her patio. At first I assumed the storm did it. Ike must have thought so, too, because he didn't mention it when he checked her place for me. She was fond of the silly thing. Call me crazy, but if she watched it break in the storm, or she accidentally broke it while trying to secure something…well that could have had a powerful emotional effect.''

Yancy's eyes, usually a stormy, cooler gray than her own, warmed, but not with intellectual appreciation. ''Belle, listen to yourself. I'm proud of your thoroughness. Just don't be quick to assume responsibility in any of this. If Maida didn't take her medication, that was her choice. If she left the premises instead of calling you at the gate to ask for EMS help, again, so be it. What I'd like you to consider is that she confided only as much as she did so you would cut her some slack regarding rules and regulations. Are you sure she's not involved with some guy?''

Campbell's initial reaction was indignation. ''She's not a teenager whose brain has logic gaps as wide as the Gulf. In any case, if she was involved with someone, I think he would be on the premises. Maida doesn't often leave the Trails these days. I've told you that, or has your medication affected your memory?''

Yancy snorted and reached for his coffee. ''Calm down. I just want to know we're all on the same page when we hit that big alarm button.''

''Punch it, Dad, because I am alarmed, and I'm trained not to be,'' she replied quietly.

''We've had a perfect record here providing security to the property—no burglary, no assaults, no murders.''

But they'd had a few stalkings and embezzlements. ''As I said before,'' Campbell replied, ''her family is the type to push litigation if something goes wrong. Maida has said enough about their lifestyle to suggest their debt situation would benefit from a quick cash settlement.''

''Parasites.'' As he spoke, Yancy massaged his abdomen. ''Well, you'd better get to it, then.''

His growing paleness troubled her. ''You've had a

difficult night yourself, worrying about me on top of the others.''

''I'm just reminded that we need to hire new staff, that's all.''

But they couldn't afford to without new clients. Naturally, they couldn't take on new clients without more employees, and for that they needed some interim financing. Right now, no bank was going to give them a loan until Yancy's next physical certified a clean bill of health. Adding to their problems were 9/11 regulations to incorporate into their daily procedure—as was the case for everyone in the law enforcement and security business. They'd also lost a small bundle putting two employees on full-time debris search after the *Columbia* shuttle tragedy.

Campbell moistened her lips, preparing to broach a subject she'd been debating privately. ''Have you considered taking on another partner, Dad?''

''I have the one I want, that's enough.''

His tone left no room for discussion. As touched as she was, Campbell couldn't help feeling that her father had made the legal changes to the corporation merely as a gesture to keep her psychologically afloat. For her part, she didn't feel she brought enough to the company to warrant such pride and defense, aside from six years' experience as a Longview police officer, which had yielded no savings, no legitimate investigative experience—just the academy training.

''Nothing has changed over at LPD that I know of,'' she continued. ''I'm still a greater liability than an asset to you. If you considered that offer from National—''

''Not today, Belle.''

The nation-wide security firm had approached him just before her resignation from the LPD and his surgery. Even then Yancy declared he would close before surrendering his company to them. But a person could change his perspective.

''Dad, I was pulled over again on Friday. There wasn't any ticket or anything, but the officer took his damned time, especially after I told him I was on my way to a dental appointment. He just goaded me in the hopes that I'd do something foolish.''

''Bastard. Who was it this time?''

''That's irrelevant. The point is, I'll continue to be harassed until I physically make myself scarce, or they get the backbone to do that for me.''

The word ''permanently'' didn't need to be spoken.

Yancy slapped his hand down on the desk blotter so hard that his coffee mug almost went flying. ''Dammit! You're moving in here. If you didn't see the need before—''

''I'm not going to let a handful of ignorant bullies control me.''

''Bullies with badges. Come on, move in. You know this place feels like a museum half the time.''

''Invite Cheralyn to move in with you.'' He'd ended his budding relationship with Cheralyn Eastman the same day he'd returned from the clinic with his diagnosis. When the suggestion earned her a glowering look, she countered it with a one-shouldered shrug. "You're alive. You're going to be around awhile. Why deny yourself good company?"

"Your love life is off-limits, but you get to give me advice?"

Campbell averted her gaze. "It's only been a year."

"Fourteen months, and that's a lifetime when the guy proves to be a—"

"Dad." In no shape to go three rounds with the champ, Campbell saluted him with her can of soda. "Message received. I'll let you know what I learn from Maida's family."

5

7:30 a.m.

The Saunders lived in an upscale development, a spare mile northwest of Maple Trails. New roads framed by concrete curbing as white as fresh-squeezed toothpaste stretched around groves of dog-wood, live oak and a relatively new planting of native pine. Safe ground for Campbell, since this area was also outside of LPD jurisdiction and private security systems were the fashion.

Locating the correct address, she parked in front of the two-story Tudor, badly designed in gray brick. As she approached the leaded glass and oak front door, she took special note of the teal-colored Ford compact with the battered front end tucked in the upper corner of the driveway. It reminded her of Maida's concerns about her granddaughter's poor driving record to date. Right now, though, all she cared about was that the senior Saunderes's vehicles were still in the two-car garage.

A considerable amount of noise from inside the

house reassured her. She rang the front doorbell, waited a good half a minute and rang again.

Suddenly she saw blurred movement beyond the thick glass, then the door swung open and Dwayne Saunders scowled at her. He was dressed in the uniform of an executive—starched white shirt, red tie, soft-leather gray loafers and belted gray slacks that did little to conceal a slight paunch momentarily sucked in. Campbell allowed that he cleaned up well. She was less impressed with his puffy face and unhealthy coloring.

"Yes?" he demanded.

Amazons weren't his type; she could see it by the stiffness entering his features as he registered her uniform and that they stood eye to eye. In turn she schooled her expression into what she hoped was something less icy than her usual countenance of late. Maybe he remembered her from Maida's last birthday party—or maybe not, since he'd behaved like a petulant teenager dragged to a family event against his will. She had not forgotten that sullen mouth and close-set eyes.

"Sorry to intrude, Mr. Saunders, but I'm—"

"Yes, yes. I remember."

"Good. I need to ask you about your mother."

"What? Why? Is she sick?"

"I hope not, sir. We're being thorough, nonetheless. Are you aware that she left the estate late last night in a rush and hasn't returned?"

"My mother? She never drives after dark. She has night blindness."

Jerk, she thought. He clearly had forgotten about

the cataracts. "I witnessed it myself, sir. And although it was quite stormy—"

He shook his head and began shifting, ready to close the door. "It didn't get bad until late, what…midnight? She would have been asleep for hours. You must be mistaken."

Campbell softened her tone. "There's nothing wrong with my vision, Mr. Saunders. Have you been in touch with your mother?"

Before he could answer, a svelte blonde dressed in chilled-peach satin appeared at his side followed by a waft of Organza perfume. "What's going on, Dwayne? You promised you'd take Debra and Marc to school so I can make my hair appointment. They have to leave. Now."

"I *said* I'd do it, Patsy."

Campbell pretended not to notice the rising notch of tension in his voice. "Hello again, Mrs. Saunders. I'm Campbell Cody with Cody Security. I'm sorry for the inconvenience, but we're concerned about Maida."

Despite the early hour, the woman looked fresh and fashionable even in a house robe. In contrast, Campbell was never more aware of her appearance— stained and torn uniform and frizzing hair. Whatever mascara and lip gloss she'd put on last night had been bitten off or washed away hours ago. Add to that, she was almost half a foot taller than the woman. No amount of slouching would improve that contrast, so she stood tall and let Maida's son and daughter-in-law think what they would.

"What's she done now?" Blue-eyed Patsy sighed.

Campbell was aware of Dwayne momentarily shutting his eyes.

"I swear, that woman should sell that house once and for all before we all go as loopy as she is."

"She's *missing*, Patsy."

Bristling at the subtle rebuke from her husband, Patsy directed new disdain at Campbell. "Excuse me? How can she be missing in her own house with security all around her? You mean you've lost her."

"She's not ours to lose." Campbell had met her type too often to be annoyed. "She is a free citizen, fully cognizant and deserving the respect due to anyone her age. That said, she left the estate under unusual circumstances last night and hasn't returned. We're hoping you might know something about the matter."

"Unbelievable," Patsy drawled. "In the same breath you insist she's of sound mind and then have the gall to admit—"

A sudden crash in the kitchen followed by a pained cry had both husband and wife racing into the interior of the house. Since they didn't slam the door in her face, Campbell followed.

In the middle of the kitchen, amid shattered glass and splattered orange juice, Debra Saunders, Maida's seventeen-year-old granddaughter, stood staring at the TV. On the screen was Wanda White of KLTV, the Longview-Tyler station, sharing the overnight tragedy regarding the teenage girl found mortally wounded behind a local restaurant.

"EMTs worked valiantly to save the teenager, but

Stacie Holms was pronounced dead shortly after arriving at Good Shepherd Medical Center.''

"Stace." The word was both an anguished whisper and a protest. Then with a wrenching sob, Debra Saunders covered her face with her hands. "Oh, my God. Oh, no…''

Campbell felt for the teen. She couldn't forget that she herself had crossed paths with the victim last night at Good Shepherd. A girl who, as luck would have it, had driven the same car Maida did. Was there information here that needed to be reported to the investigating team?

"You're a good friend of Stacie Holms, Debra?'' Campbell asked.

Patsy Saunders spun around. "What do you think you're doing? You need to leave, Ms.—Officer. This is a family moment."

"Mrs. Saunders, I'll make this as brief as possible, but I'd like to ask Debra—''

"Get out!" An adamant Patsy pointed with fierce determination to the door.

Knowing she was way out on thin ice jurisdiction-wise, Campbell held up her hands and obeyed, with a veneer of calm that vanished once she was back in the car.

"Dammit!" She struck the steering wheel with the palm of her hand.

She'd had no business trying to quiz the kid. Not only was she overreaching her authority, she was jeopardizing any form of cooperation with the adults. At this point she doubted Dwayne or Patsy would ever talk to her unless it was to press charges for neglect.

6

"**W**hy didn't you call?"

Back at the offices, Campbell took her father's annoyance as the minimum penance due. "I thought what I had to report was better said in person."

Ushering her in, Yancy shut the door to his office, leaving Beth Greer, his efficient though curious young receptionist-dispatcher to wonder. Normally, he had an open-door policy, unless he was interviewing a prospective client, or was on a conference call, or was lying down when it didn't pay to fib about his weakened state. This didn't look like one of those.

"So?"

Campbell eyed the TV remote in his hand. "Have you heard anything more from Maple Trails while I was gone?"

"There's additional damage to the houses down from the marina. Never mind that, what did the Saunders say? Was the daughter there by chance?"

As he spoke, Yancy aimed the remote at the unit behind his desk. When Campbell saw the screen go blue and read Video, she understood. He'd seen the news, too.

"Debra, yes. She was watching TV in the kitchen. She took the news hard."

"Figures. There may be about twenty-five hundred students at the high school this year, but I reckon, by the time they're seniors, the kids all have a good idea who everyone else is in the class."

Campbell wondered if his instincts had meandered down the same path as hers. "I tried to find out how well Debra knew the Holms girl after questioning her parents about Maida, but Patsy turned alpha female. Sorry. It would have been helpful for us to have something to offer the authorities if we need to ask them to bump up a search for Maida."

Yancy signaled his agreement of that with a slight shift of his thick eyebrows. "What did her loving son have to say about his mother's whereabouts?"

"He doesn't have a clue. That is, he *says* he hasn't a clue. The commotion with Debra prevented me from probing his memory a little further."

"So, for the moment, Maida has been forgotten? Maybe conveniently?"

The VCR tape momentarily captured her attention. Campbell knew what was coming. Even so, she experienced a pang at the sight of the crime scene, the white Grand Am behind the news anchor. "That's it. That's the 911 I heard on the scanner last night. Look at the car—see what I mean? That's why I let you and Ike talk me into going to the hospital. When I heard that the victim was being rushed to Emergency,

I wanted to check on her myself. Don't ask me why I didn't listen for a better ID to make sure it was Maida.''

''It's definitely one of those freak situations. Sorry as I am for the kid, I can't help feeling this is buying us time.''

Campbell understood. This brought them back to Dwayne. But before she could say anything, the intercom buzzed.

Yancy stopped the VCR and hit the TV's mute button before reaching across his desk. ''Yes, Beth?'' he said into the machine.

''State police on line one, sir.''

Yancy grabbed the receiver. ''Dolan—good of you to get back to me so fast.''

Exhausted in too many ways to count, Campbell was slow to figure out who Yancy was talking to. Wondering what he was up to, she watched his narrow-eyed stare as he looked beyond the miniblinds out to the street. As a state trooper, Yancy had cut a distinguished figure in his uniform, intimidating enough for most of her friends to give their old home a wide berth—a reaction he encouraged, since there were a number of pranksters in her circle.

''Okay, thanks. I'd appreciate that, Dolan. We'll get it faxed to you as soon as I get the additional information confirmed.''

The moment he hung up, Campbell was already leaning across the desk. ''You called Captain Wheat?''

''Didn't think it could do us any harm. He always

said he owed me for finding his boy's Harley before that chop shop spread the parts across the country. He checked on overnight activity in our area. Says so far there are no reports of anyone matching Maida's description, and no one's called in to check on anything bearing her car's plates. I guess you could call that good news.''

To a point. They could be reasonably sure she hadn't had an accident or been stopped for reckless driving or speeding. But that left plenty of other possibilities.

''At least we can delay talking to Tyndell.''

Campbell couldn't believe Yancy was suggesting that. ''How do you figure? Patsy may stay preoccupied with their daughter's emotional state, but I'd be surprised if Dwayne hasn't already gone back to wondering about my visit. I'll bet there's already a call from him on Maida's answering machine, and another on the main office's switchboard.''

''He'll wait, thinking she might be in the shower, and try again.''

''Listen to me. He may not be the son Maida hoped for, but he knows what she expects from her chief beneficiary. I'm the one who's going to shower and change. Then I'm going back to the Trails and track down Bryce. I'd rather suffer his company than watch him in a TV press conference with Dwayne.''

''Well, while you're burning all cylinders, start making a list of Maida's friends and the places you know she frequented when she did leave Maple

Trails. If it turns out that we do have to make this an all-out search, that will save us some time.''

''Good point. By the way, I'll get cleaned up here so you don't have to nag me about doing more driving.''

''I'm overwhelmed.''

Less than an hour later Campbell found Yancy sitting on the edge of Beth's desk. Between his guilty look and her big calf eyes, Campbell suspected she'd been their prime topic of conversation.

''You have a big mouth,'' she said, certain Yancy was the guiltier of the two.

''I was only telling Beth a little about Maida. Remember the time she was baby-sitting for her grandson—oh, heck, it was three years ago—and she intentionally ran over that rattlesnake?''

Campbell didn't believe his story for a second—she knew he'd told Beth about her latest lightning experience—but the snake story was an amusing one. Maida's aim was way off and she'd only broken off the snake's rattles. Her grandson had been so upset that Maida asked one of the security guards to take the creature to the vet to see if they could reattach them.

Shaking her head, Campbell headed toward the door.

''Hey—if you're going back to Maple Trails, why aren't you in uniform?'' Yancy called after her.

She simply lifted a hand in farewell, not yet ready to explain.

7

Certain the ceiling would rot and collapse on him
before he would sleep, Blade kicked free of the tangled sheet and blanket, and swung his legs to the
floor. The room spun before him in a dusky blur
thanks to the combination of fatigue and the bourbon
he'd downed to block out what he'd seen last night.
Beyond the closed drapes the birds outside sounded
as if they were in serious competition for screen time
in a Hitchock remake.

Food. Slowly, it registered that they must be impatient for their day's ration of seeds, especially since
the storm had returned winter to Texas. On the heels
of that realization came a taste of February chill
against his bare skin and he glanced around, wondering what new damage the storm had caused on the
roof or a window. Nothing would surprise him, since
he'd made no improvements and only the most man-
datory repairs to this three-room shack since taking
on the lease almost a year ago.

Blade had decided on this remote eyesore for a reason other than economics; it also ensured protection and relief from all but the most determined solicitors. The place was a far cry from his roots, but then that was what set black sheep apart from others. He owned few creature comforts—a king-size bed obtained at a furniture closeout sale, and a thirteen-inch TV found in a closet that he'd pounded and shaken until it gave him enough picture to check on the news and the weather. His existence made Thoreau appear like the Hugh Hefner of his day.

Before he turned into something from the Ice Age, Blade directed his weary self into the pea-green bathroom in search of a revitalizing hot shower.

Minutes later, in the fifties-style white-and-black-tiled kitchen, he put on water for coffee. Dressed in worn jeans and a black sweatshirt, he dragged on boots, preparing to feed his raucous wake-up service. But as he approached the door, he locked gazes with the four-legged squatter who'd arrived between Thanksgiving and Christmas. Blade suspected people who expected Santa to bring them a cute, cuddly puppy had dumped the beast in the country.

The brindled behemoth was neither cute nor cuddly, and when it growled, it sounded like gargling. Glaring at him out of one topaz eye, it peered through the window of the kitchen door, then launched itself into the air, leaping onto the picnic table, causing the dilapidated remains of rotting redwood to groan as it teetered.

Issuing his own throaty response, Blade backtracked and hoisted the fifty-pound sack of dog food from the pantry. "Shit," he muttered at its depleted weight. It was only Wednesday and it was already half empty. He'd bought the stuff over the weekend.

As he emerged from the house, the dog greeted him by throwing back his basketball-size head and making another of those drowning growls. Then he shook his head, shooting mucus from his flapping jowls like skeet at a firing range.

Blade tried to duck behind the bag. "You ugly piece of—knock it off!"

Once the assault was over, he slammed the bag on the patio and folded back the top until the crunchy pellets were exposed. "There. The Four Seasons Special of the Day. Knock yourself out."

Circling to the back of the house, Blade opened the vinyl garbage can and picked up the other fifty-pound sack—almost as depleted—of birdseed and filled the two feeders at opposite sides of the unfenced yard. Returning to the kitchen, he gave the mutt a wide berth, but even with its head thrust inside the sack, the dog growled.

Once back in the kitchen, Blade removed the .9 mm stuck in the back of his jeans and set it on the counter. He hoped not to need the weapon out here— the animal seemed to be repaying his kindness by acting as a self-proclaimed security guard—but he wasn't big on trust. It was misplaced trust and bad judgment that had landed him here in the first place.

His coffee ready, he turned on the TV and sipped the scalding liquid while waiting for the static and snow to clear. As he eyed the date on the calendar, Blade realized yesterday had been a childhood friend's birthday.

"—We now join Troy Boreman at Longview High," the no-nonsense news anchor began. "Troy, what's the latest there? Have any of the students come forward to add new information on Stacie Holms?"

The reporter in the windbreaker shrunk deeper into his thin jacket. "Carmen, as you can imagine, students and staff remain in shock. These kids went home yesterday focused on their basketball team's division play-off chances, and possible spring break excursions for the seniors. This morning those same seniors have been hit with the tragic reality that one of their own will not be graduating with them in May.

"From those I've spoken to so far," the reporter continued, "eighteen-year-old Stacie Holms was a quiet girl who, while not part of the sports or academic scene, had a close circle of friends. We're hoping to speak with them later."

"Troy, are the police on the premises to ensure the students' safety, since we don't know why this terrible thing happened?"

"As you can see behind me, Carmen, police presence is strong—here for crowd control as much as for safety concerns. But as you know, the school already has a full-time member of the LPD based here, as does each of the middle schools—part of the department's proactive methods of law enforcement."

Nodding, Carmen murmured, "Good report, Troy. Keep in touch."

Blade switched off the TV and leaned back against the counter to finish his coffee, and to think. Ordinarily, he didn't pay much attention to the juvie stuff. Tough as this episode was, it didn't compare to the number of lives snuffed out daily where he came from due to poverty, drugs, gang activity and plain old domestic violence. Kids here tended to die from sports accidents or from reckless or drunken driving. And yet he had been aware of Stacie Holms and her group for a while now; in fact, he'd seen them earlier last evening.

The teens were memorable, what the good old boys called "show ponies"—miles of hair and makeup as expertly applied as any runway model's, their nubile bodies shown off to distraction by skin-tight jeans and T-shirts. The middle-class Four Musketeers were regulars at Point East, a pizza-and-pool joint off Highway 80 frequented by an older crowd. The girls' bravado and serious approach to the game of pool made them seem older, allowing the manager to give them an occasional break. They were good for business, inducing male customers to linger, which meant the booze flowed and the cash register sang.

Blade had been increasingly aware of them as the group's apparent leader, Ashley, started spending more time flirting with a piece of bad news on his list. Luckily, bartender-manager, Truitt Hurley chased the kids out by 11:00 p.m.—earlier if he caught them trying to steal or sneak the harder stuff. Last night they stayed on the restaurant side and left immediately after dinner. Blade figured they'd heard about the bad weather due in from Dallas and decided to play it smart and dash for home. Now he wondered.

By the time he rinsed the mug and reclaimed the sack of dog food from the homesteading mongrel, Blade knew what he needed to do. It was time to see what people at HQ were saying. Daylight, however, was no friend.

Lieutenant Scott McBrill, the District C night patrol watch commander, and his boss, would be long gone by now. Day Command was handled by District A on the north side of town. Blade didn't have much use for their lieutenant, aka Mr. Hollywood, but he doubted Ted Glass knew he existed. On the other hand, at 2:00 p.m. command transferred to District B in the heart of the city. That shift continued until 10:00 p.m. and was under Lieutenant Gene Poteet, who *did* know him and who saw Blade as a way to climb over McBrill promotion-wise. Blade would detour entire neighborhoods to stay out of Poteet's reach.

Everything in the LPD was portioned into threes. The three districts were also divided into three patrol beats: 10, 20, 30 for A, 40, 50, 60 for B, and 70, 80 and 90 for C. The theory was that neighborhoods should get to know the officers watching over them and vice versa. It was an inspiring and ambitious attempt to reestablish the nostalgia of the foot cop of days gone by. Blade supposed it was working in the outer neighborhoods fairly well, where some officers actually lived around the people they protected. But undercutting that were the major highways running through the south and east sides, bringing traffic that inevitably chiseled away at the community's stability.

Minutes later, he backed a dusty, two-tone brown pickup out from behind the detached garage. The rusting eighties-model Ford was his camouflage, so common in the rural south that it passed virtually unnoticed on the streets. Exactly what Blade wanted when he had to leave his hideout without the cover of darkness.

Fifteen minutes later, he pulled into the rear of District C station. Taking no chances, he passed empty spots near the doors and parked behind a couple of transport vans, opting for exercise and caution over convenience.

Like his truck, his clothes offered a chameleon's protection. Gone was the look-at-me leather jacket, the macho gold necklace and scuffed Tony Lamas. For this trip he wore his oldest jeans with the ragged hems, a plaid flannel shirt that had never seen an iron and that was left open over a ripped undershirt. Add the cheap athletic shoes, and he could pass for any poor yokel trying to figure out where the city had towed his wreck, or hoping a stolen trailer had, indeed, been found. With the excess gel showered away, his overgrown black hair fell low over his brow, another way to alter the shape of his face and avoid eye contact. Blade tried not to expose his eyes, aware their near aqua color were his most distinguishable feature; however, there were times when wearing shades drew more attention, and visiting a police station was one of them.

"Hey."

His gaze first locked on black leather loafers. Glancing up, he saw a pair of tan Dockers, a navy sports jacket with a matching tie over a blue shirt. He met the wary scrutiny of Detective Alan Lefevre. Fair-skinned and blond-haired, the cop always appeared slightly sickly under fluorescent lights. While no friend, Blade had helped him solve a few cases— a significant one only last month.

"Slow morning?" he replied. "You're usually out hustling by now."

"One of my cases is going to trial today," Lefevre replied.

"That explains the conservative attire." Usually a flashy dresser, today Lefevre could pass for a discount department store manager.

"The defendant is Sonny Lykstra, the asshole who raped and murdered his ex-girlfriend's daughter. I'm not taking any chances on this case. You got something for me?"

"When was I designated your personal bloodhound?"

"You said you had a lead on Longo."

Ferrell Longo was another rotten apple in a depressingly bottomless barrel. "His name has come up a few times. If the roach crosses my path, I'll step on him for you. I'm here to talk to Snow."

"He's out in the field."

Probably interviewing the Holms family, Blade guessed. Since the hallway remained empty, he lingered. "What's the consensus about the kid found shot last night?"

"They're looking for a boyfriend, though they haven't discounted an attempted carjacking. Depends what all comes up on the computer from the fingerprints lifted off the vehicle."

The rain would have hurt there, but forensics should have something from the interior already. Either Lefevre didn't know what or didn't care, not being the case detective.

"Stacie Holms had a record."

Although annoyed by the cop's smug expression, Blade encouraged him with a lift of his eyebrows.

"Let me think what they said in this morning's meeting…two misdemeanors and a felony. Shoplifting and vandalizing private property."

As bad as the shoplifting was, it didn't interest Blade. The vandalizing was another matter. He would bet anything it was the most recent charge; the question was, had it been a prank that got out of hand, or an escalation of violent tendencies? "How long ago?" he asked.

"I forget. Before Labor Day last year. My head is swimming with dates thanks to those goddamn lawyers. Snow did say the felony involved messing up some guy's boat." He snickered and his face grew flushed. "Little bitches must have downed a case of beer beforehand to do that kind of damage, if you catch my drift."

Blade figured he might eat something after leaving

here, so he chose not to ask for details. Still, stupid stunts were a far cry from murder.

A patrolman who used to work the night shift passed and shot him a condescending look. Blade decided it was time to move to a less-visible location. "Thanks for the update. If I can't see Snow, I've gotta find a lonesome computer."

As he began to pass, Lefevre asked, "Are you sure you don't have anything for me?"

"Let me use your machine for five minutes and I might remember something."

Lefevre swore. "You'd charge your own mother for toilet paper." But he gestured for Blade to enter his office.

By the time he closed the door, Blade was sitting behind the detective's desk and typing in Lefevre's password.

"Feel free to help yourself," the detective muttered.

"Just thought I'd save us both time."

"I'm gonna change my password and then you'll show more respect."

"I doubt it."

Lefevre pushed at a cuticle with his thumbnail. "Don't be too sure. Even you may find yourself needing backup one day."

"Not likely. Just tell the EMTs to bring an extra body bag."

The cop's taunting eyes lost their competitive gleam. "Doesn't anything hit a nerve, Blade?"

"Not anymore. Relax, Lefevre. That also means I don't have any plans to challenge you for lieutenant."

"Like you'd stand a chance."

Lefevre seemed buoyed by the reassurance, but already bored with the conversation, Blade was glad when the newest homicide file came up on the screen. "Stacie Rayann Holms. Born—an Aquarius. Figures."

"You believe in that crap?"

"Uh-uh."

"Then why did you—" The detective swore again. "You complain about wasting time. I don't know why I bother with you."

"Because having an extra pair of eyes and ears on the street pays off. Or have you convinced yourself that you found that murdering swine Pollard on your own?"

"Okay, okay. Why don't you find me the Brown brothers instead of sticking your nose in this," Lefevre said, nodding to the computer. "I suspect Snow will bring in her murderer before you hit the streets tonight."

Blade barely heard him; he was absorbing new data on the deceased. "This could be interesting…there's a father but no mother."

"So? Maybe she's dead."

Possibly. Knowing for sure would shed some light on the situation. For instance, her car wasn't something a father would buy a daughter when he was constantly being called down to the police station to pick her up. Had he been generous because she'd achieved good grades and had straightened up her act—at least at school—or was it to cover his own neglect? Or some abuse? The kid had managed to amass five speeding tickets since receiving the car, three of them remained unpaid. Blade didn't like the vibes that came along with this information.

He also learned a .380 casing had been removed from the car. The initial consensus was that Stacie had exhibited little resistance to her attacker, but the autopsy report would confirm or refute that. At the moment, though, it did suggest she had known her killer, which would encourage Snow to grill her family, as well as her closest circle of friends. Or, could be that she'd picked up someone else after she dropped off the other girls.

"Come on, Blade, give me a break," Lefevre said, checking his watch. "I'm due in court at one-thirty and I have to stop at the hospital for one of my own investigations, not to mention grab something to eat."

Deciding he had the few facts available at the moment, Blade exited the file and the program and thought about what lay ahead. The other three of the Four Musketeers' DNA had to be all over the car, making evidence analysis tedious for Forensics. And for Snow also, since it was logical to assume if Stacie had a record, they did, too. What a media field day this would turn into—kids who reject and rebel against society.

Preoccupied, he followed Lefevre out of the building. They were at the second set of glass exit doors when the detective suddenly swore, punched them open, and raced across the parking lot. As he slammed his hand on the Cody Security SUV, Blade ducked his head and quickly veered right until he was hidden behind a van.

Had he been spotted?

His concern proved unnecessary. Glancing around the van, he saw that Ms. Cody Security had her hands full with Lefevre.

"What're you doing here?" the detective demanded.

8

Nuts, Campbell thought. She'd known this trip would be risky, that's why she had arranged to wait out here. But to be caught so fast...

One of the few friends she had left in the LPD had been transferred to District C. Campbell hoped she could convince her to share what was known regarding Stacie Holms. She thought it would help her work with the Saunders family. Politics. Networking. She hated everything that stood for, but it was the technique du jour and it was her only other brainstorm since Bryce Tyndell remained WU like Maida— whereabouts unknown in Cody speak—having yet to show up at the office or to respond to her page.

She'd changed for this meeting thinking she would meet her friend at the mall, and wore the typical shopper attire—jeans, T-shirt and jogging shoes. Then she learned Taneeka's car was being serviced and she would have to pick her up at the station. Campbell had hoped to meet her in the back parking area where there were few windows and fewer vehicles, but it was impossible to hide her Cody Security vehicle—especially from someone like the cop charging across the parking lot.

"I said hold it!"

Intimidating as Lefevre's voice could be, it was the hard slap on the truck's hood that had Campbell hitting the brakes. With sickly certainty, she knew her streak of bad luck had yet to change.

Detective Alan Lefevre stepped over to the driver's window. All she knew of the big-boned and loud-mouthed detective was that he'd been Greg's distant relation through marriage. The scene he'd caused at Greg's funeral made him a permanent part of that bad dream. Of all the people to run into…

"I said, why are you here?" he demanded.

"That's none of your business."

"You? On these premises? Guess again."

She had a choice—create a bigger scene or cut her losses and opt for a hasty retreat. As loud as he was, if she drug this out, they were bound to attract an audience. Yet she didn't quit easily.

"I don't want any trouble. Five minutes is all I need."

"To do what? Everyone knows you have an ax to grind."

"If I did, I'd be at District B."

"We've had transfers and realignments, something I suspect you know."

She refused to respond to that. Getting a friend in trouble wasn't an option, and accepting that she'd made a mistake in coming here, she let off the brake and jammed her foot onto the accelerator.

The launch into street traffic was almost as unnerving as running into Lefevre, and she barely missed a FedEx truck while, in her rearview mirror, she saw smoke rising as a minivan struggled not to rear-end her.

"I'm sorry," she said, gripping the steering wheel. "I'm sorry!"

Damn Lefevre. How was she supposed to know he'd been transferred? What were the odds that he would be leaving the building as she was arriving?

9

As soon as the coast was clear, Blade joined Lefevre in the parking lot and asked, "What was that all about?"

"You tell me."

He wasn't admitting to anything until he had to. "What are you talking about?"

"I can't decide whether you were hoping she'd shoot me or if you were hiding from her."

Blade knew better than to respond to either part of that observation. "You know, the less I'm recognized around here the safer it is for everyone."

"It looked like you were hiding from *her.*"

"Never met her before. What's your beef with the woman anyway?" He knew Lefevre usually salivated over the long-legged type, and Ms. Cody Security had the figure to be a Las Vegas showgirl.

Beneath his neatly trimmed mustache, Lefevre's mouth twisted into a sneer. "Campbell Cody is poison. Got one of our guys killed—her partner. My wife's stepbrother. It happened a short while before you arrived, though people talk about it even today."

"Now that you mention it, I do remember hearing

something." But back then he'd been preoccupied with his own misery, and with learning a new job. What intrigued him was the intensity of Lefevre's anger. Maybe Campbell Cody deserved it, but for someone who didn't work too hard at hiding that he cheated on his wife, Alan Lefevre seemed somewhat overzealous. "So, she was a cop?"

"Please. More like a bitch with a gun. Greg found out the hard way."

"Her partner?"

"Yeah, Greg Gerrard."

"What happened?"

"She didn't watch his back when she should have. She turned chicken, that's what she did. Talks a tough game, but I wouldn't trust her to cover my ass against a toddler with a water pistol."

Blade thought about last night. She'd seemed pretty dedicated to him. "Why do you suppose she was here? If she knows she's not welcome, she took a big risk."

"I don't know, but I'm going to find out. Only—" he checked his watch and made a face "—not now."

"Yeah, I have to get moving, too."

"You owe me."

Lefevre pointed a finger at him as though punctuating the statement made it written in stone. Blade merely raised his hand, letting him wonder if the gesture signaled an agreement or farewell. It didn't matter; the detective was in his issued sedan and gunning the engine. Seconds later, with tires spinning on the still-damp asphalt, he pulled into traffic and sped away.

Grateful for the reprieve from the inquisition, Blade started for his truck, only to see a white SUV with a light bar on top pull around the corner of the building. Impressed with Campbell Cody's nerve, Blade ducked behind the van nearest his truck and watched her pause while a young African-American woman in uniform ran out of the building and got into her truck.

10

As the petite officer hurried around the front of the truck and climbed in on the passenger's side of the SUV, Campbell watched for onlookers. Visibility on this side of the building was minimal, but she thought she'd glimpsed movement by a van parked a few vehicles away. Right then a sheet of cardboard came tumbling across the asphalt and she decided it must have been debris tossed by the wind that spooked her. Even so, the instant she heard the passenger door slam she hit the accelerator.

"I thought I'd missed you." Taneeka Rawley shivered and stretched her hands toward the vents blowing warm air. She wore no jacket over her uniform, exposing her elegant neck and delicate ears to the bitter bite of the wind. "I saw Romeo confronting you and hoped you wouldn't be so rattled that you wouldn't circle the block and try again. That's why I didn't take time to dash back to my office and grab my jacket."

Campbell flipped the fan to high, then darted across traffic to head in the opposite direction of where Lefevre had gone. "Sorry about that." She remained shaken from the experience, and resentful that Lefevre thought he had a right to confront her. "I should have known that oversexed yahoo wasn't out doing what they pay him to do."

"At least his taste in his victims is improving," Taneeka said with a wicked grin. "I swear, I don't know how his wife stands him."

"Who knows that she does?" Campbell had met Beverly Lefevre once at a baby shower for another of Greg's relations. She wanted to believe the attractive and intelligent woman, who worked in a commercial bank's trust department, was too smart to be easily conned for too long. "Maybe she's the city's next time bomb. People like Lefevre always think they're immune from repercussions, especially when it comes to paying for their behavior."

"Campbell… I would have come to you sooner if you'd given the word. I do know where your office is."

Despite the gentle tone, Taneeka's words retained a rebuke for Campbell's self-isolation. She was one of the few who had the right. They'd met in college and had gone through the academy together.

"You don't need to be seen there any more than I needed to be spotted by someone from our old division," Campbell replied. "It's enough to have to drive this thing."

"Remember our first year on the force and the guy who asked if you were trying to be the Longview version of Dirty Harry?"

"Paulk. His glasses were so thick, I doubt he knew if he was watching Clint Eastwood or *Miami Vice*."

"But man, did he know the recipes for explosives. Scary. So where is that sexy car of yours?"

Campbell had a moment of nostalgia over the classic Shelby Mustang that she would wash and wax every week. "In California, or so I was told. I sold it to pay my legal fees. You never want to find out how much money it costs to stop people from trying to suck the last ounce of blood out of you."

"All the more reason for you to have called."

The soft words forced Campbell to take a breath to ease the tightening in her throat. People she would have bet the Shelby on for support had turned MIA faster than she could dial 911. But not Taneeka— Taneeka, who had her hands full with her family and paid her own price for being a solid friend.

Spotting something she didn't like, she made an abrupt turn at the first opportunity. "What I want is for you to make Internal Affairs someday and nail the Lefevres of the world to a wall."

"Consider it an IOU. So what's happened?"

This was why they had hit it off so well. Both valued action and getting results over brooding and bitterness. "I think a friend is missing," Campbell began. Careful to avoid prejudice or innuendo, she went on to explain last night's strange occurrences, all the while maneuvering through traffic.

It wasn't long before Taneeka was twisting in her seat. Only her seat belt kept her from doing a full ninety-degree turn, but she did manage to tuck a leg under the other. "Are you serious? Lightning? Girl, you are living under one dark cloud."

"Won't argue with you there." A cloud that had a wide reach. If life hadn't taken the nosedive it did, she would now be living in a four-bedroom house with a cheery yellow kitchen, a hot tub on the patio and perusing wallpaper books for the nursery. Or maybe not. At the end, all had not been bliss between her and Greg. The night he'd been killed, she'd stopped kidding herself and told him that they needed to have a serious talk.

"I know the story about Maida sounds vague and incidental," she said, forcing herself to get back on track. "But I swear she would have stopped and asked me for advice if she'd had some problem."

Taneeka nodded acceptance. "Then again, older folks can act pretty strange at times. My great-aunt and grandmother got into a shouting match last Sunday that had dogs three blocks away howling—at six in the morning. You know what it was about? A stupid shawl that showed up in the drawer under the one where Aunt Petty usually puts her scarves and stuff."

Campbell remembered other tales about the infamous Petty, named in error when her mother misspelled *Pretty* to the midwife filling out the birth certificate. "Sounds like you still have your hands full over there."

"Girl, the one thing worse than a house full of women is a house full of *southern* women."

Campbell enjoyed Taneeka's rich barbecue-sauce drawl, but knew there was a message under the humor. Jokes aside, she remained passionately protective of her family. "I hear you. My father said something similar about Maida. And I understand how subtle the early stages of dementia can be, but those conditions don't occur overnight. Not to this extent."

"Tell you what…as soon as I get back, I can check to see if she or her car shows up on the computer anywhere."

"Yancy has notified the state police. They'll put her license and plate number in the NCIC system. If there is anything, he should know by now."

"Good. So why am I here?"

Campbell dealt with an inner pinch. Her friend hadn't asked, "How can I help?"

"I'm glad to see you're still on top of your game." In school, one instructor had suggested that Taneeka consider a career in Vice because of her ability to follow the thinking patterns of the devious.

"Don't get me wrong. I understand you're concerned about a senior citizen under your care, who happens to be a friend. Now answer the question."

Campbell stopped for a traffic signal. "The Holms murder. The kid was a schoolmate of Debra Saunders, Maida's granddaughter."

"Why am I surprised? Were the girls close?"

"I'm trying to figure that out. I was at the Saunderses' house this morning to ask what they knew about Maida and I saw their kid learn about the shooting on TV. If they're not pals, they have to at least share a few of the same classes."

Taneeka's fine features hardened as she shifted into

her own no-nonsense mode. "You think there could be a connection because your friend and the Holms kid drove the same car?"

"Hey, I didn't say—" Campbell paused, hearing what fatigue and pain were doing to her control. "My goal is to find Maida alive and well sitting at a bus station or something. Troubling as that would be, I'd take it over any of the other options. What I was hoping you'd do is tell me what you have on the Holms case. I have to return to the Saunderses' and hopefully get them to let me into Maida's house."

"You don't want to do that."

"I feel if I can look around, I'll get a clue as to what happened."

Taneeka shot another studious glance her way. "You know it that well?"

"I'm over there at least once a week, so if you're worried about my DNA being left behind, it's too late." Maybe it was because she'd missed out knowing her grandparents, but she liked to help Maida with errands and projects, and to listen to her talk about her youth and her views on life in general. "I know what you're going to say—it's a pretty good guess that Dwayne Saunders is going to try to blame Cody Security for his mother's disappearance, making me the last person he'd want in her house. So tell me, how hard I can push back?"

"I don't follow," Taneeka replied.

"If it looks like the LPD will wrap up this case fast and no one else from the school is involved, I can appeal for the Saunderses' full attention. If they're pulled in two different directions because their daughter lost a close friend *and* the police are hounding her for information and possible leads, it's going to make my job even tougher.''

Tankeeka looked pensive. ''Please say you're not asking for—''

''No privileged information. Absolutely not.''

''Well, it'll be this evening or maybe even tomorrow before Detective Snow gives our shift the next briefing—unless he suddenly brings in someone. Don't you think Mr. Saunders will call the sheriff himself and then this will be out of your hands?''

''One would hope, only he didn't sound all that concerned to me when we spoke a while ago. Either way, I'm going to do what I can until I find her.''

''All right, I'm in, too,'' Taneeka replied. ''Hey, have you got a picture of her?''

''Down on the console.'' The wallet-size photo had an index card attached with some personal information on Maida.

''Aw,'' Taneeka said softly. ''She's sweet. She looks like she should be on a jar of pasta or something.''

''Make that chicken soup. She's half Jewish, on her mother's side. Her first husband was a Southern Baptist, though. Then twenty years ago, after his death, she married Arthur Livingstone. He passed four years ago.''

Taneeka read the data on the card. ''Well, you'd better drive me back. I'll see what I can do for you.''

Although grateful, Campbell took her indebtedness

seriously. "I know it's still early, but I was going to buy you lunch."

"Honey, I saw how you froze when we passed that patrol car a minute ago," Taneeka drawled. "And to be honest, I'd rather paint a bull's-eye on my back than be seen in this rolling advertisement for abuse. Let me take a rain check. And hopefully we'll have something to celebrate."

Relieved, Campbell cut a U-turn in a bank parking lot. "I like the sound of that."

The change of plans turned out to be a blessing. It was just as well that Campbell's offer for lunch didn't work out. Only minutes after saying goodbye to Taneeka, she heard her pager sound. She checked the display window and the brief surge of hope she'd felt after her visit with her friend vanished. Her father— sounding as serious as she'd ever heard him—was advising that he had news and didn't want to tell her over the radio or phone.

11

Campbell grabbed her phone and punched the number one on the keypad. As soon as she heard Yancy's voice, she asked, "What's happened?"

"You'd better get back here pronto."

"Hang the security concerns, what's going on?"

"Maida's Dwayne connected with Administration at Maple Trails," Yancy replied. "Unfortunately, he spoke with the wrong person, and when that ditz at the front desk said she didn't know anything about the situation with his mother, he blew a gasket. He's filing a complaint against us for not keeping them informed."

"Are we surprised?" However, Campbell was relieved that she'd left the voice messages for Bryce, despite not wanting to leave that kind of sensitive and worrisome information on a machine. "So where's Bryce?"

"Barbie said he's down inspecting the marina and the rest of the area. You know him, he'll leave us all hanging while he makes the village believe he's on top of things. Self-serving son of a—"

"I'm almost at the turnoff to go there. I'll see what

damage control I can do.'' Campbell didn't like the tension in her father's voice. With things going from bad to worse, they couldn't risk him having a relapse.

"I thought you *were* there."

"When I learned Bryce still hadn't arrived, I got another brainstorm and went to check into that."

"That's uncomfortably vague."

"It's the best I can do at the moment. Like you, this isn't something I want to discuss over the wires."

"How convenient."

It reassured Campbell to hear a bit of the grump return to Yancy's tone. "Would it help to know that I culled a resource?"

"It helps knowing you have any left."

"Try to lie down for an hour," she said as she entered the village. "I'll bring lunch as soon as I finish with Bryce."

When she pulled up to the booth, she greeted Kelsey with "I heard Bryce has arrived?"

Mischief lit the sunny blonde's eyes. "Prepare yourself. Mr. Executive is minus a tie for the first time that I can remember, and he's hiding those bedroombrown eyes behind the darkest shades. I'll bet you a bottle of tequila that he's got a hickey under that turtleneck."

There were too many Lefevres and Tyndells in the world for Campbell's taste. "Remind me to suggest we wear gloves from now on whenever going into the administration building."

"That's an idea that's bound to get you a standing ovation."

Campbell nodded to the fork in the road. "Last I heard, he was down by the marina."

"He's moved from there. During our last radio check the boys said he's schmoozing with the chairman of the Residents' Committee."

That would be Charles Denby, who also lived on the east side of the lake. "No doubt his house is one of those damaged." Campbell suspected his insider knowledge of the job list allowed him to be at the top of the repair schedule. "Thanks for the warning. I'd like the minimum audience possible."

"Interesting. Planning to go after a few jugulars?"

"Mostly in my mind. Barbie didn't relay my calls this morning regarding Maida. Maida's son now thinks we're trying to hide something and is filing a complaint citing negligence—which is just the kind of opportunity Tyndell is looking for to replace us."

"May all his children grow up to be rap enthusiasts."

The only thing that kept Campbell from smiling was thinking of Bryce as a father. "To add to the cheery atmosphere, we're trying to figure out whether or not he received my secondary emergency messages on his pager."

"Gotcha. You're saying staff needs to be aiming for sainthood at this point."

"Oh, at the least." Adding a droll salute, Campbell continued on.

Traffic remained light despite the approach of the lunch hour. Some residents were busy picking up debris, while others stood with neighbors, apparently discussing their night of interrupted rest. She waved frequently, but kept on course.

Bryce Tyndell's black Lexus stood where Kelsey said it would be—in Denby's driveway. Campbell pulled in and parked behind the glistening sedan, leaving just enough room for the GM of Maple Trails to maneuver around her—if he wanted to risk flattening Denby's pampered azaleas. She found Bryce and Charles in the back studying the torn deck awning. One glance told her it wouldn't be wise to ask why Charles hadn't rolled it up last night when the first storm warnings were announced.

"Ah. Here's our girl," Bryce said upon spotting her. "We thought you went home for a nap."

"Having been up for over twenty-four hours, who would blame me?" she replied in the same conversational tone. To Denby she added, "I'm sorry to see you caught a bad edge of that wind. Ike came by here after the worst of the storm passed and checked to make sure nothing inside was exposed to rain and that doors were secure. I suppose you were in another part of the house or back in bed by then."

The retired golf pro with the eternal tan responded with a diplomat's smoothness. "I saw someone out there. Bryce, did I mention seeing a guard? Remind me to note Security's diligence at our next meeting with management. Campbell, do tell your people we're grateful."

"I'll be happy to," she replied. "Are you aware your neighbors beyond the point were hit even harder? Have you inspected the area, Bryce? Aside from the phone messages, we left Barbie a report taped to the office door advising you of the need to call your contract people first thing. There are entire windows and doors blown out over there. We also reminded her to notify those living out of town so they can advise their insurance companies.''

Bryce adjusted his aviator sunglasses. ''As a matter of fact, I'm heading to that area next.''

On his way to daydreaming about managing a high-rise hotel in a happening town like Las Vegas or Los Angeles, Campbell wondered what it would take to make him admit where he was last night? ''There's more I need to go over with you. Maybe my direct messages didn't get through?''

He made a show of pulling his pager off his belt. ''It seems to be working.''

Campbell was willing to allow him to save face in front of Denby, but not at the expense of the company. ''If you're finished here, I could fill you in as we move on?''

''You're the boss.'' While he shook hands with Charles Denby, his smile was stiff. ''We'll get this cleaned up in no time. Let me know if you're not satisfied with the results.''

Once out of earshot, Bryce said to her, ''Please don't do that again.''

''What? Refuse to let you make Cody Security look incompetent to cover your own negligence?''

''That's a strong term for what happened. I swear I haven't received any messages.''

He sounded sincere enough, but Campbell had seen

him burn Cody people before. "Management never gets to play victim, Bryce. Switch phone systems—or Barbies. I do not know what's going on in your life, nor do I care, but you will not save your reputation at the expense of ours. Trust me, we can document everything that happened last night. Can you?"

Suddenly he looked as if he wanted to hurt something. Campbell hoped he was smart enough to aim his temper at his Lexus.

Surprisingly, as quickly as the anger appeared, it vanished. "Tell me about your biggest problem. The resident you called Barbara about—"

"I called *you*. And the lady's name is Maida Livingstone. She lives at 577 Dogwood Lane and last night she raced out of here faster than you can think of a reason why she should have."

"Why didn't you call the sheriff right then?"

Because she'd had the lightning encounter. Because she knew how overwhelmed they would be from problems due to the storm and how they would treat a "what if?" call like that—all reasons her father echoed. Because she'd panicked and dashed to the hospital to check on that shooting victim she'd heard about on the police scanner. Because Yancy had convinced her that she was nuts and that Maida would return and explain all. None of this was anything she wanted to go over again with Bryce.

"This isn't a prison, it's not a mental institution," she said with the same give-nothing-away expression she would use with a reporter. "People have the right to leave, even at an unusual hour, even in a manner we might not like.''

Bryce drew his well-formed upper lip between his teeth. ''All right. What do you recommend we do?''

''I'd like you to call Dwayne Saunders and assure him that we have contacted the sheriff. She and her car are already on the NCIC system.''

''That's it?''

''We've made some other calls.''

''To whom?''

''The day you give me your networking list, I'll give you mine. What you can assure Mr. Saunders of is that when the car has been spotted anywhere, we'll hear about it. Also, we'll know of any admissions to the hospital.''

''Okay. So our ass is covered. What else are you leading to?''

Campbell knew she had to ask, although he wasn't in the right mood to hear the question. ''I'd like to check inside her house.''

''No. Absolutely not. If her car was on the premises, that would be different, but we're not going to risk setting off her son any more than he already is.''

Campbell knew not to argue at this stage. ''Then I'll follow you up the road to look at the other residences and reset alarms if necessary.''

''Thank you. I appreciate you staying beyond your shift. You do look tired.''

''I'll head for home as soon as I'm assured things are as set here as they can be.''

That unfailing politeness was their code for the

next hour. By the time Campbell returned to the front gate, she was operating on automatic pilot.

"What a morning," she said, entering the gatehouse. She needed to make a photocopy of her notes for Kelsey and the front office.

Kelsey rose from behind the desk. "I've got one more headache for you, or rather for Maintenance. Bobby Waldrop located a big branch down on the service road behind Dogwood Lane."

The street name won Campbell's full attention and she frowned at the sheet. "I was there earlier. I didn't see anything like that."

"It's about four houses up from Maida's place. Here's the map he drew. It wouldn't have been visible from where you were due to the curve in the road and the privacy fence the Leytons put up last summer. Bobby was able to push the limb aside to give access if there's an emergency. The bad news is the limb apparently clipped the back fence as it fell."

That was definitely bad news. The perimeter fence also provided privacy as well as security, because the county road was not fifty feet beyond it. "I'm going to bypass Barbie and go directly to Maintenance with this," Campbell said. "That repair has to be given as much priority as anything else. Once word gets around that we don't know where Maida is, the folks in that area are going to get nervous. Having a gaping hole in the security fence isn't going to reassure them."

12

Blade's eyes burned from the fluorescent lighting as much as from fatigue, and although he'd only had two beers—and had nursed the hell out of each over the last few hours—his head pounded as though he'd spent the night lying under a keg's wide-open spout. Come on, he thought, staring into the back of the guy bent over the pool table preparing for a shot. Point East would be closing in another fifteen minutes. The waitress had just announced "Last call." The faster he made his move, the sooner the game would be over. At this point Blade didn't care if he won the third twenty-dollar bill at the end of the table or not. Tonight, his idea of winning was to get outside where he could make another call without anyone seeing him do it, and before the person he was really inter-ested in moved on.

"Hey, John. Did you hear about what happened

last night? I mean about the little blonde who hung out here with her friends?''

Keeping his expression bored, Blade glanced at the waitress who'd finished taking orders and paused before returning to the bar. Her name was Deirdre and she cleaned up in tips due to her low-cut tops, as much as for her efficiency. ''Can't hardly miss it. It's all that's on TV.''

''Yeah, and the radio. Tough break, though. I told Truitt nothing good would come of letting those kids in here.''

Allowing limited concern into his expression, Blade replied, ''Hurley's not getting hassled by the cops, is he? I can't see any connection.''

''Maybe I'm worrying over nothing, but if the girls tell the police where they all were last night, he could catch hell.''

Blade frowned as he watched his challenger check the shot from yet another angle. ''So, they say they came here for a pizza. That's not illegal. Sure, they try to mooch a drink once in a while. Tell me what kid doesn't at their age? It's not like Hurley didn't threaten to evict them if they didn't knock it off.''

''What if someone from here killed her? I heard one of them who bummed a cigarette from a guy say she wished it was something better. Do you think they were hustling elsewhere and got in over their heads?'' Deirdre asked.

''They wouldn't be the first. Listen, I drive trucks and hustle a game of pool once in a while, I don't figure odds or try to rationalize kids, let alone aspiring junkies. I do know no one gets shot over a smoke.''

Deirdre sighed. ''What kind of parents let their babies out at all hours of the night like that?''

Every variety, Blade thought, including some who worked sixty- or seventy-hour weeks. He nodded toward the bar. ''Hurley's signaling you.''

The brunette sighed. ''Sure I can't get you a last brew, John?''

Even after a year, the name he used for this work sounded strange—John Blake. But it was blander than his own name, and the majority of people forgot it as soon as they heard it.

''No, thanks. I've got to pick up a rig in Dallas tomorrow.''

''Drive safe, Blue Eyes.''

Winking, she flicked her dark braid over her shoulder and left. It wasn't a serious flirtation; Deirdre was nuts about her Gulf War-vet husband. To keep the family afloat while they battled to get him treatment for post-traumatic stress disorder, she worked at what paid best. But seeing that braid had Blade's thoughts drifting to someone else with even longer hair and legs like nobody's business. Glancing up, he rested his gaze on a drug courier sitting at the darkest end of the bar.

Hustling the new waitress, the guy was getting the hint she didn't like him. Unless he came up with six winning lottery numbers, Hurley was bound to suggest he move on. Considering the hour, Blade figured the guy was heading for either Texarkana or Dallas, destinations cleverly achieved by using back roads if avoiding the law was the goal.

Blade couldn't afford to botch his timing. Whatever was at stake was probably nothing close to a record shipment—the courier didn't act urgent enough. But it would help ease his grim mood over not having gleaned any new information about the teen murder by stopping a few hundred pounds of marijuana, and who knew what else, from getting to the street.

Switching his attention back to his pool partner, he saw the poor slug had yet to shoot. "Hell—" he replaced his cue stick "—put us both out of our misery, take the money and spend it on a how-to book."

The man glanced up, confused. "Huh?"

He'd disliked his slack-jawed, lizard-slim opponent on sight, and marked him as a genuine redneck. Lizard had spit his chew into an empty drink glass shortly upon arrival and after four beers hadn't improved on his manners or his conversation. Blade imagined him with a pregnant girlfriend waiting up for him at some trailer, and an ex-wife wanting his ass in jail for being a deadbeat dad. The only reason Blade had accepted the match was because Point East was empty tonight and he'd needed an excuse to hang around.

Missing the shot, Lizard snapped, "Fuck. Hey, that's your fault!"

Deciding the man was even too stupid to accept a gift when he saw it, he set his unfinished beer on the nearest table. "Sure it is. And I'm the guy who said 'No thanks' to your mother the night she made you."

He'd had enough and walked out of the grill, merely nodding to Hurley and Deirdre. In the near-empty parking lot he dug for his keys, noting again how bad news had affected business at the bar. Nevertheless, it worked in his favor, as he determined he wasn't being watched.

As soon as he started the El Camino he drove across the street to the convenience store and called the number issued to him earlier.

Then he waited...two minutes stretched into four. When the courier emerged from the grill, Blade cursed himself for not breaking one of the taillights on the white service van with the vague electrical contractor logo on the door. At least that could be an excuse for police to pull him over elsewhere.

Just as he accepted that tonight's team had dropped the ball, three squad cars pulled into the lot, followed by an unmarked car and surrounded the van. Seeing Lefevre emerge from his car, Blade started the El Camino and drove away.

It would be a long night for the detective after a long day in court, but he didn't feel sorry for him. Lefevre would be the one slapped on the back tomorrow. Blade's work would remain unknown to the majority of the force. That's the way it had to be, and that's the way he wanted it. Once he'd been the one cheered, but he'd learned the hard way, it just made the descent to reality a harder one.

To keep from sliding into a full-fledged pity party, he let himself think of a smoky-eyed woman...and this time when he imagined her there was no fear in her eyes.

13

The ringing might as well have been a sonic boom in an eggshell. Campbell almost fell out of bed grabbing for the phone and gasping "Hello!" before her brain registered where she was, who she was, or what day and time she'd reentered consciousness.

"You'd better come in."

"Dad." No other voice could ground her faster. In the same instant that she checked her alarm clock and the watch lying beside it on the night table, her mind was assimilating and shifting toward worst-case scenarios. That wasn't paranoia; she knew her father would never wake her unless it was bad news. "What's happened?"

"Sorry, Belle. Time to get strong again."

Shit. She took a quick breath and quickly purged it. It was a technique he'd taught her years ago, similar to the one recommended for surviving a heart attack. "I'm ready."

"I'd prefer to wait till you're here."

"Tell me."

"A vehicle has been located," Yancy said reluctantly.

A part of her had expected this news, but Campbell dealt with the jarring results, anyway. "Maida."

"It appears she drove off the road and into the woods. A trucker broke down. He's the one who spotted her. I'm sorry."

A part of her noted that neither of them said the word *dead.* Then she was on her feet. "I'll be ready to roll in ten minutes."

It took her several more, but she was wholly focused when she pulled the Blazer into the street and keyed her radio. "Cody Two to Cody One. Are you there?"

Her father came on immediately. "Cody One. Coffee's on."

"Tell me where they found her."

There was a pause, a click, and then Yancy said, "Come home. There's nothing for you to see out there."

"Give me the address or I'll call the sheriff for directions."

"You would."

"Damn straight."

Listening to his directions, she recognized the farm-to-market road a few miles north and had to deal with a new wave of disbelief. "Are they sure it's her? There's nothing up there that she would be interested in. No reason—"

"Belle, listen to me. They must have removed the body by now and have it in transit to Dallas."

The body. It. Although the heater had started blowing warm air, Campbell shivered, certain she would never feel warm again. "I'm going. I have to. Don't worry, I'll be back with you ASAP. Radio's on."

Her father was right, though; by the time Campbell arrived at the scene only two vehicles remained, one a deputy patrol car, and the other an unmarked SUV down by the site. It was a good guess that the SUV was Gregg County's forensic specialist.

The sun was easing above the pines in the cloudless sky as she emerged from her own vehicle. It was going to be a gorgeous, if crisp day, the kind Maida would have adored.

Grimly, she showed her ID to the deputy. "Mrs. Livingstone lived in Maple Trails. Can you tell me who's in charge down there?"

"Detective Chuck Archer, Gregg County. I'm not sure he wants anyone in there yet, ma'am."

"I'll be mindful of that and back off if he says so, but I do need to ask him a few questions."

With a polite nod to the pink-cheeked deputy, Campbell eased down the grass-covered slope, mindful that the morning dew and rain-soaked red clay would make things slick. The detective was working out of the back of his black Chevy Suburban, leaning over his toolbox-style case. His back was turned to her and the bright yellow Gregg County Sheriff's Dept. logo on his navy-blue windbreaker was impossible to miss, even from the road. As she drew closer, she noted he was of average height and build, though his strong legs—encased in black jeans—were on the short side, giving him a stocky look. Not surprisingly, his hair, a shade darker than hers with ash tones, was cropped short. The grim fact was that just as his jeans were meant to hide any signs of a messy crime scene, anything that got on his skin or hair could quickly be showered off.

Moistening her dry lips, Campbell hoped she wasn't going to be instantly rejected by Chuck Archer. "Detective? I'm Campbell Cody, Cody Security. Mrs. Livingstone lived in—"

"I know."

Turning, the square-faced man with calm, expose-nothing hazel eyes considered her from behind steel-framed glasses. They, as much as his expression, added to his aura of maturity, but gauging the lack of wrinkles, Campbell guessed him to be on the south side of forty.

"What can I do for you?"

While it was probably science, not manners, that kept him from extending his latex-gloved hand, Campbell looked for any sign of rejection and sensed none. "Maida was also a friend. Can you share anything about what happened here?"

"I read the report your office faxed to ours." Shifting, he pointed back out of the brush and diagonally southeast. "From what I can tell so far, she went off the road over there."

Campbell had noticed the orange police ribbons

upon driving up. Interestingly, the ground was barely disturbed until the woods, though the rain could have covered a good deal of that. "I didn't spot skid marks on the asphalt."

Nodding in approval like a school instructor, he gestured toward the driver's side of the car. "All right. Come and see this. Maybe you can offer an opinion."

Grateful to have passed his first unacknowledged test, Campbell was careful to stay in his tracks, certain that he would be grading her on that, too. He stopped approximately two yards from the vehicle and leaned down to point into the interior, specifically at the floorboard.

"See the debris around the accelerator foot plate?"

"It looks like a crumbling brick."

"That's not exactly natural to this environment, is it?" His dry response was reflected in a brief glance of their surroundings.

Campbell could feel her blood pressure crank up a notch. "Are you asking if it could have come from the bottom of her shoe? She uses bricks to edge her rose garden in her backyard, and she wears somewhat thick-soled Sas shoes because she has sensitive feet. But she's meticulous, Detective. She wouldn't use broken bricks, and she wouldn't bring this much debris into her car."

"Thanks. That's good."

But he sounded more troubled than pleased with the new information, and that increased Campbell's unease as she followed him back to his Suburban. "I mean it. Maida is a white-glove housekeeper."

He picked up his clipboard and reached into his windbreaker for a pen. "A regular neatnik, huh?"

"Exactly. As a rule, the floorboard of her car was as spotless as her kitchen. I'm not discounting the weather, but she kept her vehicle in the garage, making it unlikely that it would have that mess in there."

Archer finished jotting down some notes before speaking again. "On the other hand, you said in your report that she left Maple Trails in a clear state of distress."

"That's true," she replied, unhappy with the conflict in her own testimony.

"Could she have gone out back before she got into the car?"

"I suppose. There's a ceramic figurine broken on her patio. I guessed it was damaged during a wind gust."

Archer wrote more notes. "What about inside the house?"

Campbell had to shrug. "I don't know. I haven't been there yet."

He glanced up. "You're the bonded security firm for the property. You have access."

"Only in cases of extreme emergency. Administration keeps a set of keys locked in their safe." Because she felt he was being up front with her, she decided to tell him the rest. "In Maida's case, I happen to have a personal key. As I said, we're friends." Her voice cracked and she had to clear her throat as she dealt with a new rush of emotion. "Sorry. I help her out with chores that are too strenuous or technical for her."

That seemed to surprise the detective, and Archer subtly lifted his eyebrows as though he wasn't certain he'd heard correctly. "My data indicates she has family." He flipped back a few pages. "Quite close."

"Dwayne Saunders, yes. He's an only child from her first marriage. He's married with a son and daughter. Unfortunately, theirs is no longer the most harmonious of relationships."

Archer glanced back up to the road. "It isn't possible she was headed to her son's place and got confused during the storm and took a wrong turn?"

"I'd hoped myself that she was there. She isn't in love with Dwayne's wife, but she tries to maintain a relationship with her son and grandchildren." Campbell told him about her trip there.

"Hmm. Rough day for all of you." Archer's shrewd gaze held hers. "But you must be able to understand how the Saunderses are somewhat resentful of you?"

"They shouldn't be. It's not like I was taking anything from them. In fact, in a way, I was doing tasks Dwayne should be handling."

"It wouldn't be the first time someone resented another person for doing the right thing and making them look bad. Are you in her will?" he added casually.

The question stunned and angered her. "Of course not. Well, I've never seen it, but I'm sure I'm not. I wouldn't even take money from her when she tried to pay me for my time."

"Fine. So am I going to find any of your DNA in the house?"

Campbell was beginning to regret coming out here. "It's likely, although Monday is her serious cleaning day. I was last there Saturday to replace her garbage disposal."

Chuck Archer rubbed at his jaw with his sleeve. "Do you give home improvement lessons? My wife is challenged by the dryer's lint trap. Okay—" he scanned his notes "—if you'd draft me a sketch of the rooms you've been in, I'd appreciate it."

"As soon as I return to headquarters. I'm officially off duty until Saturday, but we're shorthanded, so I'm filling in wherever necessary. When do you think you'll be going over to her house?" She knew better than to ask if he was coming to the conclusion that this was a crime scene. Even if he believed they were dealing with a heart attack or some other physiological impairment, he would continue to treat this situation carefully until the autopsy proved otherwise.

"I have to get all of these samples logged and meet with the sheriff, who's probably still with the Saunderses. Would you be available to answer more questions later this afternoon?"

"Absolutely."

The detective glanced toward the road again. "We're fortunate that the trucker had the breakdown where he did. As quiet as it is on this road, it could have been days before she was spotted in here…not that that made any difference in her chances of survival.''

Campbell appreciated the opening—but also dreaded it. "Are you saying she died upon impact?" She gestured toward the car. "The air bag deployed.''

"But when? It could have happened after the crash due to some malfunction. And she wasn't wearing a seat belt.''

"She wasn't?" Frowning, Campbell tried to remember those brief seconds when Maida raced by. "It was raining so hard, I can't say with full certainty, but she was good about fastening it.''

"That again speaks to her distressed state.''

It did, and Campbell hated to think what her friend had endured during those last moments. She allowed frustration to replace her pain. "Dammit, why? What happened?" She told Archer about Maida's aversion to driving after dark.

"The toxicology report should help us there. I understand she took several prescription drugs.''

"The usual for her age—high blood pressure, cholesterol, osteoporosis.'' That was in her report, too, and while it needed to be shared, what if it took Archer's attention off of other possibilities? "Are there only her prints in the vehicle? There should be. As little as she drove, the car hadn't needed servicing in a while, not since…before Thanksgiving, I believe.''

"You didn't drive it? No one else? Maybe to just move it for her? Carry in her groceries?''

The casual question didn't fool her; she recognized interrogation when she heard it. She'd endured day after day of it in the weeks following Greg's death. But the grim speculation in Archer's eyes had her shivering from an internal cold that had nothing to do with the weather.

"Oh, God…you believe she was murdered!"

14

"That's nuts," Yancy snapped as Campbell paced around his office.

"I'm telling you what I saw in his eyes. Add it to the questions he asked, the way he asked them, and you know I'm right." Miserable and sick to her stomach, she wrapped her arms tighter around her waist. "Maida was murdered and Chuck Archer has me on his list as a potential suspect."

"You were on duty. Ike can confirm that."

"Ike is on our payroll. They could say he's being bribed to protect his job. No one else saw me that night until I arrived at the hospital. Besides that, my DNA is all over her house. And you know procedure."

Yancy pushed away the work sheet he'd been working on—a quote for a potential customer. Then he rubbed his hands over his face. "That's right, I do, so don't make more of this than it is—a temporary inconvenience. Between your heartache and getting injured yourself yesterday, I think you're forgetting that."

"Don't tell me I'm not thinking clearly. I'm thirty-two, not twelve, and I have my own share of training."

Sighing, Yancy reached for the intercom button. "Beth, get me Sheriff Glazer on the phone, would you?"

"Right away, boss."

Sitting back in his chair, Yancy met Campbell's challenging gaze. "Let's hear what he has to say."

"If Chuck Archer wasn't willing to tell me about Maida's condition when they found her, or what he found in the car, Chris Glazer isn't going to tell you. Prepare yourself, they're going to lock us out of the house."

Yancy looked as if he wanted to throw one of his memorable fits. "Tyndell will enjoy that."

Bryce had shifted to the bottom of Campbell's list of concerns. "I just want to find out what Maida experienced and endured in her last hours. I think we have a right to know what to be watching for if this is a homicide."

"And to make adjustments."

Campbell shot her father a contentious glance. "We did not err last night, and I'm not out of control."

"You're a newspaper article away from going back into the nosedive you were in fourteen months ago."

It took all her self-control not to walk out. Campbell hated that the people who should know her best were the most clueless. Maybe she wasn't born with the duck feathers her father had that allowed him to walk away more easily from emotional situations, but she knew her core strength.

Just then, Beth came on the intercom. "The sheriff is tied up right now, sir. He'll call you back."

"Thanks," Yancy said, and disconnected. The curse that followed could have stripped paint off the wall.

For her part, Campbell was dealing with mixed feelings, the satisfaction of having your hunches proved right, yet realizing those in your circle of trust had grown smaller in number. "Call Tyndell," she said. "Let him know we're aware Detective Archer will be arriving with a warrant."

"Will do. Don't even ask to be there."

Strangely rejuvenated, Campbell tossed her braid over her shoulder. "Tough. Not only would it be more conspicuous for us not to be present—particularly after asking me to make myself available—I want to see his face even if he isn't willing to tell us anything. He needs to know we have to give answers to residents, too."

She didn't get a reply. The phone rang and Beth warned that Patsy Saunders was on the line. Yancy hit the intercom button.

"Mrs. Saunders, my condolences."

"I want answers, Mr. Cody. The family is one step away from hiring an attorney."

He met Campbell's disgusted look. "For what reason, ma'am? We've reported everything we know to you."

"Somehow I doubt that. Let me make myself clear.

I intend to get into Maida's house this afternoon to rescue family heirlooms before they are stolen from us, like she was.''

If not for Yancy's signal, Campbell would have come out of her chair and told Patsy what she could do with her accusations and shortcut conclusions. "Ma'am, your husband will be informed of his rights, but we'll pass on your comments to the sheriff and Mr. Tyndell. I'm sure both will be impressed with your priorities.''

The slam of the phone on the other end of the line provided some satisfaction to Campbell.

"You think she's pissed?" Yancy asked with feigned innocence.

"You should meet her. Think angel cake laced with battery acid.'' But Campbell's amusement was short-lived as she thought of the inevitable. "We're going to have the media at our gates. No way can we handle that.''

"That's been on my mind, too. One thing for sure, we're taking you off your post. You can switch with one of the others.''

For once, Campbell didn't argue. The less exposure she had from the press, the better. "Thank goodness we've finally got some new people starting training. I can easily take over that responsibility.''

Yancy looked doubtful. "You know we give the recruits plenty of exposure. I'd rather you stay way out of sight.''

The intercom buzzed again and her father leaned forward to speak to Beth. "Yes?''

"Mr. Tyndell on three."

"Got it." Yancy punched the blinking button and put it on the speaker phone. "Bryce?"

"My phones are going nuts, Yancy. Worse, I've just had a royal ass-chewing by Mrs. Saunders."

"Then you know I only hung up with her a minute ago." Yancy winked at Campbell.

"I do. She's not happy," the general manager replied stiffly.

"That's a relief. It would be disturbing if she was."

"Let's keep the sarcasm to a minimum, shall we? And move things along. Mrs. Saunders wants to inspect Maida's house."

"You mean Mrs. Livingstone's house?" Yancy sat forward and stared into Campbell's eyes as though he was looking across the desk at Bryce. "Inspect, my ass. Do you know why I miss the old days, son? Because a pirate didn't call himself—or in this case *herself*—an environmental excavator."

Bryce cleared his throat. "How about we stay in this century? Personally, I believe she has the right. Mrs. Saunders has informed me that Mrs. Livingstone drove off the road and was killed when her vehicle struck a tree. That sounds pretty clear cut to me."

"Then I suggest you phone Sheriff Glazer," Yancy countered. "You'll learn all of us have to stay out of the place. His forensics specialist is due at the residence anytime now. We'll have to go by his directions regarding access."

"Why? It's not a crime scene."

Campbell signaled her father to caution him in his

reply. It wasn't their place to send out alarms. Besides, doing so would just make Detective Archer's job tougher, and they needed to think themselves as an extension of his team.

"Precautions are standard until after the autopsy."

He sounded almost bored and Bryce bought it. He uttered an impatient sigh.

"That's nuts. It's not as though we don't have Mrs. Saunders available to give us her prints at any time."

"You mean tie up the computers to run the whole process again? There's a smart way to spend county funds."

"Obviously, I'm unaware of procedure. What do you advise, Yancy?" Bryce asked with studied calm.

"We wait until they tell us what the verdict is. I don't like it any more than you do, but that's the way it is."

Bryce cleared his throat again. "Listen, this agent—"

"Detective Chris Archer."

"He's not going to put that yellow tape across the doors and such, is he? We can't have that. Before you know it, we'll have a convoy of ambulances rolling in here to haul off cardiac cases."

"Then prepare yourself. What we can do is put an extra person on the night shift for a day or two. That should reassure people."

"One isn't much under the circumstances."

"It's your budget to break."

"Keep me informed."

Bryce disconnected and Yancy smirked. "Notice

how fast he stopped worrying about what Patsy might say?''

''I didn't have time. I was too busy wondering who the heck you're assigning to that shift tonight.''

''I'll take it,'' Yancy said.

''Sure you will. Right after you call Cheralyn to apologize for behaving like an oaf and ask her out to dinner,'' Campbell replied.

Not surprisingly, Yancy took offense. ''Don't be ridiculous. Even if that was a good idea—and I'm conceding nothing—your timing stinks.''

Hardly intimidated, Campbell followed him when he shot up from his chair and strode to their meeting room where he stopped before the large schedule board on the wall. She knew he was pretending to study it to see if there was anyone who could fill the position, but she also knew he had the thing memorized.

Yancy pointed with his thumb toward the Disabled list. ''I'll call Doug. He can take the gatehouse and Howie can move to patrol.''

''Brilliant idea. Push a guy with walking pneumonia into working against doctor's orders. You don't think we have enough trouble aimed at us?''

''Hell, the building is heated.''

''He's on strong medication and he'll be dealing with the press trying to sneak by him or pump him for information. What if the meds get the best of him and someone takes a photo of our security guard passed out in a chair looking as if he'd had a six-pack too many? I'll take the shift,'' Campbell said, studying the chart herself.

''You're way too overexposed as it is. We could get into trouble with our insurer.''

''Give me a break. Look, we both respect the rules, but we're one step away from leaving the residents vulnerable. That's unacceptable to me. If it'll make you feel better, have Beth call one of the new people with the best clearance report and see if they're available to start training tonight. I'll use the shift to familiarize him, or her, with the place. Think about it. It'll be a freebie for management, and it'll look good to the residents, not to mention intimidate the press. Bryce will be thrilled.''

''How much sleep did you get last night, let alone in the last thirty-six hours? You're in no shape for that, even if you were able to move your left arm normally.''

Although he exhibited the body language of censure, Yancy's gray eyes were starting to gleam, which told Campbell he was warming to her idea. ''Big deal, I'm not a southpaw in a series game.''

Her father smiled. ''No, but you'd finish making yourself lame to prove me wrong.''

She placed a hand on his shoulder. ''There's no time for this. I'll be fine. Maida won't. And my heart hurts, Dad, far more than the rest of me. It would be a kindness to let me stay busy so I could forget how much.''

''Belle.'' Briefly, her father touched her hair.

"Maida was nothing like your mother. I'll never understand your strong attraction to her."

The comment left Campbell bemused. "I never thought them as similar. Maida was a character. Maybe I see myself as one, too."

"Forget it. You're conventional through and through."

Campbell knew he meant it as a compliment; nevertheless, the observation stung. "I hope I have the intelligence and backbone to stand up to the majority even if I'm the only voice in a crowd."

Her father's wan smile extinguished just as their conversation had.

"Say we try a half shift," he said, moving around a line of chrome-armed chairs to the Wall of Honor, where pictures of Cody Security staff, recognized for achievement in security, were hung. "Surely the local media isn't up to covering this 24/7?"

"No, their budgets won't allow it. But there's always the mustang reporter. And if the national networks consider this a filler in a quiet week—"

"What if things get more complicated yet?" This time Yancy framed her face with his hands. "I need you strong, kid."

Campbell could only blink her understanding and acceptance. She already knew something had drawn her friend out into the night, into conditions anyone would find terrifying. She wouldn't rest until she understood why.

15

Maple Trails
2:06 p.m.

Once Campbell knew who was scheduled to begin training that night, she drove to Maple Trails to check on the latest condition of their working environment. After navigating around two trailers and several vans with press logos, she determined that things were going to be every bit as tough as she feared. And it was still early.

"Coffee, tea or stun gun?" Kelsey asked when she entered the gatehouse.

"That tells me not to ask how many have tried to sneak past you."

Despite the challenges, Kelsey seemed eager for the next confrontation.

"It'll get worse," Campbell said, no longer confident in her own perceptions.

"Take a deep breath. It has. The fence on Maida's service road that was damaged in the storm?" Kelsey said, indicating her checklist. "It's still down. Maintenance hopes to have it repaired by sunset."

"That's critical, but believe me, there's worse." Campbell lowered her sunglasses. "Let's just hope our friends outside don't have the ability to listen in on this and get it on the five o'clock news—complete with pictures. All right, why are you fidgeting more than usual?"

Kelsey turned her back to the sliding glass door that exposed them to the entryway. "Brad in Maintenance shared this with me before heading off to lunch and a run for supplies. He's a real hard worker. I don't want him to get into trouble."

"Kels, get to the point."

"That fence over by Maida's? It wasn't downed by any limb. Someone took a crowbar to it."

As soon as she heard that, Campbell eased Kelsey away from the door and out of sight from any super lenses. "He's certain?"

"There are notches in the wood—and the nails…he said something about how they shouldn't be straight if the tree did the damage."

Campbell was starting to feel ill all over again. "Why didn't you call the office?"

"Because by the time traffic cleared again, you drove up. Brad wanted us to know they're so tied up with their A-list of repairs, they're thinking it will be midnight before they can risk quitting tonight."

"I'm glad they're putting residents' safety first. When do you expect him back? I need to talk to him and whoever else was at that spot."

"I already told you what he said."

"Yes, but I want to know everything he saw."

Their radios crackled as one of the other guards tried to call in and then apparently changed his mind. Kelsey dropped her hand from her shoulder mike and continued, "It all depends on the size of his list. I'm guessing a good ninety minutes or two hours before he gets back."

Too long. Campbell needed specifics and that information couldn't wait. "Tell me you thought to ask him how he knew it was a crowbar and not just a chunk of wood or whatever was handy?"

"He said the indentations were a perfect fit to the type he had in his truck. And there's also paint residue left on the wood."

"What color paint?"

"Fluorescent orange."

"Well done. What about that limb in the road?"

Kelsey shrugged. "Divine assistance?"

Unnatural, maybe, but certainly not divine, Campbell thought grimly. "Have any of the residents in that area phoned in to report anything?"

"Not a one." Kelsey referred to her notes. "The Fredericks are in Denver—their daughter is due to give birth to twins. The Hassetts are in Dallas for a few days. Mr. H. is undergoing medical tests."

These people would have been in the most likely position to witness anything unusual in their vicinity despite their privacy fences, since both houses were two stories. "Are the alarms set and working at each address?"

Kelsey gave her a funny look. "No alarms have been set off."

"That's not what I asked."

"Well…with everything else going on, we haven't done a door-to-door check yet

"How soon before your team can get to that?"

Her color deepening, Kelsey gestured broadly. "I'll add it to their list as soon as they report in again, which sounds like it's going to be any second. They're not exactly sitting on their asses."

"Come on, Kels. You know Yancy will ask, because Tyndell will ask, Charles Denby will ask, and the press—"

"*I got it.* I screwed up."

Campbell shook her head. "You think you got it. You just gave me the second-worst piece of news of the day." Aware she wasn't handling this as smoothly as she wanted to, she cleared her throat. "Has Detective Archer arrived?"

"Just before Brad delivered his good news."

Then he didn't know the latest yet. "All right. I'll update HQ through more secure channels and see if Detective Archer is going to need some assistance."

"Really?" Kelsey was clearly catching up fast. "I was hoping the fence was some ill-timed vandalism by kids."

"I would give more than you can imagine for you to be right. Unfortunately, only proved facts matter now." Seeing Kelsey mentally preparing herself, she nodded. "Yeah, I have a sledgehammer of my own— Maida is dead."

She thought she could get through the declaration without choking up, but she was wrong, and she avoided Kelsey's impulsive touch by walking around the room to regain control. She knew her reaction was partly fatigue taking its toll and wondered if there was any way in hell she could catch a nap before she went on duty tonight.

Returning to face Kelsey, she managed a tight smile. "Sorry. Still processing. Um…we're waiting for more info."

"Yeah. Yeah, of course. Damn. I'm so sorry." The younger woman bit her lower lip. "You know I have a million questions."

"None of which I can answer right now, but I promise I will shortly. Until then, you don't know anything, okay?"

"Gotcha. Wait…what about Tyndell?"

"I'm leaving him to Boss One for the moment."

Promising to give her regular updates, Campbell exited the gatehouse only to slam back into Kelsey as a silver Lexus sped by. "Son of a—sorry, Kels."

"I'm fine. Who the hell was that?"

Kelsey was reaching for her mike again, and Campbell stopped her. "That's Patsy Saunders—Maida's not-so-beloved daughter-in-law. Obviously, she doesn't understand the word *wait*. I'll handle this. Do me a favor and let HQ know what's happening. At your next opportunity put the barriers out and block off the entrance and all but one lane for exit. If anyone else thinks the rules pertain to everyone except them, they're going to have to explain their damaged vehicles to their insurance company as well as to the Sheriff's Department."

It turned out that Patsy's disrespect extended to the speed limit, and Campbell took considerable risks to catch up with her. Parking up by the garage, where she could block her in beside Detective Archer's black Suburban, Campbell got out of the SUV as Patsy burst from her Lexus.

"What the hell do you think you're doing?" Patsy snapped.

Determined to keep her cool, Campbell stood her ground at the edge of the sidewalk. "I think that's my question, ma'am. You failed to stop at the village entrance for a security pass, you broke every driving regulation on your way up here, and now you're trespassing on private property."

Patsy pointed to the house. "Clear the peroxide from your ears. This is family property and nobody, including you, is going to tell me I can't inspect it."

She pushed past Campbell, dragging her ashen-faced daughter behind her. Unfortunately, she hit Campbell's left shoulder, costing her seconds to recover from the breath-stealing jolt.

Hoping the neighbors weren't standing at their windows, Campbell caught up with them at the front door. "I suggest you stop there, Mrs. Saunders."

Dressed in a stunning red suede jacket and black leather slacks, Patsy looked as if she'd been interrupted on a shopping trip. Debra wore the teen uniform of jeans and school sweatshirt oversize to the point that the arms looked like they could tie in the back.

Glancing over her shoulder, Patsy sent a glare that

was degrees colder than the wind chill. "Do yourself a favor and get lost or I swear you'll not only hear from our attorney, you and your father will both be looking for new employment."

While bothered by the woman's insight into their situation, Campbell had no time to take exception to the insult. "Mrs. Saunders, I don't believe you comprehend the problem here. You can't go inside, because the house is being inspected."

Once again Patsy flared. "They're not done yet? This is ridiculous. I have things to do. People are already dropping off food at the house. I should be there. Our minister is coming within the hour and I've an appointment at the funeral home."

Campbell knew how the casserole parade worked and would rather undergo a root canal than endure another. She could only imagine Maida was saying a few choice words wherever she was.

"It's a difficult time for your family," she replied as civilly as she could. "What we can do is notify you as soon as we can clear your access."

"You don't understand," Patsy ground out. "I need to get an outfit to the funeral home, and I intend to do it now."

Seeing Debra shudder, Campbell tried to gentle her response. "It's still early, ma'am. It will be tomorrow at the earliest, maybe even Monday before her—before the folks at the home will need her things."

"Oh, no, it won't. I don't intend to have this hanging over my head until then."

Good grief, Campbell thought, the witch stood to

inherit a tidy sum because of this tragedy; she could at least pretend to care, to find a little flexibility. "These are difficult moments, and there's no end to how schedules and plans can be upset. Nevertheless, the law supercedes all of that. As a woman, I'm asking you to understand that we will do anything and everything we can do to expedite matters. We were very, very fond of Mrs. Livingstone."

Patsy's eyes narrowed and her lips were pursed so tight a sunburst of wrinkles formed around her mouth. "Screw you." Then she continued inside with the robotic Debra in tow.

Campbell considered grabbing one or both of them. But Patsy was the type to claim assault. Cody Security didn't need to be a secondary report on the evening news. Following on their heels, and once inside, she yelled a warning. "Archer—breach!"

Even so, Patsy and Debra made it farther than Campbell hoped. Farther than was fair to the kid—all the way to Maida's bedroom.

Campbell heard Patsy gasp and saw Debra wrench free and back out of the room.

"Mom…"

The teen's strangled whimper was obliterated by a deep-voiced "Dammit, get out!"

Debra pushed by Campbell. One glance into the room and Campbell knew why. The kid would only get far enough out of the house to lose her lunch—if she'd managed to eat any.

For her part Patsy was coping, though her complexion had taken on a sickly tinge as well. "My God," she whispered. "Is that blood?"

16

History wasn't kind to Campbell. Instead of seeing the partially-cleaned stain on the ivory-white rug that Maida vacuumed twice a week, she saw a concrete pad outside a warehouse and a glistening pool of oil. At least it had looked like oil in the poor lighting. But realizing the liquid was seeping from Greg had told her she was horribly wrong.

"Are you deaf, Cody? Get her out of here," Archer demanded.

Wrenched from her personal nightmare, Campbell gripped Patsy's arm and propelled her back toward the living room. In that lovely room decorated in mink-brown, cabernet-red and sapphire, she swung the woman to face her. She knew she should get Patsy outside to where neither of them could cause any more harm, but once again she erred on the side of privacy.

"Now, you listen to me," she ground out. "You get that child and you go home. You drive the speed limit. At the gatehouse, you pause and give Ms. Mc-Graw this." She drew a pad from her inside jacket pocket and scribbled, *Let her pass.* Then scribbled her initials in the style Kelsey would recognize.

Thrusting it at Patsy, she added, "Do not speak to the press, not those beyond the gate, not later at your house, or any who contact you by telephone. This isn't a power play, Mrs. Saunders. Officially this house has been designated as a crime scene. Do you understand?"

"Maida drove off the road. How can this be a crime scene?"

The almost childlike words compelled Campbell to ease her grip, thinking of the bruises that would probably develop, but there was no time to worry about an assault charge at this point. "Yes. That's the way it appeared. Maybe that's the way it was supposed to look, I don't know. No one knows. So if you or anyone else in your family speaks recklessly, you could make it all the harder for Detective Archer to discover the truth. Do you understand me?"

"Are we in danger?"

Only of being shaken, not stirred, by an ex-cop at the end of her patience. Campbell bought herself a precious second to glance outside to where Debra was wiping at her mouth with the back of her hand. "Competent people are on this case," she told the woman. "Dedicated people who are trained to put your family's safety before their own."

Clutching the small piece of paper, Patsy nodded and without another word went to get her daughter.

"I'm sorry, mama. I'm—"

"Hush. We'll go home. It'll be all right."

Sadly, Patsy didn't put a protective or sustaining arm around the girl. Wondering more about the family dynamics going on there, Campbell watched as she saw the Lexus succeed in squeezing through the tight spot on the driveway. Upon closing the front door, she turned to find Chris Archer at the entrance of the hall.

"What the hell did you think you were doing letting them in here?" he demanded.

"Guess again, Detective. She drove through the entrance. When I caught up with her out here, she told me to kiss off. What did you want me to do, shoot her in front of her kid and the neighbors?"

"That's not a question to ask me right now." Archer swept at his damp brow with his forearm. "You think she'll keep her mouth shut?"

"It would probably be a first. At the very least I'm betting she goes straight to her husband, Dwayne, who may well call their lawyer. Maybe that'll be a good thing. He might convince them to stay muzzled for another hour or two while he leaks his own version of so-called facts."

"Didn't anyone warn you that I don't have a sense of humor, Cody?"

Tired of being the communal doormat, Campbell was ready to agree to being Elvis's latest illegitimate daughter if it got her a reprieve. "You know what, Archer? I don't care if you tinkle diamonds every morning. When we first met and parted a few hours ago, I realized a friend was dead. We meet again and

I get to see what appears to be blood in her bedroom.''

"It's blood. Someone tried to wash it out. Tried hard. When that didn't work, they placed throw rugs over it. I don't know how much time they thought they were buying themselves. They had to know the game was up as soon as we found the body.''

"Wait a minute. I saw her. Maida drove by me that night.''

"Are you suggesting the blood isn't hers?''

"I'm saying I don't know how it can be.''

"Then she accidentally or intentionally hurt someone and tried to cover it up.''

"That's ridiculous!''

"You said she all but ran you over. Sounds to me like someone is trying to hide a terrible mistake.''

"Not Maida. If something happened, she would face up to it. Hell, she drives back to a store to return incorrect change if it's over a dollar or two.''

Archer just stood there, his gloved hands at his sides. "I wanted to agree with you.''

Wanted?

"I'm waiting for verification," he said quietly, "but she died from a violent blow to the head, and I'm sure now it happened here.''

The car…there hadn't been as much blood as there should have been for that kind of wreck. Shock had prevented Campbell from acknowledging that fact. Campbell began breathing like someone trapped in a room and running out of oxygen. She gripped her left arm, thinking she might have to sit down.

"That stain. It's not big enough, is it?" Campbell questioned.

"No, but that tells us more. Someone reacted fast. They got a blanket or another rug."

"Head wounds cause intense bleeding," she said, unable to block the flashbacks from the scene in the warehouse again. "It would soak through fast. Did you find stains in the back seat?"

"Not anything beyond splatters."

"The trunk…"

"They must have used some plastic. Our next job is to find it and the rest of the covering. My hunch is it's in the river."

Murdered in her own home where she was supposed to feel safe, in a community patrolled around the clock. "But I saw her," Campbell whispered, trying to figure it all out.

"You saw someone dressed to *look* like her. You said Maida wore a wig?"

"Yes."

"Does she own only one?"

Under different circumstances, the question would have been amusing. "Hardly. She alternates them and she even had names for them…Ruth, Sophie and Dolly."

"I can figure out Dolly. Which was Ruth and which was Sophie?"

"Ruth was her homemaker one. Sophie was slightly more sophisticated for going to the bank and grocery, styled after the comedian Sophie Tucker. I guess that was before your time."

"I've heard my parents talk about her. Which did you see as the car sped by?"

"I don't know." Frowning, Campbell tried to remember some detail, but too little sleep and too many shocks were taking their toll. "Wait. She was wearing a scarf or rain hat."

"Which was it?"

"It was pouring, and one second I was blinded by her headlights and in the next trying not to get run over."

"But you knew her…you were here as often as anyone. You said so yourself. Do you know where she keeps the wigs? Could you tell what was missing? Could you speculate about what a killer would hit her with if they wanted to murder her?"

"Stop it. Of course I'll help, but why are you asking me that way? My God…do you think I could hurt her?"

"No, but you could have taken advantage of an old woman."

Campbell had to clench her hands to keep from doing something stupid. "Archer…if it wasn't for a lot of lives relying on me, I'd make sure it would take more money than you have to fix your face."

Archer held her gaze for several seconds, then nodded. "I believe you. I also believe you had nothing to do with what happened here. But you cared and that means you have insight I might find useful. Come on. I want your eyes."

17

Northwest of the city
5:00 p.m.

Wrapped in a towel, Blade entered the kitchen and poured water for coffee before turning on the TV. Usually, the rough-around-the-edges look served him better for his work and he only showered in the morning. But he was feeling particularly soiled and unhappy with his circumstances today, and yet a second shower hadn't helped much.

He turned on the TV, then went through the motions of measuring coffee into the mug and listening to the sounds outside. The dog was stretched across the picnic table, enjoying the last bit of daylight. Except for the slight rise and fall of his massive rib cage, Blade could have believed him dead. He'd never seen anything sleep so much. No doubt it was only a pose, a trick to get fed sooner than usual, but Blade wouldn't be giving him dinner until minutes before leaving tonight.

"Shocking developments regarding a traffic acci-

dent and a resident in a prestigious retirement community.''

The surprisingly crisp volume had Blade returning to look at the TV. The picture wasn't bad, either, and to his amazement he saw another white Grand Am, this time wrecked in the woods.

''Seventy-nine-year-old Maida Livingstone was declared dead at the scene of this unusual accident,'' the on-site reporter announced. ''Authorities first reported that Mrs. Livingstone, a widow and resident of Maple Trails, had died as a result of driving off a farm-to-market road north of the city during the rough storm early Wednesday morning. But KLTV has learned through unnamed sources that Mrs. Livingstone was killed in her home earlier that same evening. We have requested a statement from both Tristar Property Management, the company that oversees Maple Trails, and Cody Security, hired to provide twenty-four-hour security to the residents. Both companies have refused comment at this time.''

Blade frowned at the screen, thinking this vehicle had to be the Grand Am Ms. Cody Security was looking for. It was a rough break. Whether the company was wholly innocent or had one hand tied behind its back due to management constraints, it was in for it now. People could accept someone getting killed on a city street and not blame the police, but one death like this in a high-priced community of vulnerable seniors not only made the residents nervous, it compromised their pocketbooks by jeopardizing property values.

"Mrs. Livingstone is survived by a son, Longview businessman Dwayne Saunders. Mr. Saunders is married and has two children. Adding to the tragedy of this event, Mr. Saunders's teenage daughter was a friend of the girl killed the same night as Mrs. Livingstone. This latest act of violence will undoubtedly compound concerns in our community for the safety of residents of all ages. This is Amy Wellington for KLTV."

She had that right, Blade thought, running his hand over his whiskered jaw. Both the LPD and sheriff would be expected to produce answers and results, or people would return to the habit of carrying concealed weapons, with or without registering them. Things were tough enough on the streets; cops didn't need the added threat of a blue-haired granny pulling a six-gun out of her purse.

Something was very wrong about this whole thing. This was supposed to be coincidence? Sure, if two people in the same broad circle tried real hard they could end up dead within twenty-four hours, but they had to be in the middle of a war or on the same crashing plane. That was about the extent of Blade's belief in coincidence. Pouring the boiling water into the mug, he listened to the rest of the report....

"A memorial service has been organized for the friends and family of Stacie Holms at the Meadows Fellowship Church at seven-thirty tonight."

As the news anchor went on to other stories, Blade found that minor public announcement sticking in his mind. He questioned why. It sure as hell wasn't due to any great desire to step inside a church after all this time…but it could be because he figured the other girls would be there. He wanted to observe them out of their usual habitat…or maybe it was *in* their usual surroundings…? He still wasn't sure whether they were just mixed-up, restless kids without direction and looking for kicks, or were actually self-destructive enough to be intentionally lobbying for a trafficking position in the drug business. That's what he'd been seeing at Point East and elsewhere.

Blade rubbed at his whiskers again. It would screw up everything, but he needed to shave.

18

Maple Trails
5:11 p.m.

By the time Campbell left Maple Trails, she knew
there was no chance for a nap before leading the training shift she'd promised to take care of. It didn't matter, though. At this stage she didn't need it. She was
pumped, she was focused...but she was also heart-
sick.

At the gatehouse, she slowed as Kelsey stepped
outside. "I'll be in touch," she told the keen-eyed
guard.

"Don't be a martyr. If you need someone to do
another shift, I'm your girl. Even a half shift."

Grateful, Campbell could have hugged her. It was
only the thought of the cameras peeking out of the
RVs parked out on the road that cautioned her to re-
think all impulses, especially those exposing her battered emotions. "I need a shower and I have to brief
Yancy. Then I'll be back. Let me save your offer for
a time when I have to lay low."

"That's a grim thought." Kelsey casually stepped

onto the pavement and stood in front of the truck's side-view mirror so that she blocked any cameras from seeing Campbell's face. "How did it go up there?"

"Short of learning Baton Rouge's serial killer had relocated here, I don't know how it can get any worse. Whatever happened, happened there."

"Shit."

"You can say that again. Did a woman called Taneeka happen to leave a message for me?"

Kelsey shook her head. "Maybe it's the press keeping the lines clogged. Every resident who has made it through, trying to find out what's up with the investigation, is complaining about how long it's taken."

"Could be. About the queries—you still know nothing, got it? This is going to get out fast enough as it is."

"What about questions from our own people?"

"Tell them we're on high alert. That'll be enough for them to know to keep their eyes open and to watch their backs."

Promising to be more informative when she returned, Campbell pulled out into the road, negotiating around reporters, who rushed forward to ask for a statement. She didn't make any.

As she crossed Highway 259, her phone rang. "Please," she murmured as she flipped open the palm-size unit. "Cody."

"Did you give up on me?"

"No," she told Taneeka. "But I'm glad you heard my mental nudge."

"What I heard was that your friend was found. I'm really sorry."

"It gets worse. Can you talk?"

"Lay it on me. I just got home."

"I've just left her house and I'm going to HQ. The county's forensics guy was over at Maida's doing the sweep. He found blood."

For a second there was dead silence. Then Taneeka exhaled, whispering, "Oh, Campbell…"

"Yeah." Sensing this could take a minute, Campbell pulled over to the side of the road—as much for the strong cellular signal as to contain her emotions.

"Tell me he's got some strong leads?"

"If he does, he didn't share them with me. It didn't help that Maida's daughter-in-law forced her way in with daughter in tow," Campbell added grimly. "That's how I got inside myself. I had to chase her down."

"I swear somebody must be putting something in nail polish that turns the bitches into witches," Taneeka muttered. "Did she compromise things much?"

"No, thank goodness. But she saw the stain and she's not the type to keep her mouth shut. It's the kid that worries me more, though. She saw it, too, and she barely got outside in time before she lost her lunch."

"Uh-huh. You know, she's why I'm calling. I haven't been able to find out much about her friend.

Snow spent most of the day with the Holms family, Stacie's teachers, and her closest friends, but they haven't brought anyone in for formal questioning. I don't think we're looking at a fast resolution here.''

Campbell sighed. ''That's not good, either. At least I can let you off the hook. Now that I've been inside the house, you don't need to risk your neck for me anymore.''

''I can't say I'm not relieved—not because I minded—I just didn't have much for you except what you probably heard yourself.''

''I don't follow. Things have been so intense here, I was going to check the news when I got to the office.'' Campbell kept one eye on her side-view mirror, checking to make sure she wasn't being followed by a reporter, or that a squad car had pulled in behind her.

''All I was going to suggest if you were still looking for access to the family was to attend the service tonight.'' Taneeka gave her the details for Stacie's prayer vigil.

While appreciative, Campbell remained doubtful. ''I can't imagine Debra will be in any condition to leave home, even for that. And what with a second murderer on the loose, do you really think her parents would let her out of their sight?''

''They haven't exactly been able to control her so far, have they?'' Taneeka drawled. ''Something's bothering me between what you've told me and what I'm hearing here. Are you sure your kid is as fragile as she appears?''

If this had been anyone else, Campbell would have immediately argued on behalf of Maida's blood; however, Taneeka didn't insinuate, let alone make rash statements without having a reason. That had her gripping the phone tighter. "I'm not blind to the fact that Maida was concerned about her and disappointed that they'd grown apart."

"The kid we're hearing about is closer to being a juvie parolee than a suburbia princess."

"Wait a second. Are we talking peer gossip or something on file?" Campbell understood off-the-record testimony could be invaluable, but she also knew firsthand what gossip, based on jealousy and malice, could do.

"To be fair, I don't know what she's guilty of. But the gang she's hooked up with is a different story."

"Gang...you're using the word loosely, right?"

"I wish."

"Including Stacie? Stacie Holms had a record?"

"And she'd only turned eighteen a week ago. What I saw in her file is a lot of undirected energy, and a deep anger that's increasingly being tapped into pulling more dangerous stunts."

Campbell didn't want to listen to any more. The impulse went beyond wanting to protect Maida's memory from hurt. She knew if she heard any more she would be obliged to dig deeper herself, and she was drowning in responsibility and obligations as it was.

"Hey...you still there?"

"Yeah. I'm just—Taneeka, Debra was shattered

when she saw her grandmother's blood. There wasn't any tough-guy behavior or snotty attitude. She even apologized to her mother for making a mess in the flower box. Maybe she was going down the wrong path, but hopefully this has scared her enough to re-think that.''

"Okay. I hope you're right. Gotta go. You take care, girlfriend, and keep in touch.''

"I will—and thanks, Taneeka.''

Closing the phone, Campbell went through the motions of checking traffic to ease back into the road, but her thoughts remained on what she'd just heard. She was still disturbed as she approached headquarters and her mood wasn't helped when she saw two vehicles parked at the entrance to the property. More reporters on stakeout, she thought. As she turned into the parking lot they emerged from their vehicles.

"Ms. Cody, can we ask you a few questions?" A woman in jeans and a corduroy blazer jogged toward her.

"No." With long strides, Campbell hurried to the front door.

"Just a statement?" the man called, catching up fast.

"You're trespassing."

Hoping Beth had spotted her on the closed circuit monitor and released the electronic door lock, she grabbed the doorknob. It turned and she rushed inside, slamming the door behind her.

"Thanks." She sighed with relief and eyed the

younger woman, who was looking frazzled herself. "Why haven't you escaped? It's past time."

Headphone in place, Beth nodded at the state-of-the-art switchboard where every incoming line was either lit or flashing. "Too much activity. And with my luck, one of those turkeys outside is apt to follow me home and offer me a juicy bonus for spilling a secret, so I figure why throw myself in front of temptation?"

Knowing she lived at home with her widowed mother, helping to raise her three siblings—all boys under twenty-one—Campbell's respect for the young woman grew. "Does Yancy know about Maida?"

"I thought he'd figure it out eventually. You know he won't ask."

"What about your family?" she asked.

"I checked to make sure Mom will be home from work on time and then ordered three large pizzas on my credit card to be delivered—" Beth checked her watch "—right about now. It was my turn to cook."

"I bet your brothers adore you. Try to find a second to nuke something from the freezer. This won't be a good evening to risk deliveries here." She managed a crooked smile. "And check the first aid cabinet for something for your throat. You sound like you need relief."

"What about you, can I get you something? You look… I'm sorry about Mrs. Livingstone."

"Thank you. And thanks for the thought, but what I could use I can't have because I'll be on duty this evening. Holler if things outside get too rowdy."

Campbell found her father in his office leaning back in his chair, his feet up on his desk, his hands covering his face. "If you're sending messages Upstairs, add one from me," she said as she quietly closed the door.

"Line's busy." Yancy dropped his hands onto his lap and studied her as she settled on the corner of his desk. "My poor Belle. No need to ask how you are. I sure F'd this one, didn't I?"

"It's the leader's job to stay positive." Campbell moved aside a stack of unopened mail and settled on the edge of his desk.

"Piss on positive. I urged you to doubt your intuition…and now you've lost a friend and there'll be hell to pay."

The need to physically steel herself in order to stay outwardly calm almost had Campbell gripping her left arm again. The only reason she succeeded was to spare her father from increased worry. "I'm sorry I asked Archer to have Sheriff Glazer call you with the news, but risking using the radios or cell phone—"

Sitting up Yancy leaned forward to touch her knee. "Security first. You did the right thing." Just as quickly, he cleared his throat and sat back again. "How's Archer treating you?"

"Decent enough after the inevitable dressing-down for not keeping Patsy and Debra from making it into the house."

"What could you do without risking the kid's safety, or causing a scene that would further upset others in the neighborhood?"

"Exactly. Nevertheless, he was right to defend his area of responsibility."

"All right, all right… What did the killer hit her with—did you find the weapon? Chris didn't say."

"It was the marble vase she bought on her last trip with her second husband. It had been scrubbed, like the carpet, but Archer found trace evidence with his UV equipment."

"Ah, hell," Yancy muttered.

"Worse yet, she had a special attachment to the piece." Massaging the spasms at the back of her neck, Campbell tried to recap the best theory thus far. "We believe her killer put on one of her wigs and drove her car out to relocate the body in an attempt to make it appear that she died due to poor driving conditions."

"Clever, but not carried through with much thoroughness."

"He was successful enough." Campbell checked herself. "Or she. In any case, I was fooled, and if it wasn't for that trucker breaking down, that car might not have been spotted before the killer got back to the house to finish cleaning up."

"You think that was the plan?"

It would help if they knew the motive behind the incident. Campbell had seen enough crimes to conclude that a fair number occurred because there was only one of two options, and the perpetrator didn't take—or didn't have—the time to think of the second. "It had to be," she said. "With luck, when the car was eventually found, maybe—thanks to varmints—

the body would no longer be there, or there wouldn't be enough of it left to allow forensics to determine the cause of death…or to sustain the sheriff's department's and the D.A.'s interest." As terrible as Maida's death had been, Campbell was grateful that she hadn't endured that indignity.

"At least that reassures us that one of our own isn't a killer," Yancy said, clearly recapping.

"Now the challenge will be to make sure residents at Maple Trails and our other clients continue to remember how carefully we choose our people, and how strict our requirements are."

"I'll draft a memo to all employees to take every opportunity to make that clear," Yancy replied. "And then a letter to our customers to restate our high hiring standards and strict requirements, as well as our unwavering commitment to serve and protect."

Something in his proud countenance stirred Campbell's suspicions. "Do not mention me by name, or the lightning. It'll just tempt Tyndell to make his own negative comments behind our backs."

"Have a little faith. I'll be sufficiently restrained, but I'll be damned if I keep it hidden that one of our own was injured in the line of duty." Yancy jotted himself a few notes. "Moving on…give me your best hunch—are we looking at another Trails resident as a suspect?"

Campbell moistened her dry lips. "I'm increasingly convinced that the killer or killers got in through the fence."

"The fence that went down because of the storm?"

In a way this theory was worse than a neighbor committing the crime, as it opened all residents to a new threat and it would add to the criticism that Cody Security was not doing its job. "The tree limb barely brushed it. The section came down because it was—" Campbell saw Yancy's expression change "—Dad, there are crowbar markings."

"Are you sure?"

"The crowbar was painted, and there is orange paint in the dents in the wood."

"Wait a minute. Maintenance would have set out cones to warn anyone driving back there. Those cones are orange, aren't they?"

"True, but the cones are an after-the-fact issue. Also, the coloring is baked in, not sprayed on."

"What did Archer say?"

"He took my notes. Then I let him check my truck."

"Are you crazy?"

"You know it was inevitable." Campbell leaned over and patted his hand, moved that he couldn't be anything but a father at the moment. "There was nothing for him to find, Dad. Maida has never been in the truck."

"Well, what if the killer had planted something in there? Don't do that again. If the sheriff can't make an arrest soon, you can bet attention will come back to you."

Or someone else on their team. But Campbell had been thinking since talking to Taneeka. "I want your input on something. I've learned the Saunderses have other problems. Their daughter is apparently having more trouble than Maida knew about. She's hooked up with a pretty tough group.''

"Are you going to suggest—"

"No." Campbell felt a familiar queasiness at the suggestion, just as she had when Taneeka had outlined what she knew of Debra's background. "Nevertheless I have to be one hundred percent certain, don't I? And I hate living with this seed of doubt that's been planted in my mind. Also, I can't deny any dirt we have on the Saunderses could give us leverage down the road."

"Where's this leading?" Yancy asked.

"I want to delay my training by an hour or two and check out the memorial at Meadows Fellowship Church." She told her father about the service.

"I heard something about that on the news. You think the Saunders girl will be there?"

"I don't know. If she's anything like what I've heard, I can't see why she would show, and I can't see her parents letting her out of the house knowing her grandmother has been murdered. If she's not there, I'll be back on duty by eight o'clock. At the latest, by nine-thirty."

"And what are we supposed to do with the new guy in the meantime?" Yancy leaned forward and glanced at the file on his desk. "Raynor, Andrew. It would help if you'd read this before you meet him."

"Make me a copy. In the meantime, start breaking him in at the gate. He has to learn the post, anyway. Tell Howie he goes on patrol for now and call the gate and take Kelsey up on her offer to stay a little longer.''

''I won't pretend I'm following all of this, let alone agreeing with it, but I owe you.'' Yancy reached for the phone.

19

The church was packed when Blade slipped in with the stragglers and tucked into an inconspicuous spot behind the last row of benches. Organ music muffled what little conversation there was. In fact, as he scanned the room, he saw much stiffness and unease, and some people were openly checking their watches. He doubted Stacie Holms would be offended. She wouldn't have shown up for something like this herself…and she definitely would have hated the flowers.

There were no more than a dozen arrangements spread along either side of the podium, a modest display by any standard, and all but one pink. Blade wondered if Stacie liked pink; somehow he didn't think so. The one that was different was a dark, fan-shaped burst of deep purple gladiolas mixed with evergreen. He could imagine who had sent it and he scanned the church looking for three familiar heads. He spotted them on his side in the first row. Stacie's friends were huddled together as though they were welded at the hip. All of their heads were bowed. The rest of the bench was empty. Stacie's father and two younger sisters were on the opposite side of the aisle, along with another couple. No one from that row looked across the aisle at the other side.

Blade noticed that there was still plenty of seating and no one needed to be standing back here. Interesting. The place could easily hold three hundred, but he doubted a hundred people were present. Was this the size of the church membership, or a reflection of the girl and her family?

As a cell phone beeped to his left, he glanced over and spotted an embarrassed reporter hurriedly turn it off. Blade knew the guy wouldn't know him by name, but there was a chance he'd recognize him even though he was dressed differently. Thinking this might not have been a great idea after all, he turned his head to the right and looked straight into a pair of gorgeous eyes. *Shit*, he thought.

After the first shock, he quickly refocused on the front of the church. The choir, dressed in burgundy-red robes, stood and began to sing. As the congregation rose and joined in. Blade didn't hesitate; he eased his way back to the door and slipped out as quietly as he'd entered.

With quick strides, he retraced his steps to the parking lot, exhaling sharply in frustration. His breath was transformed into a cloud of white in the bitterly cold night air.

What the hell was she doing here? Did she recognize me?

No doubt she would have if he had lingered. Blade's thoughts raced faster than traffic out on Loop 281, escape the ultimate conclusion. But he wasn't even at the end of the sidewalk when he heard the door of the church open.

20

Campbell made it outside in time to see the subject of her interest break into a run and disappear into the unlit parking lot. Any doubts she had that the clean-shaven man in the gray wool blazer and sexy black T-shirt was the scuzzy biker-type from the other night vanished. They had to be one and the same.

Despite her high heels, she started running, too. When she reached the first row of cars, she hiked up her already short skirt and stepped on the fender of a Dodge pickup in the hopes of spotting him. Just as her foot began to slide, she saw him three rows ahead.

Relieved that the parking area was paved instead of graveled, Campbell resumed the chase. Although she had to dodge an obstacle course of side-view mirrors, she fumbled in her bag for her small Beretta. Now the brainstorm to bring along the small automatic that usually stayed under her pillow made as much sense as leaving the .9 mm in the SUV with her uniform and boots. Unfortunately, the .25 caliber was smaller than her wallet, ID, phone and pager, and grappling around for it cost her as much speed as the heels did.

She continued scanning the area for the flash of an interior light going on in a car or truck—but there wasn't any. That triggered a new surge of adrenaline. Under most circumstances she wouldn't have been so quick to reach for her weapon, but he was using the darkness and this maze of vehicles to hide from her. That was warning enough to approach with caution.

Grateful to close her fingers around the automatic, Campbell shoved the bag strap high on her shoulder and glanced over to the street to see if she'd been wrong about an LPD presence. No, there were no police to help with traffic once the service ended. That also meant she couldn't hope for any backup if things got touchy out here. At least, she told herself, she wouldn't have to answer a bunch of antagonizing questions once they recognized her…that is, if she was capable of talking after this was over.

At the last row she gripped another tailgate. About to climb up on the truck's fender, she hesitated. He might be carrying, too. Checking the spaces between the next few cars, she crouched to peer beneath both vehicles.

Where the devil was he?

Her blood pounding in her ears, she rose and brushed her skirt back in place. Wearing a suit had seemed a gesture of respect and smart camouflage, but it now annoyed her with its impracticality. Worse, the brief pause cost her a precious second, long enough to sense air shifting behind her.

Suddenly, a powerful hand closed on her left wrist and her arm was yanked behind her back while her gun hand was trapped in another vise of powerful fingers. Before she could begin a defense, she was shoved facedown over the hood of a Mercedes.

"Don't fight me," a low, slightly rough voice warned. "You'll scratch the paint."

The ludicrous order was lost on her. The hot breath at her neck failed to intimidate. All Campbell could think about was a dire need to escape the blinding pain in her left arm. Fighting not to sob, she rocked her forehead against the ice-cold metal willing the frigid night air to numb her.

"Stop it!" her captor snapped. "And release the gun."

As he spoke he used his body to press her harder against the car. Campbell should have been seething with rage at the blatant insult behind the intimate contact of this stranger nestled between her legs. But all she could focus on was getting past the agony.

"My arm," she gasped.

"I'll stop as soon as you let go."

"My *arm*. The lightning," she ground out. Didn't he remember or was her original impression right about him being a complete asshole?

As quickly as he'd overpowered her, he wrenched the gun from her hand and released her left arm.

Freed, Campbell moaned and shakily eased herself up. Although she managed to face her attacker, she had to lean back on the Mercedes as her nervous system dealt with this latest trauma. It did, however, give her a chance to study the stranger leaning against the SUV that hid them from the street.

"Sorry about the rough stuff," he told her. "But I don't feel like getting shot tonight."

She saw neither hate nor madness in his too-blue eyes. "I didn't intend to shoot you. Not unless you gave me no choice."

"But, as we discovered the other night, accidents happen."

How appropriate that the man of mystery continued to weave a riddle to thwart her. "What do you want?"

"That's my question. You came after me."

"You ran. I figured you had a lot to hide." Thanks to the heels, she could almost look straight into his eyes. Framed by enviable lashes that matched his near-black hair, those eyes were undeniable attention-getters, though there was something grim and fatalistic about the expression in their depths. But she had to give him points for cleaning up well. She'd gauged him as street slime—one of the lowlifes that made work ever more dangerous for those in law enforcement. How often did lowlifes act with consideration? "Who are you?"

"No one you need to waste your time with."

As someone who enjoyed listening to people, Campbell zeroed in on his accent, realizing it was a detail she'd been sensitive to from the moment he'd crashed into her. "You're not a local."

"No."

"No…that's a Yankee accent. New York?"

He simply crossed his arms.

Campbell could have seen that as a gesture of rejection, except that the movement did redirect the barrel of the Beretta. "What was your relationship to Stacie Holms?" she said, pressing on.

"Who said I had one?"

"I do, because you're here. Because you were running in after the gurney when the EMTs were wheeling her into Good Shepherd."

"What's your relationship to her?"

"I think this is where I say quid pro quo."

"Not if you want your Beretta back." He glanced at the automatic, which looked like a toy in his hand, and shook his head. "Why the hell are you carrying this? Unless you've got the stomach to walk straight up to someone and put a bullet in the back of his head, this is a joke."

"Between his eyes...or his balls," she replied. "Not that it's any of your business. I also didn't think it would be appreciated if I walked in wearing my uniform with the .9 mm on my hip."

"Screw the .9 mm. You want to make doughnut holes, stay in the kitchen. If you're serious about stopping your opponent and can handle the monster, you'd be better off going back to a .45." The man's gaze did another slow drift over her. "I do approve of the uniform modification, though."

Her mind spurned the sexual innuendo, but her body betrayed her. It was almost a relief to have her attention drawn away by a flash of headlights. Looking across the parking lot, Campbell saw a police car pulling in at the first entrance. Then to her surprise, the stranger swore softly and handed her back the gun.

"Try to stay out of trouble, Ms. Cody Security."

Did he actually believe he could walk away? Campbell brought up the gun and aimed at his back. "Freeze, pal."

He stopped, eased up his hands, and slowly turned to face her again. "That's not exactly quid pro quo."

"I think you'd better tell me who you are and what's going on, or we'll just flag down that patrol car and you can share it with the officer," Campbell replied.

The stranger met her gaze without blinking. "I have to leave now. You want to talk, follow me."

"Where to?"

"Worried?"

"I may not want to kill you—yet—but I don't have a problem slowing you down."

Signaling his intentions, he eased his hand into his blazer, drew out a billfold and dropped it open to expose a badge. "You worried?" he asked again.

"Yeah," she muttered. "Now I am."

21

Blade used the entire trip to his house to call himself every kind of fool. It had been asinine to call Campbell Cody's bluff when he had pretty much determined the woman didn't have the sense to lay low when stalked by a small but vengeful army of good old boys in uniform. At the same time, he had to protect himself and didn't want to keep hanging around the church parking lot with that squad car so near. He told himself that since he was leading her to the far side of District A—as far as he could tell, she didn't have the notoriety there that she had in Districts B or C—she was better off, too. But now she would know what only one or two others did—his hiding ground and sanctuary from the world at large. How genius was that?

When he pulled into his driveway and parked, he saw her hesitate at the entrance. He didn't blame her. The place looked bad enough by day. At night a stranger in the rural areas needed to understand that trespassing was taken seriously. You could be shot at for simply coming too close to someone's illegal hooch camp or amphetamine lab, just as easily as you could be invited to have a cup of coffee. Blade decided to let her make up her own mind. After all, she'd screwed up his plans; why should he make it easy for her?

As he slid out of the pickup and unlocked the kitchen door, the growling dog sat up on the picnic table. The big oaf was looking from him to the end of the drive and the idling SUV, as though trying to figure out whether to pounce on him or use the Cody vehicle's tires as a teething ring. Turning on the kitchen light, Blade cut the mutt's choices in half and went inside, where he put on water to boil. By the time he found a second, though chipped mug, he heard the SUV pull up behind his truck, then the sound of the picnic table rocking. The dog had decided to investigate…or worse.

His conscience got the best of him and he returned outside to act as interference, but he was too late. "Son of a bitch," he muttered.

The big hulk had his front paws on Campbell's shoulders and was making guttural sounds of gratification as she rubbed his ears and cooed to him.

"You're such a big, sweet boy. What's your name?"

"Douche." That earned Blade a sidelong glance of disapproval. "Well, look at him."

She scratched the dog's chest with the back of her fingers and then took hold of his paws to ease him down. "Okay, I need a break. You're no feather pillow."

"You shouldn't let him do that, especially in your condition."

"He needs a collar," she replied. "I didn't see a fence."

"He's not my dog." Blade returned inside.

A moment later, Campbell followed. "He obviously thinks otherwise."

"He doesn't think. He eats and sleeps. That's all I've ever seen him do since the day he showed up. The only reason I started feeding him was because he seems to like guarding the place. I hope you don't take milk or sugar because I don't have either," Blade added, reaching for the jar of instant coffee.

"No problem." Campbell glanced around and drawled, "I'm surprised you have one coffee mug, let alone two. Where are we, in a safe house?"

Blade grunted. "The ones I've seen are mansions compared to this. If you don't mind, close the door. It's okay," he said at her doubtful look. "Heaven will run out of halos long before I ever earn one, but my word is good. In any case, the place is drafty enough without the help."

She raised her eyebrows. Finely arched, they were slightly darker than her hair, which she wore loose tonight. That was almost more temptation than he could stand. Half of the reason he'd thrown her over the hood of the Mercedes was to find out if she felt and smelled as good as she looked.

"Go ahead, ask," Blade said. "I've already broken all of my rules by bringing you here."

"Why did you?"

He spooned the granules into each mug. "I figure it's a smaller risk to trust you than it is to deal with you blindly sticking your nose where it doesn't belong, compromising my work."

"Which is?"

"I work undercover. Meaning if our paths happen to cross again, I'd appreciate it if you'd pretend I'm the cockroach you thought I was last night."

"I didn't—" Campbell had the grace to look embarrassed when he shot her a level look. "Okay, I did. But it wasn't all because of you."

Once you got past the professionalism, she was softhearted. Blade didn't want to know that, it made her all the more attractive. "Thank you," he murmured, frowning into the mugs.

"The thing is, we did meet and there were witnesses, so what do people who know you on the street call you?"

"John Blake."

"And what's your real name? I can identify a badge in the dark. I can't read the fine print on an ID."

Shifting, he leaned back against the counter and crossed his arms over his chest. She had yet to move from the door, but she'd already decided she trusted him—even worse, was attracted to him.

Christ, he thought, things were going from bad to dangerous. "Blade. Jackson Blade."

The corners of her glistening lips twitched. "That sounds like something from an Aaron Spelling nighttime soap."

"No one with the name Campbell Cody should criticize," Blade drawled.

"Campbell Bond Cody."

His own smile came with surprising speed. "That's almost as bad as Jackson Jordan Blade. There should be a codicil attached to all birth certificates that allows kids to alter their names at the same time they get their driver's licenses."

"Works for me. What do I call you while I'm here?"

"Blade. You?"

"Anything except Belle. I once sent a guy to the dentist for trying 'Wild Belle Cody.'"

Blade decided he could spend the rest of the night watching her stand there in her sophisticated black ensemble that showed off her womanly curves and exposed her great legs to the point of distraction. He nodded to her arm. "I meant what I said about hurting you. How are you doing?"

"Compared to Maida and Stacie, I'm fine."

"Okay, then let me try this route—how did you get injured?"

"I was at my post at the gatehouse at Maple Trails," she began.

He learned that since leaving the LPD, she had handled the night shift at the prestigious retirement community. Blade thought it a lonely occupation for a young woman with so much of her life before her. The news about the old lady and the ironic aftermath had him wincing inside. But he only said, "Tough break."

"That's part of the reason I was so ungracious when you tried to help me up after we bumped into each other," she said in conclusion.

He liked her voice, mellow and without rough edges. "No lasting damage done. I was too busy admiring your eyes and hair."

"Right," she drawled. "You were in a hurry to get inside and check on Stacie."

"It didn't take us long to get to the heart of the matter, did it?"

"That's why I'm here. Did you know her?"

No one could accuse her of using her sexuality to gain an advantage. Blade wondered what had made her repress it so deeply? "Slightly. You?"

"Not at all. As I explained, the only reason I was at the hospital was because of that Grand Am. Maida had just purchased the same model in the same color. Her granddaughter, Debra, asked her to because Maida was going to give it to her as a reward if she graduated with grades good enough to get her into a decent college. I only learned today that Debra and Stacie were more than schoolmates. I shouldn't have been surprised. It's common for kids to mimic a close friend's buying habits. Have they been friends long?"

"I've only been in the area about a year and they didn't start coming into Point East until a few weeks ago."

"Aren't they underage for that place?" Campbell asked, clearly confused.

Blade shrugged. "Not if they stick to the restaurant

side. On a slow night the manager lets them play pool as long as they behave.''

''And how often can you go there without arousing suspicion?''

''I'm supposed to be a trucker. In between contracts, I hustle a little pool. That makes it easier. On days when I'm supposed to be on the road, I check on leads and study new case files.''

''Can you handle an eighteen-wheeler?''

''Enough to bluff my way through a conversation or a challenge.'' His brother-in-law, Sam Martini, used to drive a rig from Buffalo to Chicago and Blade had accompanied him a few times as a teenager.

Campbell glanced at her watch. She seemed to be waging a battle within herself.

''Have a seat,'' Blade said, pouring the water into the mugs.

She checked her watch again.

''If you need to call and let your dinner date know you'll be late—''

''I'm training new personnel tonight,'' Campbell replied coolly. But she did cross over to sit on the single stool on the other side of the counter, settling her bag on her lap.

Blade shouldn't have been so pleased with that information. He knew about the pitfalls of mixing his work with his private life, and considering the life he'd chosen for himself, he had no business entertaining the thought of getting involved with any woman. Nevertheless, he had only to look at her and that's the route his thoughts took.

"If I do the math, you've been putting in a lot of hours since this mess began," he said, sliding his mug toward her.

She stared at him, a slow dawning registering in the smoky depths of her eyes. "Where else have you seen me?"

So, he thought, she might appear emotionally and physically wounded; however, she could still think on her feet. "District C Headquarters."

A slight flush crept into her cheeks. "Are you setting me up for Lefevre?"

"No."

"I don't believe you." She slid the strap of her bag over her arm.

Blade knew he would have to talk fast and with total honesty or she would do more than leave, she would put up such a defensive wall between them he might never break through it. "Yes, you do," he said bluntly. "That's why you came in here when all of your training told you it was too risky. That's also why I invited you, even though few besides Lieutenant McBrill know where I live. Like you, I'm no advocate of trust, and I don't necessarily think telling you all of this is smart. Denial just seems a bigger waste of energy."

Campbell studied him a moment longer before letting the strap slip back down her arm. "How well *do* you know Lefevre?"

"He uses me, I use him. I happened to be in his office this morning when you arrived. I won't deny I fished for information about you."

"You told him we met?"

"I wouldn't—that son of a bitch." Blade's blood chilled as he saw fear shadow her eyes. "Has he touched you?"

All but shuddering, Campbell replied, "If he thought he could get away with it, I think he would try, though I swear it would be his worst and last mistake."

"I would help you get rid of the body." His conviction and the speed of his declaration shocked him, and he could easily understand the new fear dawning in her eyes.

"I can't do this," she murmured, rising from the stool.

Blade gripped the edge of the counter to keep from going after her, but he spoke quickly. "Wait. I apologize. I won't lie and tell you that wasn't an honest reaction, or deny I'm strongly attracted to you. But I am a big boy. I know what lines not to cross."

Keeping her gaze on the floor, Campbell replied, "You said you would give me answers. That's the only reason I'm here. If you thought otherwise—"

"I didn't. And I will share what I know, just please—sit. Take a sip of that coffee, you're shaking with cold."

Actually, she was trembling from emotional overload, only he knew better than to shoot himself in the other foot by mentioning it. Relieved that she at least stepped back to the counter, he began, "Stacie and her gang came on to my radar sweep when one of the girls started flirting with a serious drug trafficker."

"'Gang'…that's the second time I've heard that word tonight in reference to them."

"Your friend didn't give you a summary of the girls' rap sheet? Don't take offense to that," he said, noticing how her expression turned stony. "Yes, I saw you pull around the building and pick her up after Lefevre left. It's my job to notice things—and I shouldn't be in law enforcement if I didn't have at least some resources."

"Just don't cause my friend any trouble."

"You have my word."

Seemingly reassured, Campbell said, "I'd heard Stacie had gotten into some trouble, but I didn't think things had progressed to where it did."

"I'm afraid it's true. Why anyone should be surprised, I don't know. The percentage of female offenders involved in juvenile crime has risen to well over the twenty-five-percent mark. I've watched these girls night after night and I know the behavioral signs. They're increasingly aggressive, and every time they succeed in getting away with something it emboldens them. I think a lot of the momentum belongs to their self-appointed leader, Ashley Mize."

Although she remained standing, Campbell placed her black leather bag on the counter and wrapped her hands around the steaming mug. "I don't know that name. Tonight was the first time I saw the girls together. Is she the tall, striking one?"

"Yeah."

"She's beautiful. Any other girl her age with her bones and height would race to the nearest modeling studio," she mused. "Do you know what her problem is?"

Blade leaned his forearms on the counter and picked up the chipped mug. "I'm not entirely sure, but I suspect part of it is that her state trooper daddy is a disciplinarian and maybe not a fair one. What I do know is that she seems intent on breaking down the system any and every way she can."

"My God. Of course." Considering the information, Campbell took a careful sip of her coffee. "Yancy was with the state police. My father," she amended when Blade frowned. "I'll ask him if he knows him, or can get some feedback on the trooper. Do you know his full name?"

"Donald, I think. You call your father Yancy?"

"Sometimes. We're business partners and it's hard to be seen as a professional if you tell a prospective client, 'Let me get back to you as soon as I confer with Daddy.' But it really began years earlier. He's never coddled me."

"That's a pity," Blade murmured, briefly thinking back to his own childhood happiness. "Every child deserves that."

"And yet not every adult should be a parent. But it's okay, he's a good man and I love him, limitations and all." Her eyes lit with faint amusement. "It gives me a good negotiation position when he gets overly paternalistic."

That small insight into her background aroused his curiosity even more and once again, Blade had to consciously keep himself focused. "Well, if you find out anything about Mize, I'd appreciate a call."

"Is that why you went to the church tonight?" Campbell asked. "To see if you could unearth some useful background information?"

"To a degree. Mostly I wanted to see how the girls act under public scrutiny. Plus there was a chance that someone who's considering mentoring them in their criminal career would show."

"I can't see a drug supplier taking that kind of risk."

"Unless he's their phys ed coach or math teacher," Blade countered. "Or one of their mothers' latest boyfriends." Once he had her attention, he added, "No, I don't presume to know anything like that is true, just as I can only guess where these young women are willing to take their anger and growing appetite for mischief. Every night I cross the path of car thieves, chop-shop operatives, prostitutes and your basic thugs, and you know what? Occasionally I've spotted some of them shopping at Wal-Mart like everybody else. You bet they could have been there tonight."

Campbell bowed her head until her hair veiled her face. "Then I'm doubly sorry I caused you trouble."

"I'm not. This is important, too."

"I'm beginning to agree with you." She rubbed the smooth skin between her eyebrows. "You're making me think that I've come into this with too narrow a focus."

"You couldn't help it. Under normal conditions,

your job is to police what—a five- or seven-square-mile area? Except what's the rule about normal?''

"Don't remind me." Campbell drew a sustaining breath and eased back onto the edge of the stool. "You probably already know we're under scrutiny for Maida's death, but new evidence collected today will initiate accusations of negligence against Cody Security. Since it all happened under my watch, you might want to keep your distance from me.''

A veteran of trouble, Blade heard all of the signals warning him to distance himself from this woman. He might have gotten through his probation period with the LPD, but he was by no means considered invaluable. The smart thing would be to heed Campbell's generous invitation to run and hope she forgot his address.

"You have my attention," he told her.

"I spent a good part of the day with Detective Archer of the Gregg County Sheriff's Department as he worked through Maida's house," Campbell began.

Blade didn't pretend to be ignorant of the status change in the case. "I heard her death was reclassified as a homicide."

"I think we also found the murderer's access point." Campbell told him about the downed fence. "It was only during repairs that one of our Maintenance people noticed crowbar marks and the residue of orange paint proving the fence didn't go down because of weather."

"You're convinced there's a connection?"

"Archer doesn't seem to think so, not completely,

but I do. In the history of the property we've had only two minor incidents of vandalism, both of them quickly resolved. That's why property there is bought up as soon as it's available, and why our contract has been repeatedly renewed—although there's no great love lost between us and the property manager.'' Campbell put down the mug and tapped on the counter with her neatly clipped, unvarnished fingernail. "Someone took down that section of fence Tuesday night with the intent to get to Maida. If they were looking to do a B and E there were two houses closer that were vacant. Both sets of owners were out of town.''

Blade felt a flicker of excitement. "Did they leave lights on?''

"Only night-lights or accent lighting here and there. Generally, we recommend against too much of it so those on patrol can tell who's awake and whether someone needs our attention.''

"And your guards didn't notice anything abnormal during their patrols?''

"Nothing.''

"Severe weather came into play. Did you experience any electrical outages in the area?''

Campbell shook her head. "The damage we did incur is over by the lake.''

Blade thought about what she was suggesting. "So what's your best guess? Are you thinking one person could be responsible?''

"I'm not ready to say. It would depend on who— his size and strength.''

"Maida's son?"

"They had their differences, but she hadn't mentioned anything to suggest that things had deteriorated to that extent." She paused, her expression increasingly introspective. "Things were definitely touchy between Maida and her daughter-in-law, Patsy, and yet I can't believe Patsy would risk ruining her manicure. If it was either of them, neither would have wanted to enter the property through the front gate because there'd be a record of their presence. That said, family often knows things, like which neighbor is out of town."

"Meaning either of them could have hired someone to do their dirty work. There are addicts who'll murder for twenty-five bucks."

"Sure, if it's some other loser lying in an alley. No one stupid enough to risk the death penalty in Texas for a lousy twenty-five is smart enough to have put as much thought into a crime as this perp did."

Watching her closely, Blade replied, "There's always young Debra."

Campbell closed her eyes. "Please, God, no. Despite recent strains, Maida adored her. That kind of faith in another person has to count for something. And as I said, the girl was shattered when she saw the stained carpet."

"Or overwhelmed with guilt? Didn't you say she apologized to her mother? What if that wasn't about getting sick to her stomach? What if it was a confession?"

"Wait a minute." Campbell reviewed what he'd said. "Weren't the girls at Point East?"

"For a brief time only. They left around seven. Stacie was found at what? One? Where were they for the next six hours?"

Appearing tortured herself, Campbell raked her hands through her hair. "There's my fatal flaw. Maybe it's a good thing I didn't stay in the force, I can't open my mind to what you're suggesting."

Blade understood only too well. "You wouldn't be the first. That's why there are such wealthy trial lawyers." But for the moment he had to play devil's advocate. "If you don't come up with some viable suspects, you know what that leaves, don't you?"

Campbell met his gaze. "Yes. Me. Or rather me and Ike Crenshaw, who's my patrol. But we stayed in radio contact and I knew where he was virtually all the time. Plus I let Archer use his UV light on my truck to clear myself."

Blade couldn't believe she'd allowed that. Like many who wore uniforms, she still didn't fully comprehend how easy it was to contaminate a site…or the cunning of someone intent on transferring evidence. "That was risky. What if someone wanted to set you up? Didn't you say something about ill will between Cody and others in authority?"

"It would be riskier to let the press start trying this case on TV and in the paper. I have ulterior motives, Blade. My father's health doesn't need the burden of prolonged stress. He's just been through prostate cancer surgery."

The Codys had been through their share of problems. This newest confidence made Blade all the more admiring of Campbell's ability to keep it all together as well as she was. "I didn't know. How's he doing?"

"The prognosis is excellent, but he needs time to regain his strength, and my continued problems with the LPD—you know about that, don't you?"

"I know you left the LPD one step ahead of being stripped of your badge and that you lost your partner—Lefevre's wife's stepbrother? I didn't dig deeper because I didn't intend for our paths to cross again. When you're ready, you can tell me yourself."

Once again their gazes locked. Blade decided the cliché about moments when the world stops were a weak analogy. Nothing stopped. Everything accelerated, magnified and merged—his senses, his thoughts, his desires. This time he was grateful for Campbell rising and breaking the connection.

"I really have to go. We called in a new employee even before we finished his background check because we're already seriously shorthanded without the added strain the press is causing."

"How do I contact you if I need to pass on information?"

She hesitated. "Can't I contact you?"

"I don't carry your communication equipment just as I don't carry my real ID on me. It would be a shortcut to a bullet in the head."

Without further comment, she unzipped a compartment in her bag and drew out her business card and a pen, then she wrote her pager and cell phone numbers on the back. "Can I count on you to keep this private?"

Blade reached over and ripped a paper towel from a roll and wrote down two numbers, an unlisted one and his cell number. "It goes both ways," he said, handing it over. "And the cell phone is rarely on. Like I said, it stays in my El Camino—I drive a gray '82 model—and I keep my legit ID and stuff in there when I'm working."

"I understand," she said quietly. "I'll never use these unless it's critical." Folding the napkin, Campbell put it in her pocket. "Hopefully I'll have some good news the next time we talk. About my hours…they're erratic and will probably be worse the next few days. I'm supposed to be off duty, but under the circumstances that's changed and I'll be training in between whatever else comes at us."

In a way Blade thought that was healthier for her. Staying busy would keep her from brooding about her friend's death. Yet he'd been through the process of loss himself and knew better than to lecture. "I make my own hours, but they're usually from around seven in the evening to anytime after two in the morning, depending on what's going down. If we need to talk about specific people, will you come by here again? I'm paranoid about wireless feed."

"And I don't have a backup vehicle anymore. Do you think it would be smart to have the Cody SUV in your driveway?"

"Borrow something."

Murmuring, "All right," she left.

The dog followed her to her truck. From the door, Blade watched with a mixture of disbelief and envy as she gave the lug another good petting. Then it stood there watching her until she drove away.

With a hefty sigh, it wandered over to his truck, pissed on the rear wheel and, giving what Blade swore was a smug look, went back to his post on the table.

The only reason he didn't shoot the bastard then and there was because he knew Campbell would be back, and he didn't want to see fear or pain in her eyes again.

22

"**W**here are we?"

As Campbell brought the SUV to a halt, Andy Raynor peered out into the darkness. Snapping on his penlight, he checked his notes and map. "Uh…Magnolia Parkway?"

"Magnolia Parkway is our loop around the innermost section of the development where the recreation center, health club and gym, and the golf course clubhouse are located," she replied. "Imagine you've just broken down and you need to advise the gate that you're stranded here."

"Do I have a flat tire? I can change a flat in less than ten minutes."

"I'll call you the next time I have one," Campbell drawled. "Check your landmarks. Remember the order in which the buildings are located."

"Right! We've just passed the golf course clubhouse…that row of lights up ahead should be the sidewalk to the health club…so that means if it was daylight, I'd see the eighth hole flag beyond my right shoulder.''

"Is that east, south, what?" Campbell asked, quickly reaching up on the dash to block his view of the compass.

"It's…the center.''

"Try again. You always have to keep your directions clear because you're dealing with senior citizens who rely on specifics or they can get confused. If the sun was up, you could use it to pinpoint your east-west line. But at night, sometimes it's so overcast you can't see any stars, let alone the moon. Even if your compass is broken, your map and landmarks tell you what?''

"That eighth hole flag is set due east. So I'm at the east end of the loop. You enter the development from the west end of the development.''

"Great, and where's the lake?''

"Um…north. If you were just entering the property, you take the first left, north, on Lakeshore Drive.''

Campbell sat back in her seat and unbuckled her seat belt, pleased with his eye and memory, particularly at this hour. "Terrific. Let's switch seats and you can drive us back.''

As they passed each other between the beams of the truck, not even the cold night air helped Campbell's fatigue. She'd been teaching Andy the layout of Maple Trails for the last four hours. Her voice was getting scratchy and her eyes were burning so badly, she doubted eye drops would help. She needed to call it a night.

"Radio the gate that you're coming," she said. "We'll turn in our radio, sign our daily log, and since you've done so well, you can surprise your wife by coming home before dawn."

He grinned as if he'd been given a bonus and reached for the mike. "Great. Thanks. Marti's still a little nervous about the idea of being by herself at night."

Six-foot-four and free-range thin, Andrew Raynor lived in a world that was already full of responsibility, and he was only twenty-three. He and wife, Marti, were about to celebrate six months of wedded bliss. Their son, Andy Jr., called Drew, had been born four weeks ago. With a hospital bill to settle and the prospect of numerous future medical checkups for the little one, he was anxious to find employment with more of a future than managing a convenience store. He'd eagerly accepted the offer to start training tonight, especially when told it meant he was officially on the payroll.

"Are the apartments where you live well lit?" Campbell asked after his exchange with Howie Johnson at the gatehouse. She wanted to get a feel for whether Marti just needed to adjust to being a new wife and mother, or was the spoiled princess type, or whether they were residing in a bad location. Any of those things could create a conflict, making it difficult for Andy to perform his job.

"Oh, it's okay. We're practically across the street

from a fire department," he replied. "But it's an older place and there are a lot of noises that sound creepier when she's alone. I'll be able to move us into one of the nicer places as soon as I'm through my probation period and my medical coverage kicks in."

"Good for you." Campbell stifled a yawn and tried to keep herself alert by thinking of what she hadn't yet taught him. "Now you'll park your patrol vehicle where you left your pickup truck. You saw the two white SUVs there?" When he nodded she continued, "Make sure you've taken any cups or food wrappers out and drop them in the gatehouse trash can. Every shift is responsible for cleaning up after themselves. You turn in the keys at the same time you do the rest, then you sign out and you're done."

"What about gas?"

"That's the day shift's responsibility. They fill up over at the maintenance barn. That's also where they wash the vehicles, air up the tires, and do other minor repairs. Oh, and all maintenance vehicles—except for the big dump truck—are olive green and they have roof lights, too. Theirs flash yellow, though. You shouldn't see any during your shift, unless there's another bad storm like the one the other night."

By three, Campbell was shaking hands with Andy, saying her farewells to Howie and climbing back into her truck. Ahead of her, she saw that only one of the local media trucks remained out front. The rest had pulled out after they'd done their reports for the ten o'clock news.

As she exited the property, she saw the silhouette

of a figure in the small side window of the RV and assumed she was having her picture taken again. She considered flashing her high beams to ruin some of the photographer's film, but decided against it. There was no point in antagonizing members of the press, since they were simply doing their jobs, too. But after turning out of the property, she was relieved to look in her rearview mirror and notice the RV wasn't following her.

Small gifts, she thought, navigating the serpentine turns. She wondered if things were quiet back at headquarters. Probably so, since Yancy hadn't responded when she'd radioed to say she was leaving the Trails. She hoped that meant he'd finally turned in.

Was Blade asleep? A faint, shivery something ran through her as she finally allowed him to invade her consciousness. She'd been fighting that while she'd worked with Andy; however, now that she was alone, the events of the day came at her with the energy of a blue norther storm.

She'd never met anyone quite like him before, and she hoped trusting him wasn't going to prove a huge mistake. But he was right—for some reason she did trust him. He was also right about the chemistry between them, but the timing couldn't be worse, and professionally it was entirely inappropriate. Having been in a similar position once before, she continued to pay a price for it. Never again, she'd vowed to herself. And yet she missed being held, missed the intimacy, but not at the cost of breaking her heart.

The buzz of the cell phone startled her and Campbell fumbled with it before successfully flipping it open. Surely it wasn't Blade...?

"Yes?" she said cautiously.

"How'd it go?" Yancy asked.

She exhaled in relief before demanding, "What are you doing up? I've a good mind to let your doctor know that his 'get plenty of rest' directive has been summarily ignored."

"Keep it up, and you'll lose what's left of your voice. For your information I was up getting a drink of water and heard you on the radio. That TV dinner Beth insisted I eat had enough sodium in it to turn me into jerky." At that, he paused to take a sip from his water bottle. "So? How's the new recruit?"

"He's a nice guy and as quick a study as Kelsey."

"Then let's hope we can keep him. I remember him admitting his dream was to become a homicide detective someday."

"Isn't that the standard for everyone who wants to carry a badge and a gun?"

"You never said it."

"Maybe not to you. You always made it clear I was supposed to take over the company." Yancy didn't respond right away and Campbell wanted to kick herself for her candor.

"You don't want my business?"

"I didn't say that." But he'd spoken the one word that made her uncertain. It was *his* business despite having made her a partner, and would be until his last breath. "Dad, it's almost three in the morning. Have pity."

"A helluva hour to learn you've wasted your life."

Campbell had to change the subject or end the call. Her head was beginning to throb. "Go back to bed or I'll call Cheralyn and tell her you want to see her."

"You do that and you won't have to worry about inheriting a dime," Yancy growled.

"Grouch. When did Beth finally go home?"

"After our fan club outside did their evening reports and returned to their stations. I told her to wear dark sunglasses when she comes in this morning or they'll accuse us of abusing her."

Campbell saw the humor in the statement, but also the concern. "We have to pace our people. I know most of them are dedicated. The thing is, you can wear out that dedication."

"I don't have to worry, I have you to correct me."

Zing. Sometimes she thought her father was like a .45 attached to a minicomputer. It struck automatically based on key words. "Well, I'm glad you phoned," she said, slipping into her diplomatic tone. "I'd like you to check into something for me in the morning with your state trooper friend about a fellow officer. I don't know his rank, but the name is Mize, first name Donald."

"Who is he?"

The spontaneous query told Campbell this would be a more complicated process than she'd hoped. "The father of Ashley Mize. She's a classmate and friend of Debra Saunders."

"And we give a damn because…?"

"I'm asking."

"What are you up to?" Yancy's demand held a new edge.

"Connecting dots."

"I can damn well figure that out, the question is whose?"

"A wild card," Campbell replied, almost soothingly. "We get it out of the way early and we don't have to waste any more time in that direction."

"What's going on, Belle?"

She kept things succinct. "Stacie has a record. Maybe the queenly Ashley does, too."

"Are you going to suggest Maida's granddaughter—"

"That's enough over the phone." It might be late and few people were likely to be up and accidentally eavesdropping; on the other hand, it only took one attentive soul to create utter chaos. "Just do me that favor and see what information you can get, okay?"

Yancy grumbled a bit more. It was usually as effective as his roars. "You never said much about the church service. Something must've happened to initiate this. It sure lasted long enough."

"It was educational." Campbell's dulled senses were making it increasingly hard to even form the words coming out of her mouth. In another minute, she was bound to start slurring like a drunk. "We'll talk when I get in. See you between nine and ten."

"You're not coming over here?"

"There are things I need to take care of. Get some rest. Night."

She disconnected and shortly thereafter pulled into

the parking lot of her complex. It was one of those newer ones Andy had mentioned. She couldn't think of anything she yearned for with as much relish, except maybe having her good reputation back.

After parking, she wearily collected the outfit she'd worn to the service, and the rest of her things, locked up and climbed the stairs as quietly as she could. Even exhaustion didn't let her forget there were three other neighbors needing rest around her own one-bedroom unit. It was the little things in life that mattered, simple courtesies. Maida used to speak of that.

A deeper sadness joined her fatigue so that the last three steps might as well have been another entire flight to scale. She fumbled with the keys in her hand and heard something hit the stair, then fall between the next slat and drop to the concrete entryway of the apartment below hers. Glancing between the cracks Campbell saw it was one of her high heels.

"Dammit," she whispered.

Unlocking her door at the top of the second floor, she dropped everything but her keys onto the chair just inside the apartment. Then, she went to reclaim her shoe.

Straightening, she looked out the other end of the entryway to see an LPD patrol car making a security check. The cop driving had spotted her and braked. Please God, she prayed, bending to pick up the shoe, don't let them be anyone who recognized her. Standing up, she lifted the hand holding her keys to wave and tried to mount the stairs without exposing her dread.

At the top of the stairs, she glanced over the wrought-iron railing. The cop in the driver's seat waved and continued onward out of the parking lot.

Anyone else would have been relieved at the reprieve. Campbell could barely keep her hands steady enough to secure the two dead bolts. Her vision already blurred by tears, she missed placing the keys on the TV and they knocked something else to the carpet as they fell, but she continued on to her bedroom, guided by the night-light glowing in her bathroom.

Dropping facedown on her queen-size bed, she muffled her choked cry in the quilted comforter. She was finally able to let down her guard—the stress and heartbreak of the past twenty-four-plus hours refused to be contained another minute. Yielding to her grief, Campbell gripped the bedding and sobbed.

23

Friday, February 7
8:54 a.m.

Not even sunglasses helped ease the pain behind
Campbell's eyes as she headed toward headquarters.
Whoever said a good cry was therapeutic had never
done it in one of the allergy capitals of the south,
where migraine-level pain was as commonplace as
black eyes on a boxer. Tea bags and a cold washcloth
had improved things to where she'd been able to add
a quick sweep of mascara, but otherwise she was
doomed to mimic an MTV star.

Wishing she could delay going to headquarters, she
groaned when her phone buzzed. It had to be Yancy.
She wished she could have these few minutes of driving to prepare herself for the interrogation that was
all but a sure thing once he saw her.

Flipping open the phone, she snapped, "You're
early."

"I don't know how I can be," a male voice replied,
somewhat uncertain. "I only got the information myself minutes ago."

Campbell mouthed the S epithet. "Detective Archer. My apologies. I thought you were Yancy with a stopwatch in his hand."

"Then I'm going to add to your stress. Can you come over here to my office? I need to run something by you."

He, too, was cautious about the security of wireless calls. Appreciating that, she made a sharp right at the next intersection to head toward the heart of town. "I'm on my way."

Was this a clever trick? As she entered the municipal building, Campbell wondered if she should have given Yancy a heads-up call. Seconds later it was too late to worry; upon introducing herself to the desk officer, she was directed up to Archer's office.

He wasn't there. She found him a few doors down in the lab. Wearing a lab coat over his dress shirt and tie, the straight-faced Archer indicated his gloved hands and apologized for not shaking hands. "Are you okay?"

She'd weighed wisdom against ego and had taken off her sunglasses. "It was another long night. Combined with allergies, I'm a great candidate for a 'before' model for the latest pharmaceutical miracle."

"Then a double thanks for coming so quickly. We have what might be a strong lead. I'd like your input. It's a long strand of hair found in the trunk of Mrs. Livingstone's car."

The half mug of coffee she'd managed to drink shifted uneasily in her stomach. She had been set up. When was the last time she had helped Maida haul or unpack something? To the best of her recollections, she usually insisted they use her truck in order to protect Maida's vehicle.

Following Archer to his desk, she waited for him to open the manila envelope and lift out the seemingly empty plastic bag. She had to blink several times to clear her vision enough to see what he held up...and almost went weak-kneed from relief.

The strand was black and not as long as her own hair.

"Can you tell me of anyone you know who had contact with Mrs. Livingstone that has hair resembling this?" Archer asked politely. "I admit I was upset and didn't study Mrs. Livingstone's granddaughter as well as I should have, but I seem to remember the color is wrong for her."

Campbell didn't believe that for a second. "You're certain it's human? It looks like something from one of those fancy dust brushes for intricate chandeliers."

"Surely Mrs. Livingstone didn't need one of those for her modest dinette fixture? Was she ever around anyone's pets?"

That would have been the logical next guess, but she wasn't going to fall for it. "Detective, I missed several meals after cutting up frogs and various animal organs in biology, but I have great faith *you* can tell a human hair from a silky-haired retriever or some manufactured dust mop without losing your morning doughnut and coffee."

Archer actually smiled. "I think I like you, Ms. Cody."

"Now you're scaring me."

"That's human hair."

Of course it was, but at that moment Campbell could only think of one person it could belong to. Ashley Mize. That meant she had to be experiencing some kind of mental-processing glitch. She'd seen her yesterday, had discussed her with Blade.

Struggling to focus on Maple Trails people, she looked straight at Archer. "The secretary over in Administration. She had this length and color of hair."

"Natural or dyed?"

"Natural, I think."

"What's the past tense mean? She cut it?"

"Yes. Maybe a week ago. It's now about four to six inches shorter."

"Do you know if she had reason to be with Mrs. Livingstone for some reason before her hair appointment? Maybe they attended a benefit together or perhaps Mrs. Livingstone delivered something to the office for some reason?"

"I just don't know. If she did, she didn't tell me."

Archer looked dejected but not crushed. "I'll have to talk to the woman, nonetheless. Even if she had it cut, it doesn't mean she wasn't with Mrs. Livingstone the night she died. It would suggest a longer relationship. What kind of person is she?"

Campbell tried to be fair. "Attractive, talkative, she knows most of the residents by their first names." The men, anyway. Some of the more reserved residents had taken offense to that habit. "I'm afraid she isn't exactly my idea of efficient, but she seems to please Mr. Tyndell.''

Hazel eyes studied her calmly. ''Could you see her as the type to blackmail a resident?''

''No. Barbie isn't smart enough.''

''Does she have a temper?''

Already feeling the fatigue she thought she'd slept off from last night, Campbell rubbed her forehead. ''Detective, I tend to avoid Barbie as much as I do men wearing a lot of jewelry. Just talking to her on the phone works on my nerves like nails on a chalkboard.''

Archer bowed his head. If he was smiling, his pursed lips hid it. ''Anyone else who could match this sample? Neighbors or neighbors' children? Any of your personnel?''

''No, and thank heavens, no. Besides me, the only other CS female guard at the premises is Kelsey McGraw, and her hair is lighter and shorter than mine.'' No way would Campbell bring herself to mention Ashley Mize, even if the girl was the first to come to mind. Archer would laugh in her face. She might as well say she'd seen a girl with black hair crossing Main Street. But she had a strong urge to talk to Blade.

''I'll be returning to the house today,'' Archer told her. ''Can I count on you to warn your person at the gate?''

''I'll phone them as soon as I leave here. Can I give them a possible ETA so they can have the barriers removed for you?''

He glanced at his stainless steel watch. "Within the hour. I trust we'll be more successful this time in keeping out the family."

As far as she knew, they hadn't heard from any of the Saunderses, let alone Bryce Tyndell, since yesterday afternoon's fiasco. That didn't leave her feeling anything close to reassured. "If there is trouble, our guard will ring the house immediately to warn you. Would you mind if I check in with you after I finish at headquarters and with Mr. Tyndell?"

"Not at all. But I'd prefer you don't warn—what is her name?"

"Name…oh. Barbie. Excuse me, Barbara Young. No, I have no intention of divulging anything to her." Campbell needed fresh air and sunlight. She didn't feel comfortable about this conversation at all. "The thing is, Detective, that hair could easily belong to anyone…the bagger at the grocery store."

"True enough." Archer replaced the bag in the envelope and nodded to her. "I'll see you later, then."

Discipline helped Campbell wait until she was out of the parking lot before she reached for her phone. The first call she made was to Kelsey to advise of Archer's pending arrival. Right afterward, she punched in the number she'd committed to memory. As it began to ring, she prayed she was doing the right thing.

On the third ring he answered.

"Yeah, umm…it's me," she said, suddenly self-conscious. "Is this a bad time?"

"No," Blade replied. "Are you okay?"

OFFICIAL OPINION POLL

Dear Reader,

Since you are a book enthusiast, we would like to know what you think.

Inside you will find a short Opinion Poll. Please participate in our poll by sharing your opinion on 3 subjects that are very important to all of us.

To thank you for your participation, we would like to send you your choice of **2 FREE BOOKS** and a **FREE GIFT!**

Please enjoy them with our compliments,

Sincerely,

Pam Powers

Editor

P.S. Don't forget to indicate which books you prefer so we can send your FREE gifts today!

What's your pleasure...

Romance?

Enjoy 2 FREE BOOKS that will fuel your imagination with intensely moving stories about life, love and relationships.

OR

Suspense?

Enjoy 2 FREE BOOKS that will thrill you with a spine-tingling blend of suspense and mystery.

✓ Whichever category you select, your **2 FREE BOOKS** have a combined cover price of $11.98 or more in the U.S. and $13.98 or more in Canada.

Simply place the sticker next to your preferred choice of books, complete the poll on the right page and you'll automatically receive **2 FREE BOOKS** and a **FREE GIFT** with no obligation to purchase anything!

YOUR OPINION POLL
THANK-YOU FREE GIFTS INCLUDE

▶ **2 ROMANCE OR 2 SUSPENSE BOOKS**

▶ **A LOVELY SURPRISE GIFT**

DETACH AND MAIL CARD TODAY!

OFFICIAL OPINION POLL

YOUR OPINION COUNTS!

Please check TRUE or FALSE below to express your opinion about the following statements:

Q1 Do you believe in "true love"?

"TRUE LOVE HAPPENS ONLY ONCE IN A LIFETIME."
○ TRUE
○ FALSE

Q2 Do you think marriage has any value in today's world?

"YOU CAN BE TOTALLY COMMITTED TO SOMEONE WITHOUT BEING MARRIED."
○ TRUE
○ FALSE

Q3 What kind of books do you enjoy?

"A GREAT NOVEL MUST HAVE A HAPPY ENDING."
○ TRUE
○ FALSE

Place the sticker next to one of the selections below to receive your **2 FREE BOOKS** and **FREE GIFT**.
I understand that I am under no obligation to purchase anything as explained on the back of this card.

Romance

193 MDL DVFS
393 MDL DVFU

Suspense

192 MDL DVFR
392 MDL DVFT

0074823 ‖‖‖‖‖‖ ‖‖‖‖ ‖‖‖‖ **FREE GIFT CLAIM #** **3622**

FIRST NAME

LAST NAME

ADDRESS

APT.#

CITY

(BB3-04)

STATE/PROV.

ZIP/POSTAL CODE

The Reader Service — Here's How It Works:

Accepting your 2 free books and gift places you under no obligation to buy anything. You may keep the books and gift and return the shipping statement marked "cancel." If you do not cancel, about a month later we'll send you 3 additional books and bill you just $4.74 each in the U.S., or $5.24 each in Canada, plus 25¢ shipping & handling per book and applicable taxes if any.* That's the complete price, and — compared to cover prices of $5.99 or more each in the U.S. and $6.99 or more each in Canada — it's quite a bargain! You may cancel at any time, but if you choose to continue, every month we'll send you 3 more books, which you may either purchase at the discount price...or return to us and cancel your subscription.

*Terms and prices subject to change without notice. Sales tax applicable in N.Y.
Canadian residents will be charged applicable provincial taxes and GST.

"Compared to what? Listen, I was wondering if you're coming into town in the next few minutes? I'd like to get your input on something."

Blade hesitated. "It would be smarter for both of us if you came here."

Not in the Cody Blazer, it wasn't. He had put his trust in her and she wasn't going to pay him back by suddenly making his hideaway a place of speculation. "I have to change vehicles, then. It'll take me an extra few minutes."

"I'll wait."

24

9:29 a.m.

At first Yancy resisted handing over his Caddy—a Christmas present to himself. But when Campbell started to offer to rent Beth's car for two hours, he tossed the keys to her. She knew it wasn't selfishness that held him back—the car was rarely used these days and she was actually doing him a favor—he was simply leveraging to get information out of her.

"Get me that information on Officer Mize and we'll talk later after I update Tyndell and check in with Detective Archer," she told him. While she would like to skip Tyndell, it couldn't be avoided, plus she needed to fish for information on whether Dwayne Saunders was making more protests about access to his mother's property—or worse.

Thankfully, there was no sign of the press as she drove out of the parking lot. On the downside, Kelsey had warned that a significant number of them were back at the entrance to Maple Trails. No station would miss Detective Archer's return to the property—all the more reason to check in with Bryce, once she took care of other pressing business.

Understandably, at the first sight of the Cadillac, Blade's dog leaped off of the picnic table and did his best to wake not only the dead but the yet to be born, as well. Campbell reached over for the two hot dogs she'd taken out of the refrigerator and offered them to the great-jawed animal. He wrapped his tongue around them as well as her hand.

"Sure. Make me look bad."

Blade stood in the doorway unshaven, his hair wet from a shower. Dressed in another black T-shirt and jeans, he looked ready to return to his undercover world. Campbell suspected that if she checked his closet or drawers, all she would see was black.

"Sorry," she said. "It's my father's car, and I'm trying to bribe this guy not to use it like a lounge chair...or a fire hydrant for that matter."

"Nice wheels. I'm not sure it's less of an attention-getter than the Cody mobile."

At least her father had resisted the temptation of personalized tags. "It's the best I could do on short notice. I won't be here long." Giving the dog pressing against her thigh an affectionate last pat, she crossed to the house. Blade stepped aside to let her enter, and as she passed him, she caught the scent of soap and coffee.

"Can you stay long enough to have some?" he asked, gesturing to his mug on the counter. "I promise it's not last night's reheated."

Two jokes in a row. Campbell wondered if this was

a glimpse of his real personality or if she'd sounded worse on the phone than she'd imagined and he was trying to make her feel better. "Thanks, but no. I'm strung pretty tight already. Besides, I meant it, I really have to get back to—"

Blade held up a finger and approached her slowly, cautiously reaching up toward her face. When she realized he intended to take off her sunglasses, she took a step back and removed them herself—and instantly knew that the improvement in her appearance she believed she'd seen in the last hour was wishful thinking.

"What's happened now?" he asked quietly.

Wanting badly to slip the glasses back on, Campbell settled for averting her face. "Things are just piling up. I'm fine."

"How's the arm this morning?"

"Almost back to normal, thanks."

"Uh-huh."

"Listen—" she forced herself to meet his troubled gaze "—I've just come from the Sheriff's Office. Archer has a strong lead that points to a suspect."

"Not you?"

"No. But he found a strand of hair in Maida's trunk. It's black. Want to give me your first reaction?"

Instead, he leaned back against the counter and crossed his arms over his chest. "Campbell, I didn't know Maida existed until you asked about her at Good Shepherd."

It struck her that he thought she was accusing him.

With an incredulous laugh, she pointed outside. "You think I'd bother driving out here in a different vehicle if I thought it was you?"

Shrugging, he replied, "You could have thought that because I've had some contact with the girls, including Debra Saunders, that there was an outside chance I was keeping something from you." Then the hint of a smile tugged at the corners of his mouth. "My second thought is knowing the idea never crossed your mind makes me really want to kiss you."

She felt heat in her face and didn't want to think about what message he was getting from that. "It's a long hair, Blade. Twice the length of yours, but shorter than mine. Come on, who?"

"Ashley Mize," he replied, turning to pick up his mug. "Is that what you want me to say?"

"I want to know what you think."

"You're responding to a simple case of association. We saw and discussed her last night. I hope you didn't run your hunch by Archer."

"Of course not, not when I can't swear she and Maida ever met. It's possible Debra inadvertently carried the hair on her clothing and during her last visit with her grandmother somehow left it on the felt lining of the trunk. What I did feel obligated to inform him about was that the strand could belong to the secretary of the property's administrator. She cut her hair several days ago." Campbell told him about Barbie.

"Are they in frequent contact?"

"Maida lived to hold Bryce Tyndell's feet to the fire," she said dryly. "She was always telling me about charging down there or leaving irate messages for him—probably because Barbie was finally ordered to screen his calls—citing infractions around the development, and how Bryce wasn't doing his job. As cranky as that sounds, she was usually right. Bryce is more political than efficient and knows exactly who he has to keep happy and who he can leave dangling. That's one of the reasons an increasing number of residents are recommending incorporating into a town. They've been inspired by another private community near Tyler that has done exactly that."

"Maybe Archer should focus on Tyndell," Blade replied. "Is he confrontational, disrespectful toward women, does he hold a grudge and talk about what he'd like to do to people?"

Campbell thought that description better suited Lefevre. "Bryce can be a snake, but he's more apt to stab you in the back than do something directly confrontational. And as I said, he's political. He keeps his emotions in tight control."

"What about the secretary?"

"Our staff gave her the nickname Barbie after she botched one too many messages. You don't want to know how she is with losing files. She could have given Hillary Clinton lessons."

Blade contemplated her over the rim of his mug. "Why do I get the feeling she's another looker like Ashley?"

"No argument there. I understand the UPS driver

and mail carrier leave daily with their tongues hanging down to their laps. It's amazing what false eyelashes, padded bras and skirts a half size too small can do for a girl.''

''Not everyone is brought up to believe that their minds are their greatest asset.''

It wasn't the argument that annoyed her; it was the twinkle in his eyes. ''Maybe this was a mistake.''

Setting down the mug, Blade laid his hand against his chest. ''Bad timing with the cop humor.''

That she understood. She had begun to rely on it herself when she was on the force. ''Am I wrong to feel Ashley's DNA needs to be compared with Archer's evidence?''

''Maybe not. Probably not. The longer it takes for him or the LPD to make an arrest, the more the press will focus on Cody Security and law-enforcement policy, and on hints dropped by 'unknown sources.' That snake you mentioned could be sure that includes you.''

Encouraged, Campbell made her request. ''Then will you help me? It's asking a great deal, I know,'' she continued quickly at his sudden expression of doubt, ''but as you said, you've actually met her. It would be easier for you to get a strand of Ashley's hair.''

The idea sounded better in Archer's lab. She didn't want Ashley to be guilty; she didn't want this whole mess to have happened in the first place, but if she could resolve one puzzle one way or another, maybe the world would stop feeling as if it were spinning uncontrollably toward some black hole.

Blade set down the mug and wiped a hand over his mouth and beard. "Are you aware...? Campbell, for the record, I'm thirty-five. She's eighteen."

"I'm not asking you to sleep with her."

"Then what? Borrow her hairbrush?"

His words held no scorn, but they should have. She had no right to put him in this position. There was no telling what he was working on, what case or cases her request could compromise.

"Forget it. I had no right to ask." She'd just done something she swore she would never do—compromise the safety of another person.

"Hey."

Not knowing what else to do, she started to leave. Afraid of what she would see, she was slow to look back at him.

"You're thinking about your friend. When it's personal like that, wisdom is as easy to sacrifice as fear is to ignore."

How she wished he was right. But she'd been in this position before and she'd refused to sacrifice the wise choice, had refused to push aside her fear. "It's my problem. I'll figure out something else."

She had her hand on the doorknob when she heard him say, "I guess I can finally let her challenge me to a game of pool."

Campbell hesitated. "Is she any good?"

"No. But she's better than the rest of her friends.

I told her last time she asked that she needed to practice a lot more, and she has been."

Campbell accepted a kick of jealousy as her due. "Maybe I could go there, sort of drop by and pretend to spot Debra—"

"No way."

"Why not?"

"Because I'm not sure I could pretend I didn't know you. Not anymore."

Talk about a universe in chaos, she thought. This man had sucked her out of her orbit and into the unknown. She needed to leave; there wasn't enough oxygen in the room. "Then I'll wait for your call," she said, turning the knob.

Suddenly, his hand was covering hers. "Are you training staff again tonight?"

His warm breath was a caress against the back of her neck. "Yes."

"As soon as you're free, come over."

She turned her head, even though it brought his lips so close to her cheek, her skin tingled. "How do you know you'll have the sample?"

"Because I want to see you again."

25

"**I**'ll be there as soon as I can."

Campbell flipped her phone shut and wondered how to divide herself into two more pieces. For once Tyndell had arrived at the office on time and was demanding a sit-down. Archer had arrived at Maida's house and was requesting her presence ASAP. First, however, she needed to return Yancy's car and get the Blazer. She could only hope her father was tied up with personnel at one of the other clients' businesses. Blade had flustered her again, and she wasn't ready to be interrogated by anyone who read her emotions too well.

Fortunately it didn't happen. Beth informed her in between phone calls that "Boss One" was in conference with a new client. "A Fred Sheffield, vice president at Eastside State Bank."

Nice, Campbell thought, raising her eyebrows in surprise and appreciation. "What does that give us—three financial institution accounts?"

"Five," Beth intoned.

In comparison, she didn't appear all that thrilled. Campbell had only to look at the younger woman's desk to understand why. She was slowly being buried in a mass of printouts, files and unopened mail. The computer screen also told her that Beth was still working on the payroll checks, which were usually ready by noon on Fridays.

They used to have a two-clerk office, but a former employee's husband was military and had been transferred, forcing her to quit. With Yancy's illness, they'd put off searching for anyone new. He'd also taken to doing a portion of the paperwork during his convalescence. But they'd acquired another new account since then besides the bank, and it was evident that things were beginning to overwhelm Beth.

Deciding to make an executive decision, Campbell said, "Call our agency when you have a chance. Let them know what you need in an assistant and a clerk, and that you'd like to start interviewing on Monday."

"An assistant?" Beth's eyes almost doubled in size. "What does that make me?"

"Office manager, I guess." Scratching her head, she glanced down the hall. "You'll need an office and some furniture, won't you? Scavenge around and see what you can come up with, and we'll take it from there. This first room behind your desk should work."

"It's pretty loaded with files and supplies."

"Hire someone to move all of that to the next room down the hall."

"I have a cousin who has been laid off and is looking for work. His wife just found out she's pregnant. He's strong," she added eagerly.

"Fine." Campbell did a double take. "Do you

think he might be interested in security work? Give him an application while he's here.''

Yancy might fuss that she was trying to put him back in the hospital, but he would have to see this was a necessity—unless they wanted to watch Beth walk out the door due to exhaustion. "Yancy will give you the details on your raise as soon as we talk.''

"I can't thank you enough." Beth bit her lip. "Is there anything I can do for you?" she asked tentatively. "You look…''

"Yeah," Campbell replied dryly. "So I've been told. No, I'll be fine as long as you don't quit. Things will improve, I promise.''

After filling her in on where she would be, Campbell headed for the Blazer. It felt good to see Beth look happy, to know she'd done some constructive problem-solving. But her pleasure was short-lived as she approached Maple Trails and saw the area was again a swarm of RVs and satellite trucks.

Kelsey stepped out of the gatehouse to move the barriers for her. "Am I relieved to see you," she said through stiff lips.

Aware that the cameras had gone live again, Campbell understood. "If they're getting disrespectful, call the Sheriff's Office and ask for a deputy to help with traffic control.''

"Oh, this is still manageable. It's Tyndell. He has Dwayne Saunders in his office, and I guess to impress him, he's being his obnoxious worst. Right before you drove up, he phoned and said if he didn't hear from you in five minutes, he was calling the sheriff himself and having all Cody Security personnel removed from the premises.''

''Lovely. Do me a favor and call Maida's house and let Detective Archer know that's where I am, that her son is there, too, and that I'll see him as soon as I'm through.''

''Done. Good luck!''

The chill factor dropped significantly upon entering the administration building. Barbie was nowhere to be seen, the switchboard was buzzing like a beehive and she could hear Dwayne Saunders in Bryce's office lecturing at a pitch that sounded like he was grounding both of his kids until they were forty.

Bryce spotted her first. ''Here she is.'' His demeanor immediately switched from tense and worried to morally outraged. ''We've been waiting for over forty minutes, Ms. Cody.''

''So I heard. But I did get here as fast as I could.'' She made no other explanation, knowing Bryce would hate that more than an excuse. ''Mr. Saunders, how's your daughter and Mrs. Saunders?''

Chest thrust out and hands on hips, he snapped, ''How do you think they are? You had no right to expose them to such ugliness.''

Of all the things Campbell expected him to accuse her of, it wasn't that. ''Excuse me?''

Dwayne Saunders smirked at Bryce. ''You called it. She's going to pretend it didn't happen.'' He pointed his finger at Campbell. ''My wife told me what you did. You encouraged her to speak with that detective but didn't warn her that he was in my mother's bedroom where it all happened.''

''That's not true.''

''What's true is that the presence of my daughter didn't seem to matter to you—and you'd already seen she'd had a traumatic discovery earlier in the day.''

Campbell had to clear her throat to temper her own response. ''Sir, I'm going to give your wife the benefit of the doubt and suggest your family's loss has affected her memory of the event. For the record, Mrs. Saunders first drove by Security and then pushed past me and entered your mother's house after being clearly cautioned against it, because Detective Archer was still working in there. He would be entirely within his authority to file charges against her.''

''Campbell.'' Bryce sat forward in his chair, his expression aghast. ''Please do not indulge in such intimidation techniques in this office. I can't allow it any longer.''

What on earth was he suggesting now? she wondered. But refocusing on Dwayne, she said, ''No one outside of your family is more heartbroken at what has happened than I am, Mr. Saunders.''

''Save it,'' he snapped. ''My mother would be alive if you people had done your job. You're going to be hearing from my attorney, I promise you. It will be a pleasure to update him on what Cody Security will do to get attention off of yourselves.''

''What is he talking about?'' she asked Bryce.

Bryce shook his head. ''You're going to deny you stayed out of sight just long enough for Detective

Archer to stop by and all but call Barbara his chief suspect?''

''Cody Security does have other clients, Bryce. Where is she?''

''Where do you think? After he made her pull her own hair out of her head and drop it into an evidence bag, she left, practically hysterical. Heaven knows when she'll be fit to come back.'' With dramatic flair, Bryce gestured toward the reception area. ''Listen to that racket out there. Who's supposed to answer all of those calls?''

Campbell knew what she wanted to suggest, but thought it wiser to stick to her own problems. ''Detective Archer is, and has been, a complete professional. I trust he was as considerate to Barbara as he could be and explained that it was simply a formality.''

Bryce struck his desk with his fist. ''Yes, but how did he *know* she had the type of hair he was looking for if you didn't tell him? He's never met her before.''

Calmly Campbell asked, ''If an officer of the law asks you to list everyone at a location matching a certain ID, would you lie?''

Bryce settled back in his chair and looked away.

''Now…if we can focus on the facts, Mr. Saunders—''

With his lower lip jutting out, Dwayne Saunders's expression started to resemble that of a bulldog. ''The fact is that I let my mother move here because it was supposed to be safe. She paid a considerable fee for you people to protect her, and she was murdered, anyway.''

''Sir,'' Campbell replied solemnly, ''up until this week, Cody Security has never lost one person under its protection. Neither the LPD nor Gregg County Sheriff's Department can match that record.''

''That doesn't help my mother, does it?'' Dwayne snapped. ''You'd better hope that I don't find out you're in her will, lady, or so help me you will think getting kicked off the police force was a treat compared to what I'll put you through.''

''It's not wise to threaten people, Mr. Saunders,'' Campbell said, coolly. ''Particularly in front of witnesses.''

Bryce snickered. ''I didn't hear a thing.''

She shot him a withering look. ''You're beyond contempt.''

Knowing she had to leave before she lost it, she headed for the exit.

''When can we get into the house?'' Dwayne yelled after her.

''When Detective Archer says you can,'' she said over her shoulder, slamming the door behind her.

26

Completely oblivious to the glorious sunshine streaming down at her between the boughs of the pines, Campbell made short work of the sidewalk. She didn't even bother zipping her fur-collared jacket, although the wind had picked up as a weaker north front began blowing in. She was hot enough to be in her shirtsleeves.

Wishing she could take some quiet time before she went up to see Archer, Campbell climbed into the Blazer. She had just turned down her handheld radio and turned up the one in the car when her cell phone sounded.

"Perfect," she muttered, lowering the volume as Kelsey received a patrol-status check from Bobby Waldrop and Dyle Travis. She flipped open the phone.

"Yes?"

"Office manager?" Yancy asked without preamble. "Don't you think we should have discussed this first?"

At least he wasn't roaring. "We can discuss her raise. That's the best I can do for you at this stage."

Checking traffic, she backed out of the parking spot and pulled away from the administration building. If she didn't see that place again today, she would consider it a personal favor from on high. "Beth's not as dumb as I am," she drawled to her father. "She's not going to inherit this cream-puff job where she gets to work seven days a week and has the privilege of dealing with pond scum like Tyndell, or being threatened by the likes of Dwayne Saunders."

Yancy's silence told her he got the message.

"You want me to drive over there?" he finally asked.

"Hell, no. Then I'd have to visit our favorite bail bondsman to check you out of the city motel." She raised four fingers of the hand holding the steering to wave at the Jeremys, who approached from the opposite direction in their silver Lincoln Town Car. They looked like they wanted to talk and, sighing, she braked. "Hold on," she told Yancy.

Depressing her window's lever, she looked down at Mr. Jeremy in his plaid fedora and Mrs. Jeremy with her charming short haircut that made her a ringer for Dame Judi Dench.

"Campbell, we're not being told anything," the stricken-faced man said. "What's going on back there?"

She understood the confusion and fear they must be feeling. She was close to the investigation and most of the time she was confused herself. "I can't really go into anything right now, Mr. Jeremy. It's early on in the investigation."

"But Maida was found in her car out of here some-where. Why are the police taping her house?"

"They have to be thorough."

"You mean it's true what they said on TV? Her killer was across the street?"

"I hope not, Mr. Jeremy, but—"

"We've been locking our doors," Mrs. Jeremy called up to her. "In the ten years we've been living here, we've never locked our doors."

"Well, we've increased the number of patrols, as I'm sure you've noticed," Campbell said, trying to sound soothing. "But it's always a good idea to err on the side of caution. Has Detective Archer come over to interview you yet?"

"Is that the man in that black Suburban?" When Campbell nodded, Mr. Jeremy shook his head. "We don't know anything, though. We went to bed early. Connie thought she was coming down with a bug and I wanted to finish a book, and, you know, our bed-room is in the back of the house."

"The storm didn't wake you?"

"We just hunkered down deeper under the covers," Mr. Jeremy said, tugging his quilted jacket closed at the throat. "Should we go to our daughter's in Dallas, Campbell? Is it still dangerous?"

That's all they needed, fear to spread throughout the place, initiating a mass exodus. Wouldn't the press enjoy that footage? "I can't make your deci-sions for you," she replied carefully. "But I believe this is an isolated situation. Keep to your routine, but stay alert. I'll pass on what you said to Detective Archer.''

Signaling she had to go, she eased her foot off the brake. Once she was passed the Town Car, she lifted the phone to her ear. ''Did you hear that?''

''How many conversations like those have you had to deal with?''

''Enough. Kelsey's managing most of the calls so far, but Archer better lock in on a suspect soon or we're going to see *For Sale* signs in front of a bunch of houses.''

''I guess I can wait to talk to you about Beth later,'' Yancy said.

He wanted to help and didn't know what else he could do, Campbell thought. But what would help was making sure the office continued to run smoothly. ''No, let's settle this. I need to feel we're gaining some ground today and Beth deserves the assist, Dad.''

''A few weeks ago, you thought she was too young for the job.''

Campbell smiled at the dry note returning to his voice. ''What—I'm never wrong?''

''She didn't waste any time getting someone in here to move things around. He looks like a wrestler from the WWF.''

Yancy sounded as if he was covering the phone with his hand so as not to be heard. Campbell knew now was the time to reassure him. ''Sounds promising. He's a relation of hers. Been laid off due to production cuts and needs steady work. Give your best sales pitch. I hear we need a couple of new bank guards.''

''You've got an answer for everything, I see. Well, when can you get back here so we can figure out what's fair to offer her?''

''I'm on my way to meet Detective Archer at Maida's. And you're past negotiating. I've made her the commitment. You open your wallet and don't embarrass me. It wouldn't hurt to mention a year-end bonus.''

''What? She got one. Everybody got one.''

''We're talking the management variety.''

Yancy choked. ''Now, let's not get carried away.''

''You're breaking up. Besides I'm here at Maida's. Talk later,'' she said, quickly disconnecting.

She hated this property now. She hated having to go inside and see the rooms where she had had laughs and pleasure. Maida would hate the police tape and she would call it ''tacky.''

Opening the screen door, Campbell called, ''Detective? It's Campbell.''

When she didn't get a response she ventured inside—and immediately froze. There was a golf club wrapped in plastic on the floor near the hallway. Now what? she wondered.

''Archer?''

''Back here.''

He was in the garage. Campbell first saw his UV light searching the surface of the concrete around where Maida's car would have been parked.

''Nothing,'' he said, sounding dejected and not

necessarily speaking to her. "They sure wrapped her better than they cleaned up after themselves."

Campbell stayed on the doormat waiting for him to invite her farther in. "Could one person have managed this?"

He looked up, his pale face owlish in the subdued light. "Depends on his or her size. Could you have done it?"

"I'm afraid, despite her petite height, Maida weighed more than my best bench-press record."

"There you go. That's why murderers often cut up their victims." She must have made a sound of some kind because he glanced at her again. "Desperate situations, Ms. Cody. The fact that our killer didn't do that—"

"Means we're looking for a male the size of a Humvee?" Campbell asked hopefully.

"Or more than one participant."

This case was simply not going to end any less painfully than it began, no matter how much she wished otherwise. "Sir...there was only one person in her car as she passed me."

"The greenest assistant D.A. would remind you that the weather was atrocious and that you didn't get a clear view inside the vehicle. Plus there's the matter of the fence."

Campbell couldn't help but be heartened. "You're taking that seriously?"

"I take all incidentals seriously."

"Why did you take the golf club?"

"It shows blood residue."

"But you said she was struck with that urn?"

"That's what I believed. We'll see. Did Mrs. Livingstone play golf?"

"She'd begun to take lessons."

"Here?"

"Yes, we have a few retired golf pros living here and one of them teaches part-time. Um...Dean McFarland. I think his number might be in her—"

"Address book. I have it." Archer scanned the next section of the garage floor. "If the family asks, I'll return it tomorrow after I photocopy it. They may need it to contact people for the funeral."

That reminded Campbell of the queries being received over at the gatehouse. She briefed Archer about that. "I can get you a copy of the log of calls so far if you think it would be useful."

"I do. Thanks."

"And driving up here I spoke with Maida's neighbors directly across the street—the Jeremys. They're disturbed that you haven't been over to interview them yet."

"Do they have any information?"

"I'm afraid not."

"Then I trust you informed them that collecting on-site evidence is crucial at this point and that we'll move on to interviews shortly?"

"I did my best. But they are considering leaving their home and staying with family in Dallas. If we don't give them something reassuring soon, that could trigger an exodus."

"I appreciate your concern. We're moving at a fine pace, though."

Deciding not to challenge that, she tried a new approach. "I understand you met Barbara."

The way Archer pushed himself to his feet spoke of too many hours on his knees and of progressive arthritis. "She's quite a package."

"I've been informed that *package* went home sobbing."

"Not because of me she didn't." Archer switched off his equipment, casting the garage into gloom again. "She took the request for a hair sample quite well. I would have waited until her boss returned from a meeting, but when I explained this was simply a routine check, she not only offered me her hairbrush from her purse, but asked if I needed to pluck a strand directly from her head. And she requested I check Mrs. Livingstone's car for a cherub charm she's lost off her bracelet."

"Her attorney would head for the nearest happy hour after hearing that," Campbell said.

"The D.A. would buy," Archer added. "Unless that wide-eyed guilelessness is an act, somehow I doubt she's our girl."

Campbell agreed; however, she was already thinking beyond Barbie. "That lying scumbag."

Archer's light went on and off. "Excuse me?"

"Tyndell. He had Dwayne Saunders in his office. He let him think you strong-armed Barbie, and that I encouraged you because I might be in Maida's will."

"Are you?"

"Thanks for your support, Detective. Of course not."

"You're certain?"

"We discussed it twice after painful episodes with her son. I made it clear that, as touched as I was by her gesture, there was no way I could allow her to do anything of the sort, even if it wasn't against company policy."

"I'd feel better seeing a copy of the will, but since you've as much as told me the family doesn't have one, getting that isn't going to happen without involving attorneys. I'll leave it in Sheriff Glazer's hands."

Great, Campbell thought. And in the meantime she would be sweating blood until reassured that Maida had listened to her. But there was no use worrying at the moment. Archer had moved on.

She followed him until he stopped to scan the box of garbage bags.

"Just when you think you're going home with a half-empty shopping cart," he murmured.

Hoping to learn what he meant, Campbell edged closer and squinted over his shoulder. She saw the faintest smudge, as small as a tiny moth wing. If seen in sunlight she would have mistaken it for mud.

"Like I said, they probably wrapped her in garbage bags until they got her to the site," Archer said.

Campbell barely heard him. She was staring at the spot where the box was stored, half hidden by pretty ceramic pots and cleaning supplies. "Someone had to know where to find the bags,'' she told him. ''I never knew where they were until she told me.''

Looking more pleased than she'd seen him yet, Archer replied, ''We're definitely going to have to check deeper into those woods for trash...or that creek beyond where they dumped her car.''

27

The increased pressure on restaurants and clubs to discourage smoking on the premises didn't have much effect on the club's business tonight. Blade hadn't been in the place more than thirty minutes before his eyes began to burn. But it was the weekend, pockets were temporarily full of money, and the regulars were seeking an escape from the monotony of their daily lives.

He'd already pocketed forty bucks when the girls grabbed a vacated table next to his. Or rather Ashley did. The other two hung back at the booth until she chided them for being "chicken."

"I feel stupid," Debra whispered. "I don't know how to play."

"It's too soon to be back here," the other girl they called "Jules" added.

"You think that joke of a service last night was a better tribute to her?" Ashley swept her black hair behind her shoulders. "Come on, you two. We stick together and move on. I'll break. Jules, you challenge. Debutante, you watch and learn.''

"I asked you not to call me that'' came Debra's sullen reply.

As she passed her, Ashley intoned, "And I told *you* not to open your mouth when you're not with us.''

Her bead bracelets jingling as she crossed her arms, Debra tugged at the ends of her lank brown hair. "The police weren't there to interview me. They were talking to my parents.''

"*Shut up.*'' Ashley glanced around. Only when she was satisfied that no one was watching did she take her initial shot. When the red and green balls rolled into opposite pockets, she said, "Solids are mine.''

Although he continued playing by himself, Blade kept an eye on the girls. He couldn't deny Ashley had improved her game. Not that she was close to being able to try to make serious money at it, but her friends didn't stand a chance against her, and for tonight that seemed to feed the restless, ambitious teenager's ego.

"Hiya, Blade.'' Posing on the end of her table, she purred at him when he next rounded to her side. "Not much competition for you tonight.''

He went to the wall shelf and picked up his bourbon and water. Having previously established himself as someone who never responded to the obvious, he simply gave her a bored look.

The only nerves she exposed was moistening lips thick with lip gloss. Dressed in ripped jeans, a black T-shirt with a ribbon bodice that was half undone, and black suede ankle boots, she looked to be on the make, but like all novices trying too hard. "Seen Fuentes around?" she asked.

"Who?"

"The flashy dude. Buys us girls a drink whenever he's in. He wears leather, too. Not as well as you, though, I have to admit."

Blade crunched an ice cube between his molars. "The day I look at guys in leather I give you permission to shoot me."

Ashley laughed as though the comment was hilarious. "Can I have a sip of your drink? This ice tea is worse than piss."

"No."

"Come on. A tiny sip. It doesn't cost to be friendly."

"Yeah, right."

Pouting, she eyed him from beneath expertly applied false eyelashes and ignored her friends' signals to return to their table. "Be nice, Blade. We're having our own memorial here for our friend. You saw Stace in here with us plenty of times, didn't you?"

Once again he refused to respond, ever aware that although the others in the place seemed focused on their own business, he couldn't assume no one was eavesdropping.

"Be a sweetie and help us out. She loved coming here. The funeral is tomorrow, but we thought we'd send her off in style tonight."

Blade reached behind her, letting his sleeve with its buckles snag her hair. "Shit. Stay still." He quickly freed himself and showed her the chalk cube he'd been wanting.

"Now you owe me," Ashley whined in a baby-doll voice.

"I'd like to help you, kid, but not at the expense of getting my ass thrown out of here."

"What about giving me a few pointers? I promise to scram as soon as someone wants to play you for real."

Blade pretended to consider the request, ignoring the disapproving look Deirdre gave him as she delivered drinks to the table next to theirs. "You want a pointer? The first thing you need to learn is to think more and talk less."

Setting his cue stick on the table, he left his unfinished drink and headed for the exit, hoping the silky strands of hair dangling from his jacket sleeve were still there when he got to the El Camino.

28

After signing out and saying good-night to Howie and Andy, Campbell left Maple Trails. Fortunately, the sheriff's department had decided the RVs were a potential hazard in case of an emergency and ordered them to leave, allowing her some respite from hidden cameras. But that was the only good news—that and Andy's continued progress.

She was exhausted, so much so that as soon as she reached for her phone, she changed her mind. She wouldn't call. If Blade had managed to get the sample she'd requested, there was nothing she could do with it until the morning, anyway. She wanted a shower and a drink. She needed about ten hours without the phone ringing. Second best would be a dreamless sleep of any duration.

Go home.

Wise counsel, she thought. Only she didn't really have one these days. Headquarters worked for her father because the business was his life, and the apartment was simply where she parked her things. Besides, there was so much to do, so many details to analyze—details like threads that needed to be tied together, or cut away.

All of that internal coaching did her no good, and when she found herself driving toward Blade's, she decided she'd really lost it. Not only was it too early—he must still be at Point East or otherwise deep into his own work—she was also driving the Blazer.

As she turned into his driveway, she saw she was right about one thing—he wasn't there. But the table sitter came to immediate attention, his eyes a pair of glistening amber buttons in her headlights. He leaped off the table and trotted to the SUV and Campbell reached for her bribe. The offering was less impressive tonight, half of a honey bun.

"What do you think, will this do?" she asked, carefully easing out of her vehicle.

She broke off a piece and handed it to him. By the time she sat down on the picnic-table bench, the dog had inhaled the rest of it as though it was filet mignon, and was licking every trace of it off of her hand.

"Stop trying to charm me," she told him as she wiped her hands on the paper towels in which she'd carried the bun. "You know it's nuts for us to become friends. But I sure would like to give you a new name."

The dog succeeded in joining her on the bench, but his added weight proved too much for the thing, and before Campbell could get off, the seat disintegrated beneath her. She gasped, then grunted as she crashed to the hard concrete. That seemed to egg on the hulk, and he plopped himself across her lap and with a moan rolled belly up.

"You give new meaning to the term 'beached whale,'" she told him.

The lighthearted moment was short-lived though, as lights flashed when another vehicle pulled into the driveway. As it grew nearer, she raised her hands to her eyes to avoid the glare, but heard "I'll get him—don't move!"

Afraid Blade meant to shoot, Campbell quickly wrapped her arms around the beast and called back. "Don't shoot! He's just playing."

Whether the dog sensed his precarious state or saw Blade aiming the automatic at him, he retreated behind her and pressed his head between her shoulder blades.

"It's okay, Trunk," she said, reaching back to rub the rolls of skin along his neck.

"Trunk?" Slowly, Blade lowered the gun.

"He needs a better name. Doesn't he remind you of a big old tree trunk?"

Tucking the gun in the back of his jeans, Blade stopped in front of her. "I call him what he reminds me of. Do you need a hand?"

"Please." She extended hers. "And a drink if you have anything that will transfer the sting from my backside to my stomach."

He tugged her easily to her feet and unlocked the door. When the patio and kitchen lights came on,

Trunk figured out what was what and moved to block her from going inside.

"I can tell I'll pay for competing for your attention," Blade drawled.

"You should be nicer to him. He's lonesome, aren't you, sweetie?" But when Campbell intercepted Blade's less-than-amused look, she patted the dog and hurried inside. "Okay if I wash my hands in this sink?" She doubted it would matter; she figured the rusting basin hadn't seen a fresh vegetable since he moved in.

"Help yourself." Blade took a bottle of bourbon from a cabinet and two glasses. He filled the silence by cracking ice cubes from their trays.

"I should have called," she said, slipping out of her jacket. Glancing around, she used the doorknob as a hanger.

"You are off a lot earlier than I expected."

Not by her count. "Six hours of training after a full day of management duties and investigative support? I figured I'd earned it."

"I agree."

The subtle disappointment in his voice made her want to kick herself. She was so tired, she was beginning to take the simplest comments the wrong way. "Sorry. Anyway, I'm being my own efficiency manager, checking in to see if you found anything for me. Then I'm going to my apartment to sleep until the phone rings, because I sure as heck refuse to set the alarm clock."

While Blade poured, Campbell washed up, including splashing cool water on her face. A bare face didn't bother her—she was sure she'd worn off her makeup hours ago.

"Better?" Blade asked.

"Much. Thanks." Campbell sighed as she blotted her face and hands with a paper towel.

"Another rough day?" Waiting for her to toss away the towelette, he handed her a thick glass tumbler.

"Not if you're schizo. We went from bad news to someone eager to instigate a riot, to a promising yet confusing breakthrough... I've about lost track." She took an eager sip of the bourbon and closed her eyes. "Oh, this is nice...and lethal." She intended to get to the point so she wasn't tempted to finish the whole thing. "Don't keep me in suspense...did you get it?"

He unzipped his jacket and reached inside to pull out a plastic bag containing one hair. Then he slipped out of the jacket and laid it over the counter. "What did you mean by 'promising but confusing?' Is your investigation going all over the place?"

Campbell eyed the strand. "Archer found a golf club with blood on it today. Buried in the back of Maida's closet."

"Suggesting what? Two murder weapons?"

"I don't know about that, but it will make life difficult for the man she was taking lessons from. Dean McFarland is our resident pro."

"His prints are on the club?"

"Someone's, besides Maida's, are." Campbell

took another drink. "Sloppy, don't you think? Wipe the vase, but leave the club?"

"Sounds to me like someone wanting to redirect attention somewhere else."

She told him the rest of it, the scene at the office with Bryce and Dwayne, the supposed condition of Barbie. "And the people in Maida's neighborhood are putting two and two together and concluding the murder might have occurred at the house. When Dean gets hauled in for questioning, that'll be it. Head for high ground because the convoy of moving trucks will go right over you."

Campbell's gaze settled on the plastic bag again. She didn't want to think a mixed-up teenager could be the source of so much pain and danger. The single strand looked like a question mark through the plastic. True enough. Was this what she was looking for or not?

She gestured toward the bag with her glass. "The state trooper father? A hardnose—and, no, I'm not trashing him. Yancy and Archer filled me in on what they discovered. There are some problematic things in his file. As a result, he works nights in rural counties. Ashley is his one and only, and from the sound of things he's always been disappointed in her. He wanted a son."

"What about her mother?"

"Hair stylist. Her hours are as problematic as his. I don't see her as a lot of help in the civil war between father and daughter. So it's plausible that we're dealing with a kid who's been rejected, learned to disre-

spect the hypocrisy of authority, and is rebelling.''
By killing a classmate's grandmother? The thought
had her downing the rest of her drink.

"I have other news, too," Blade said, pouring her
another finger from the bottle. "You spoke of orange
paint on the fence?"

"Yeah. *Yeah*." She had temporarily forgotten it in
the wash of information. "You've uncovered something?"

"I went to see Snow this morning—well, after you
left. I asked him if he'd finished examining Stacie
Holms's car and if by chance there was a crowbar or
something similar in it. There was—with orange paint
on it. It turns out her father is in the construction
business and he marks all of his tools with fluorescent
orange paint. It's a common habit among trades
where you have several people on a job and everyone
is bringing in the same stuff."

An ice cube popped in Campbell's glass and she
blinked, then made a wry face as she wiped moisture
off her cheek. "That's my stomach right now."

"I was the same way, but don't get too excited
yet," Blade said. "You know you're going to have
to get a scraping from that fence and Snow will have
to test it against what he has. Even if we find a match
in the chemical composition, it could be challenged
as circumstantial, especially if the paint is manufactured by a company that's common at every hard-
ware, building center and discount store."

Campbell nodded to the bag on the counter. "But
if that hair matches what Archer took from Maida's

trunk, that, at least, supports the theory that both Ashley and Stacie were at Maple Trails.''

"At some point. Not necessarily the night Maida and Stacie were killed."

Rubbing the chilled rim of her glass against her lower lip, Campbell struggled to work through the next puzzle. "Debra would have to know, wouldn't she? When did she introduce her grandmother to her friends?"

"She didn't necessarily have to. It's possible she just talked about her. Bragged about the car she was going to get."

Campbell wasn't buying it. "And from that the girls knew how to pinpoint which house was Maida's and which section of fence to take down? Yeah, right. That little bitch had to have shown them. Oh, God." She pressed her other hand against the next lurch in her stomach.

"Easy." Blade laid a steadying hand on her back. "You're forgetting the golf club. Until you know what role it played, the rest remains circumstantial."

"Is that what Snow said?"

"I haven't told him everything. Not yet," Blade replied. "I know I can't hold him off for long, but when Archer gets a reading on that hair, we have to tell Gregg County and the LPD to merge their data, and then it's all out of our hands. We want to make sure all of the pieces are there to make the case and not get brushed aside or repressed to suit some financial or political agenda."

"You don't think that could happen here?"

"Every town and every state is fertilized with buried evidence and innocent bystanders proving that lesson."

They seemed to be at a fork in the road. Which was the key piece of evidence to direct their way, the hair or the club? To Campbell it didn't matter; someone Maida knew, someone whom she cared about, had betrayed her.

"Why couldn't it be a stranger?" she whispered.

"It wouldn't have made it any less final, or wrong." Blade set down his glass and stepped behind her to massage her neck and shoulders, careful of the left one. "Are you okay? You feel tight enough to snap."

Sighing, Campbell closed her eyes, aware this wasn't smart, but grateful for the ministrations. "It's the guilt mostly. I keep thinking there was something I could have, should have, done."

"When we have all the answers, maybe you'll see there probably wasn't."

His hands moved up to her neck, his fingers gentle as they massaged taut tendons and scalp. This tenderness was as unexpected as his humor, and it made him all the more seductive. When she felt his lips brush the sensitized place below her ear, her breath caught as the thrill ran through her as sharply as lightning.

Her glass struck the counter hard as she set it down. "I—I really have to go." She focused on pocketing the plastic bag in order not to meet his intense gaze.

"I know you've really put your neck out for this. Thank you."

"Campbell..."

She was reaching for her jacket when—much like last time—his arm came around her and he flattened his hand against the door to keep it shut. "Blade...no."

"Why not?"

"Because." Because she wasn't ready. Because she was.

He shifted, but only to shut off the kitchen light. While he didn't crowd her, his warm breath caressed her ear and his hands resumed their soothing massage. "Stop fighting this. Stop thinking about 'what ifs.' Kiss me."

"That's not—"

With his fingers under her chin, he coaxed her to turn toward him. "Kiss me."

No, it might not be the smart thing, the safe thing, but it was what she wanted. Offering him her mouth, she accepted that she wanted him more than she needed peace of mind. Although he felt miserably out of practice, the hunger in his kiss gave her the reassurance to continue turning until she was completely in his arms. Murmuring with pleasure at how well they fit together, she wrapped her arms around his neck and pressed herself closer yet.

Blade's arms tightened and the kiss deepened, grew a little less tame as their passion flamed like a match touched to rice paper. Everything she'd stockpiled inside to block ever feeling like this again was reduced to ash—the disappointments, the misplaced trust, and the mourning for ideals forever shattered.

When Blade lifted his head, Campbell opened her eyes, and in the softer glow of the patio light filtering into the room, she saw more than his question. She saw clear honesty and a bottomless capacity for commitment. Under different circumstances, his blue eyes could have terrified, but not now. She was willing to put her faith in them.

"Stay with me."

"Can I have a few minutes?" she asked, her fingers caressing his beard. "I need a shower."

Taking her hand, he pressed a kiss into her palm, locked the door and led her around one corner, then another to the bathroom lit by a night-light that barely softened the starkness of the place. When Blade released her at the doorway, there was apology in his gaze.

"The Ritz it's not."

"I'm fine." She kissed his cheek and closed the door.

No, the atmosphere wasn't conducive to romance; more important, though, was that he had the kind of soap to wash away the day's dust and let her feel like the woman she wanted to be for him. Minutes later when she stood in front of the mirror and unbraided her hair, she might have wished for a drop of the outrageously expensive perfume she had stopped wearing, but she approved of the new light shining in her eyes.

Walking into Blade's bedroom, she saw that he'd

turned on the lamp on his bedside table, and draped his T-shirt over it. He waited, reclining on three pillows stacked against the wood headboard. The bedcovers were drawn to his trim waist.

Sitting on the edge of the bed where he'd folded the covers back for her, Campbell fingered the deep blue towel that was the only other thing separating them. "I hope you were planning to do wash today," she told him. "I've used your backup."

"Maybe I'll go shopping."

The remark deserved a smile, but she couldn't. "Is it safe? I have plenty, I can—"

Reaching for her, Blade drew her onto his chest. "Whatever you say, whatever you want, just kiss me again."

She did want that, too, to be consumed by the fever they were discovering could be quickly ignited in each other. Despite the chill in the room, his hard body already exuded heat, and his heart pounded fiercely against her hand. Welcoming the intimacy of his tongue, she curled her fingers into the mat of black hair covering his chest.

With a groan, Blade tugged the towel free and drew her under the covers. His expression had never been more intense as his gaze moved over her. Then touching her wherever he looked, he murmured, "God, yes," as though answering some secret question.

Lowering his mouth to her breast, he slid his fingers inside her to test her readiness, prompting Campbell to close her thighs around his hand, while she arched to receive more of what his mouth had to offer.

She couldn't believe she could get this close this fast, but she could feel the tremors starting. His hard length pressing against her thigh told her he was beyond ready, too.

"Blade, could you…?"

Encouraged by her coaxing, he slid smoothly into her silky softness, completely filling her. Campbell not only felt, but watched as his strong body registered the union, relishing the pleasure rushing through him.

He eased himself down to his forearms and his hot breath caressed her lips. "*Bella Belle*…it's too good."

The raspy endearment had her wrapping her legs around his waist. "I want you so much."

It seemed all Blade needed to hear. Locking his mouth to hers, he rushed them to a peak that had them both crying out. Then, clinging to each other, they rested in that shimmering ecstasy.

29

Wishing he could prolong the experience, Blade finally yielded to concern for Campbell and his own comfort. Collapsing onto his back, he thought of one thing: if she suddenly announced she was leaving, he would have to pack his things and be gone before the sun rose. He'd known from the first that she could touch the one spot still vulnerable inside him, and if she rejected him now, he couldn't stay, not if she was within begging distance. He'd tried that once—not in the romantic sense—and had failed miserably. No, he wouldn't repeat the experience any more than he would go home again.

But he had to touch her. Rising on his elbow, he looked at her with her expression relaxed, her eyes closed. If she'd fallen asleep—as she damned well had a right—it would be cruel to disturb her, but Blade couldn't resist touching the silken hair that glowed like old gold.

Her eyelids lifted and she looked directly at him.

"I fell in lust with your hair the instant I barreled into you," he told her.

She wasn't buying it. "Please. I looked like tomorrow's bait for Gulf shrimpers, not to mention acting frantic enough to give rabies to anyone who got in my way.''

It often surprised him how people saw themselves. The disparities in opinion between the observed and the observer were often wide. ''I'm the one who wasn't exactly ready for a cover shoot.''

The right corner of her mouth twitched. ''I thought you were a lowlife biker slithering through town.''

''You were supposed to—and to keep a careful distance.'' Blade caressed the red marks on her chin and breast where his beard had taken its toll on her lovely skin. ''Look what I've done—you've already been burned.''

She looked anything but worried, at least about herself. ''Do you like what you do? Being a night wolf?''

''Night wolf?'' He was intrigued that she used a term he found equally fitting.

''Yeah, Texas performing artist Terri Hendrix even wrote a song called 'Night Wolves.' They're the people who work or live while others sleep.''

''That about describes me these days,'' Blade drawled. ''I was raised to be a cop. Come from a long line of them—my father, my grandfather, two uncles…a brother.'' He shrugged. ''But things happened and doors closed for me. This is about as close to that former life as I can get.''

When he didn't continue, Campbell said, ''Fair enough. If you ever want to tell me the why, though, I'll listen.''

Just like that? His own flesh and blood had treated

him with less respect. And he did want to tell her, only he'd discovered that after a year and hundreds of miles, the wound remained tender. But also, in hindsight, his decisions and sacrifices seemed kind of stupid now, too—or at least a wasted gesture.

"If I talk about it again, it'll be to you." The warmth in her smoky eyes went straight to his groin, and though he could happily begin making love to her again, there were questions nagging him, too. "What I'd really like is for you to tell me what Lefevre didn't."

She grimaced. "I let my partner down, isn't that what he said?"

"And you know how I don't buy into what comes out of his mouth."

"Smart man." She drew and purged a deep breath. "His name was Greg Gerrard, and we should never have been on patrol that evening, at least not together. I almost called in sick. If I had, Greg might still be alive. As it was, even his last hours were miserable." Campbell shivered and pulled up the covers.

Blade suspected her reaction wasn't only due to the drafty house, and he reached over her for the drink he'd retrieved from the kitchen while she'd been showering. He offered her the glass, which she accepted with a grateful glance.

"Thanks," she said after, taking a sip and handing it back. "I'll bet when it came time to interrogate, you played the good cop."

"If it's still too painful to talk about—"

"We were engaged," she blurted out. "No one

knew, not then, anyway. As you can imagine, it was against policy. Our relationship happened fast—'' she shot him a dry look ''—I've learned my lesson, haven't I?''

''Ouch,'' Blade drawled.

''Oh, God, I didn't mean—''

''It's okay, go on.''

''Actually, it wasn't this fast. I knew him two, maybe three months. My previous partner had just retired and Greg switched over from days. Aside from being charming and funny, he also had a problem with rules. To him they were for other people.''

''Why do I get the feeling that extended to the rules involving relationships?''

''Where were you when I needed you?''

''Swimming in my own piss pot, darlin'.'' But Blade needed a drink this time to keep himself from calling her former lover several forms of asshole. Why had the guy needed to screw around once he'd been with Campbell?

''The day before Greg was killed, I learned the poker game he'd gone to was actually a friend's bachelor party, and he thought he was entitled to the same privileges as the groom.''

''How'd you find out?'' Blade asked.

''The same way you gauge someone's maturity in the first place—the big-mouth factor. I entered the briefing room in time to hear them congratulating each other. Anyway, I returned his ring and everything else he'd had at my apartment. Second mistake. When I tried to explain what happened later, I was accused of fabricating the whole thing to play for sympathy.''

''Wasn't the ring evidence?''

Campbell smiled bitterly. ''What ring? They let Lefevre go look for it, he being family and all. He claimed he never found it. Interesting side note—his wife was sporting a pretty nice diamond pendant the last time I saw her.''

Blade swore softly then took her hand again and brushed a kiss across her knuckles. ''How'd it go down?''

''Exactly the way it does if you cease working as a team. We spotted what we thought was a warehouse burglary. There was a van with the back doors wide open. But there was a fancy Infinity with gold hubcaps, as well. I didn't like the look of that, or the fact that we didn't know how many people we were dealing with. I wanted to sit tight and radio in for heavy backup, but Gregg was angry, and he saw this as his next step up the ladder.

''He was out of the car and heading over to check out the vehicles when they emerged from the building. There were five of them, and two were carrying the best firepower that drug money can buy. The others weren't empty-handed, either.'' Campbell shook her head. ''I was already hurrying to provide backup, while still radioing in, but it was too late. They practically cut him in half.''

Blade squeezed her hand. He knew the work too well not to understand how lucky she was to still be here. ''How did you escape the same treatment?''

"I didn't think I did. While they were getting into their vehicles to haul ass, I dove behind a storage shed. Fortunately it was loaded with heavy paper goods because, as they drove by, they did their best to turn the stuff into confetti."

Blade took another swallow of bourbon and hoped Gerrard was in hell for his recklessness. "Except for the bad judgment about your relationship, you weren't the one who misstepped. Added to his previous conduct—"

"What previous conduct? A brother in blue was dead. His pals praised him as a 24-karat cop. And I wouldn't let my few friends risk their own careers supporting me. I was left to look like such an incompetent and liar that his family considered suing me in civil court." She gave him a sad smile. "Bye-bye career and virtually every penny I had, since even mediocre attorneys don't come cheap."

That explained the rest of the story behind the uniform change. "Your father must be grateful you joined him." Blade wouldn't insult her by suggesting her work was safer now. She carried a gun. The days of rapping a troublemaker on the head with a nightstick and sending him home were long gone. Today's criminals would rather shoot than answer questions, let alone face arrest—as she'd experienced firsthand.

"Sure," Campbell replied. "And strangely enough the timing was perfect, because shortly afterward he learned he'd developed cancer, and the business would have collapsed if I hadn't been available to temporarily step in. But there's a lot of life left in that old soldier and the bottom line is it's his company, his dream.''

Blade's respect for her grew. While she probably wouldn't say so, she was rebuilding her life. In turn, he had been playing craps with Death simply because he'd ceased to really give a damn about anything.

Campbell stifled a yawn and snuggled deeper under the covers. ''Are you going to let me stay the rest of the night, Blade?''

Setting down the glass, he switched off the light and drew her into his arms. ''What do you think?'' he murmured.

30

As little as a week ago, Saturdays meant catch-up for Campbell—especially catching up on sleep. But she couldn't allow herself the luxury of that today, let alone dwelling on thoughts of last night with Blade. Once she left him, she had to move at Mach speed.

By the time she paused at her apartment to change uniforms, there were four messages on her pager. Two were from Yancy—probably echoing the three on her answering machine. She phoned him while on her way to the sheriff's.

"Do you know how worried I was about you?" he demanded upon hearing her voice.

"Sorry. I'll explain as soon as I'm done in town. I hear Doug Sutton's well enough to take the gate today."

"So he says. He's as white as my socks, but insists he'll make it. I called Andy to see if he wanted the time and training, and he's over there as backup."

Campbell smiled, pleased with their newest employee's enterprising attitude. "Has Doug been briefed?"

"As far as I was able to, but then I don't know everything that's going on, do I?"

"You won't be happier when you do. Gotta go. I'm here, see you ASAP."

Considering it was the weekend, Campbell had phoned ahead to check if Chris Archer was at the office, but needn't have bothered. She found the dedicated detective in his office hunkered over Maida's case file with a large Starbucks cup in his hand.

"You don't look dressed to get muddy," he said as a greeting.

For his part, Archer looked dressed to shred a pasture—or trudge along creek banks. In denim, with an undershirt poking out, he seemed more approachable, although the shrewdness remained in his eyes as he studied her.

"I hope to join you later. I have to check into a few things first."

"Does it have something to do with what you wanted to drop off?"

"Maybe." She pulled the sample Blade had given her and laid it on top of the opened file. "Another one of those is being delivered to Detective Gordon Snow, LPD."

Frowning, Archer glanced down and read the label she'd stuck on the bag. "And who is Ashley Mize, aside from someone with black hair?"

"She's a friend of Debra Saunders...also the late Stacie Holms."

"Okay, that's closer than six degrees of separation. I know Snow is handling that case. Did this Ashley have a relationship with Mrs. Livingstone?"

"I don't know that. What I do know is that I think there's a link between the orange paint on the fence that was forced down, and the paint that was found on the crowbar in the trunk of Stacie Holms's car."

Archer's frown grew progressively grimmer. "That would be sensitive information. How did you learn that?"

"I'd rather not say. Yet," she added quickly before he could interject. "What I'd like to do is to send a sample from the fence and let Detective Snow compare it with what he has to see if we can determine a match."

"You've been busy."

But the detective didn't look wholly approving of her actions and Campbell hastened to explain. "Sir, I didn't really think there was a connection between the cases until the last twenty-four hours or so. However, recently I've met someone who has had the opportunity to watch Ms. Mize and her gang—"

"Gang…figuratively speaking or literally?"

"Stacie Holms had a record. So does Ashley, although I believe her father has succeeded in getting some of the incidents dropped from her file. He's state police, sir."

"Of course. Now I know where I've heard the name." Archer removed his glasses and pinched the bridge of his nose. "Do you realize the scandal you could be triggering with this?"

Campbell swallowed hard but held his gaze. "Having already been in the center of one myself, I do. But it doesn't change the facts. It's my understanding that those girls—Debra Saunders and Julianne Willis included—are showing increasing signs of female aggression. I don't have to give you the statistics regarding that. Maybe this is a small group and not as hard-core as some in Houston or Dallas, let alone L.A., but Stacie's death is seeming to me to look more and more like an execution, and Maida was bludgeoned to death for no apparent reason."

"Well, we haven't yet allowed her family access to tell us if anything is stolen. I was hoping to get to that today."

"I'd like to be present when you do."

Archer set down his cup and folded his hands on the desk blotter. "I'm not sure that's wise. While I can see how your knowledge of certain individuals would be helpful, I can't ignore that you're not exactly admired by some of the people I have to deal with. Mr. Tyndell, for example."

Now what? Campbell wondered. "Bryce's conduct with Dwayne Saunders has been incendiary at the least."

After glancing at his watch, Archer nodded. "I'm inclined to agree with you. All right...for the record, Barbara Young's hair sample did not match ours. Maybe that will calm him down somewhat. What may offset that is—" His phone rang and, excusing himself, he picked it up. "Archer...send him up."

Wondering if she was going to be asked to leave, Campbell lifted her eyebrows in question.

"Dean McFarland is here. As I was about to tell you, it's his print on the club."

The sinking feeling in her stomach had her lowering herself into one of the chairs facing his desk. "Does he know?"

"I wasn't about to give the man time to think of an alibi on his way here." Archer glanced over her shoulder. "Mr. McFarland—please come in." Archer rose. "I trust you know Ms. Cody?"

With his full head of snow-white hair and golfer's tan, Dean McFarland was reputed to look younger than his seventy-seven years. Campbell agreed he did—the last time she'd seen him at the ladies' tournament a few weeks ago. She was shocked to see at how he'd changed. Although he wore a well-cut navy wool blazer and gray slacks, his trim body appeared frail, his coloring was gray, and there was a dazed look in his blue-gray eyes.

Noting his breathlessness, she felt an unexpected protectiveness and rose to accept the old man's hand. "Mr. McFarland…come sit down. You didn't take the elevator up?"

"Yes. But I haven't been myself all week, and now with Mr.….Detective Archer's call—"

"It's merely a formality," Archer interjected.

Campbell sent him a look of dismay. It was wrong to have done this to Dean. Granted, he had enjoyed his celebrity in the community—which almost surpassed that of his professional life—but he'd always been a perfect gentleman treating the ladies of Maple Trails with a special consideration. If Archer believed Dean was his killer, he needed to think again.

"I don't understand," Dean replied. "You're not bringing everyone else down here. I haven't heard anyone say they've been asked to an interview."

He almost sounded like a boy. Campbell led him to a chair and urged him to sit.

"We know you were good friends with Maida, Mr. McFarland," she began.

"I loved her."

Campbell all but fell into the opposite seat. Hoping she recovered before it was too noticeable, she replied, "Many of us did."

"No, I *loved* her. She didn't care a bit about golf," he said with a ghost of a smile. "She only took lessons because she knew it meant so much to me."

Unbelievable, Campbell thought, and rose to walk to the door because she was afraid the tears in her eyes would be misconstrued. Had Maida found love again in those last days or months of her life? She'd certainly seemed content despite her concern with her family's behavior.

"Why didn't anyone tell me what happened?" Dean asked. "I had to find out from a caddy. You people couldn't make a local call? Campbell, she adored you."

Campbell returned to him, sat down and took his hands in hers. With her grip she tried to transmit to him how important it was for him to listen. "Mr. McFarland, we didn't know about you. *I* didn't know.

Apparently, this was a relationship Maida wanted to cherish by and for herself.''

Archer cleared his throat. ''Mr. McFarland, you have our deepest sympathies, but we do have to ask you a few questions. When was the last time you saw Mrs. Livingstone?''

''Tuesday,'' he said simply. ''It was a beautiful day on the golf course. Maybe a little too warm for this time of year, but we rode in the cart. I had to check the greens. We've got new mole and gopher infestation.'' He glanced at Campbell for confirmation and she smiled and nodded. ''It was a good time to give her an early Valentine's present because I was going to have to be gone that day. I was flying to Houston to watch my grandson in his first tournament.''

''How wonderful for him,'' Campbell said gently. ''Could you…do you mind me asking what kind of present?''

''The garnet bracelet. She said she'd never take it off.''

A swift glance toward Archer confirmed her worst fears. From the slight shake of his head she knew— they'd found nothing like what Dean had described on Maida's body.

As far as she was concerned they could go no further without giving the elderly gentleman the right to call for counsel. Campbell waited for Archer to tell him that, but he just sat there tapping his pen against his pad.

She stared harder.

Finally the detective asked, "Do you know where Mrs. Livingstone got her set of clubs?"

"Me." Dean replied without hesitation, though he did wring his hands together between his parted knees. "She didn't need a fancy set and I know people who don't need their equipment anymore."

"You mean they're deceased?" Campbell asked.

"Well, sometimes there's an estate sale, yes. But mostly it's players who have given up the game and know I'll do them right."

"Do you do this as a side business?" Archer asked.

"Excuse me?" Dean was appearing increasingly confused and stressed.

"Get a commission for matching equipment with people?"

Sitting back in his chair, the aging golfer smoothed a hand over his white polo shirt. "Hers were a gift," he said softly.

Not at all liking where this was going, or comfortable with Dean's weakening responses, she gave Archer another more determined look. "Could we offer Mr. McFarland some coffee? The presence of his attorney?"

That got Dean's attention. "What—why do I need an attorney?"

"Well done, Cody," Archer murmured.

Her tolerance stretched to the limit, Campbell replied stiffly, "He's not a marlin you can work to exhaustion and then reel in. Treat him with the respect he deserves!"

She knew she'd made a mistake as soon as she

spoke, but it was too late. Deciding to help where help was needed, she turned back to Dean and clasped his hands between hers. "They found your fingerprints on her clubs."

"They would. I carried them. I was teaching her."

"Dean—" Campbell had to push the words out. "Her blood, too."

If he'd been pale before, now he turned a pasty gray. "Oh…oh, no. Dear God. Oh, no."

"Let me get you something to drink. Some water." She gave Archer an entreating look.

Dean waved away the offer. "It's just that I was told…car accident and, and she didn't tell me she was going anywhere. She has her own life," he continued as though explaining it to himself. "But…it was a car accident."

Campbell didn't need a psychology degree to know the man was unraveling. She urged him to his feet. "Let's get you home, Mr. McFarland. Come with me and I'll have a deputy help us. He'll drive you and I'll take your car, then he can drive me back." Leading him into the hall she said, "Just give me a moment and I'll be with you directly."

Returning to Archer's desk, she leaned over and whispered, "Satisfied?"

"Yes," he replied quietly. "With you, too."

It was the one response she didn't expect. "What is that supposed to mean?"

"You're right, he looks bad. Get him home and let him know I doubt I'll be troubling him again. Congratulations, Cody. You do better under pressure than I'd heard.''

From behind them came a strangled gasp and then a thump. Campbell spun around and saw Dean on the floor.

''Shit,'' she and Archer said in unison.

"If they were awake during the storm and if they noticed him up and around at his place? That sort of thing."

"You bet. Um…is he a suspect?" Paula asked.

Campbell understood her doubt. It wasn't only golfers who were fond of Dean. He had a solid reputation through all of the Trails. "I'm ninety-nine percent certain he's safe from any suspicion, but he did have regular contact with Maida, and we have to be thorough. This way I can reassure him and his family that he won't be troubled further."

Things were far more upbeat at the gatehouse. Doug and Andy had taken to each other, and Doug reported that he thought Andy was just about ready to drive shotgun for a day or two in order to meet as many of the residents and employees that he could.

Campbell updated them on Dean's condition as she placed his wallet and keys in a manila envelope. The outside was labeled with son Denton McFarland's cell phone number and car information for when he eventually arrived at the gate.

She already knew Archer had been to Maida's house and had not found any sign of the bracelet. He was waiting for a call back from the Saunderses regarding other jewelry.

"How are you holding up, Doug?" she asked. "Can I borrow Andy for half an hour to drive me back to the sheriff's office? I need to pick up my vehicle."

"Oh…I might be able to survive that long if it means not hearing another one of his *you might be a redneck jokes.''* Pointing with his thumb at the vacant entryway, Doug added, ''Except for the van that did a remote for the morning news, we haven't had any press traffic.''

Once Andy dropped her off she was able to call Blade from the privacy of her own vehicle. He'd already attempted to reach her twice and she noted his concern in his pager messages.

''It feels like I've been halfway across the country and back since leaving you,'' she said when they finally connected.

''Why don't you take a lunch break and come fill me in?''

There was a secondary invitation in his voice that had her insides fluttering like a teenager with her first crush. ''Tempting, but Yancy is threatening to take my Blazer keys away if I don't physically report in. Besides, you don't need my white elephant in your driveway again.''

''You could bring the ocean liner.''

Campbell chuckled at his reference to the Cadillac. ''True, except I also promised Archer I'd try to meet him over at the wreck site. They're doing a broader sweep of the area.'' She filled him in about Dean. ''I'll call you from the office in a few minutes. We have another piece of crucial evidence to look for.''

''Sounds good. Then I'll fill you in on my meeting with the Snowman.'' Blade paused, then said gruffly, ''When *am* I going to see you again?''

She pressed her thighs together as she thought of their slower, second intimate encounter…and the third in dawn's soft light. "Don't you have to work tonight?"

"Unfortunately, yes. The natives are particularly restless on a Saturday night. But you could wait for me here. I could tie a key around the tree trunk."

When she disconnected she was still grinning. A handful of vitamins couldn't have been better for her. While she lost the smile upon entering the building, her father noticed a change in her when they met outside Beth's new office.

"Since when does ICU agree with you?" he demanded.

Ignoring the question, she complimented the two hard-working people who were nearly done painting the room. Then she gripped her father's arm and said to the two painters, "Sorry, I have to borrow your spectator—I need to update him. See you later."

Yancy allowed himself to be led to his office, but once the door to his office was closed, he said, "You're awfully bossy for being AWOL."

"If I make it through today, I'll have completed an eighty-five-hour work week, and you're going to begrudge me being incommunicado for six hours?"

"If I rephrase that and ask, as your father, will you tell me?"

"No." Slipping off her jacket, she tossed it on the couch and settled in the chair facing his desk. "Focus on this instead… Dean McFarland was romancing Maida. He gave her a nice piece of jewelry. We haven't found it yet."

"Maybe it doesn't exist." Yancy eased into his chair.

"The man makes his living in a sport where if you cheat, everyone hears about it. Anyway, you don't lie about something that's easily verified through a credit card company or bank or the jewelry store itself."

"Did you?"

"I saw the entry in his check register before I put his valuables into an envelope for his son."

"That's my girl," Yancy said as he swiveled in his chair. "So you think Maida was a victim of a burglary gone bad?"

It was a key question they couldn't dismiss. But while Maida didn't have to worry about money, there were a number of residents at Maple Trails who were much more affluent. "Maybe we'll know more soon. I'm joining Archer over at the crash site. There's a growing list of items he needs to account for and he believes they may be deeper in the woods or in the river."

"He's okay with you being so hands-on and having such privileged information?"

"He invited me, I didn't ask." When her father lifted his eyebrows, she was quick to crush any speculation. "He's married and not my type…and while we had a less-than-smooth start, I think he now sees me as an asset." She filled him in on the new twist regarding the paint markings and the latest hair sample. "The Sheriff's Department and the LPD are soon going to be working together."

Yancy stopped swiveling. "And you're staying involved? What are you, a glutton for punishment?"

"Right now you can ask me the what, but not the why, how, or who."

He studied her more intently. "This is about your vanishing act. You're working with someone else besides Archer."

"Everything is legit. He's a badge, too. Now forget you heard that," Campbell said, pointing at him.

"Bull. I thought I was the one with the connections."

"Our paths kept crossing as we were working on leads for separate cases."

"At that time of night?"

"Focus on the case or I'm leaving."

Campbell's calmness only prodded Yancy. "What if you're being set up?"

"Thanks for the confidence vote." Campbell rose. "I have to make a few calls before I head over to see Archer."

"Dammit, Belle, don't punish me for caring about you."

"Well, you know what? You can't afford to be a daddy, Daddy." Her hands on her hips, Campbell wrestled with her frustration. When she was certain she could keep her voice from shaking, she rested her hands on his desk. "Listen to me. The orange paint on the fence? There's a crowbar in Stacie Holms's trunk that appears to match it. The black hair? It's not Barbie's, so we've had to move on. This is where the two cases converge again. One of Stacie's friends has black hair. Both Archer and LPD's Detective Snow have been given strands of her hair. If we have a match, we can no longer look at the Saunderses as the surviving family, but as suspects at worst and hostile witnesses at best due to Debra's connection with her friends.''

"I apologize.'' When Campbell accepted his offered hand, he added, "And if it's permitted, I'm proud of you. Do you need to borrow my car again?''

"I was thinking of buying my own this afternoon when I finish with Archer.''

Yancy pulled open his desk drawer, picked up his car keys, and handed them over. "You'll be dusty and tired. I wouldn't want you to unsnap your holster if the salesman didn't come down enough on the price.''

32

Crash site
2:09 p.m.

The ground in most areas in East Texas had quickly soaked up the flooding rains from Tuesday's storm, but not along the riverbeds and surrounding lowlands. Campbell was glad Yancy had reminded her to take a pair of the knee-high rubber boots they kept in storage.

They had started off with four in their group, including Archer, but a serious tractor-car accident across the county had forced two of the deputies to head over there. Archer told Campbell that made him all the happier to see her.

"I have Ronnie searching straight east from where we collected evidence on Wednesday," he told her, pointing out the area in which the deputy was walking.

"I thought I'd start combing this side of the riverbank, and if you're willing, you can drive across the bridge and see what luck you'll have on the north side."

"That's fine." Campbell wasn't happy to see the condition of the water, though. "I'd hoped the mud would have settled some."

"Yeah, it's a good thing I decided to hold off on the divers. It's nothing new for them to search in poor visibility, but they need to know what they're feeling for. I just hope if we're right about this being the dumping area for evidence that it hasn't been carried too far downstream."

"Let's find out."

After returning to the Blazer, Campbell took her cue from Archer and changed out of her quilted jacket and into a bright yellow raincoat. A high-pressure weather system had formed over West Texas again and the temperatures had settled back to a comfortable fifty degrees. Besides, she wanted Archer to be able to see her as clearly as she could see him. She also slipped on the plastic gloves he'd issued her. Pocketing a few small evidence bags and a large trash bag, she began her search.

Finding garbage was easy. Despite Lady Bird Johnson's antilitter campaign in the early seventies, a whole generation had passed and little attention had been paid to the problem in recent years, except for recyclable items. Sadly, it was again common to see disposable cups and shopping bags half buried in the clay or hanging from trees and the brush. Campbell cocked an eyebrow at the relatively new condom wrapper, then dropped a rusting fishing lure caught in thick swamp grass into her pocket, hoping she'd saved a water bird or some mammal from future injury. Periodically, she had to step off the bank and into the water because of thick vegetation or a tree blocking her advance. However, where the drop-off was steep, she didn't risk losing her balance on the slick clay and falling in; instead, she opted to wrestle with vines and climb over large downed trees in order to continue.

After some fifteen minutes, she glanced back, only to find that she'd walked a mere three hundred feet or so. On his side, Archer wasn't doing much better, but he carried a gaff, and was presently using it to drag in a branch held by a dead pine that had crashed into the water. Campbell saw a flash of something dark and glossy, and found herself holding her breath.

Once he was able, Archer grabbed hold of the branch and tugged it to shore. Tangled in the web of branches was a black plastic bag. "Yes!" Campbell whispered, tempted to run back to the Blazer and drive over to inspect the thing more closely.

Noticing he had her attention, Archer held it up and pointed to the cinch ribbons. They were red. The ones in the box in Maida's garage were yellow.

Disappointed but determined, she continued searching.

She startled a kingfisher, sending it shrieking across the river to sit in a taller tree ahead of Archer. Then she came to another downed pine so wide that when she straddled it, her feet were completely off the ground. Beginning to believe that it would have been easier and faster to get a boat from the Parks and

Wildlife people, she stepped into shallow water to get around a bushy evergreen with nasty thorns.

On the other side of the pine she saw signs of the dogged and—in her opinion—the insensitive: a yo-yo line. Campbell couldn't remember if trotlines were illegal on Texas rivers, but this was the answer to them if they were—an easier method of fishing for catfish if one was harvesting alone. The line was tied to a stout limb on a tree leaning off a point that cut the distance between the two shorelines in half. She didn't want to think about how long someone spent getting the filament on the right branch without landing in the water himself.

"Some folks have way too much free time on their hands," she muttered.

The taut line and the bend in the branch suggested some poor mud cat had fallen for the trap and gotten itself hooked. Her first impulse was to get out her pocketknife and cut the unlucky thing loose, but if the hook was badly placed, the fish could suffer a slow, painful death.

"Okay, Moby," she said, reaching for the line. "You can call this your lucky day."

It was easy enough to get her hands on the line; however, she had to dig her right heel hard into the sharply sloping bank to keep from sliding into the water's mud-churned depths. Tugging, she also discovered it would take both hands to pull up the unfortunate fish.

She was guessing the weight at a minimum of five to seven pounds when the mud gave beneath her boot.

Leaning too far forward, she couldn't drop to the bank and hold on; instead, she made an ungraceful belly flop into the water. The momentum and her weight took her under and she instinctively held tighter to the line. Terrifyingly, it slid through her grasp as though greased. She couldn't feel ground, and her boots were filling with water.

The bank—reach for the bank!

Before she could react to that command, she felt a terrible stab in her forearm that had her involuntarily gasping, then panicking as something slapped against her chest. Oh, God, she thought, choking on filthy water and fighting against some clinging mass. She was going to die.

Her lungs searing and spasmodic, she kicked with all her might and managed to get her head out of the water. Although her vision was blurred, she saw and grabbed for roots jutting out of the bank like a skeletal hand. The problem was the hook that had knifed through her thin rubber jacket. It was connected to a line weighted by something that threatened to hold her in place.

"Archer—"

"Hang on!"

He was coming around to help her…but would he be fast enough? Having traversed the area herself, Campbell knew it would take him at least ten minutes. She didn't think she could hold on that long. The cold was already having its effect; her teeth were chattering and her hands were going numb.

Accepting that she had to improve her situation

herself, she pushed her left foot toward the bank with all her might in an attempt to find something to rest on. The limb yielded and she almost went under again. Using her grip on the roots, she steadied herself and tried with her right foot. For a second she thought she'd found something stable, only to feel it give and tumble deeper into the river.

The impulse to panic was growing. Coughing and spitting up a mouthful of water, she stabilized herself and tried her left foot again, aiming higher.

Her foot found a short, but hard object—a broken root. If it held her, she could use it to thrust herself farther up on the bank, but she would have to do it carefully. She didn't dare lose her grip. And she would have to remember at a crucial point in the momentum to let go of the line and push away the mass clinging to her, to keep from getting sucked back into the water.

The pain brought back the agony of being struck by lightning and she hesitated. Only for a second, though. Death would be more painful and—as she suddenly pictured Blade—unacceptable.

Shifting her body, she summoned her weakened strength and thrust herself up and to the left.

She was vaguely aware of her cry, but more conscious of her precarious position on the edge of the bank. For one heart-stopping instant, she saw the water rushing up at her. In total rejection, she flung herself onto her back.

Now she was fully conscious—her arm, the hook digging deeper into her flesh made certain of that.

Gritting her teeth against the sobs and the muck in her lungs choking her, she struggled to get out her pocketknife. Her right hand was shaking too much to be of any use, so she had to use her teeth to pull open the blade.

Then clenching the line between her teeth, she swiped and severed the nylon. The freed filament went dancing off over the water, and Campbell sat there with what looked like a large dead squid on her lap.

Suddenly her revulsion for the ugly gray mass gave way to disbelief and another coughing fit. That's how Archer found her as he burst from deeper in the woods—she was sitting there laughing and weeping.

"It's...it's Maida's sweater," she wheezed.

33

"**Y**ou really know how to make an impression on a guy," Chuck Archer said. He stood in the Emergency cubicle while Campbell waited for her release, his hands in his jacket pockets and his expression a rather endearing mixture of dismay and relief.

"I'll bet that's one trick you don't want me to teach your wife."

"You've got that right."

Campbell braced her bandaged arm in the palm of her left hand. It wasn't an ideal position, considering that the added weight put pressure on her previous injuries, but she'd rejected the offer of a sling. She did, however, hope the painkiller kicked in soon—but not before she got to her apartment and got out of her filthy clothes.

"Are you sure you don't want me to drive you home?" Archer asked.

"Nah. You've lost enough time as it is, and you have a deputy waiting outside who's on the clock, too. I do appreciate you having him bring my truck here. I'll be fine."

She'd had a tetanus shot last year, so all she'd

needed—once the doctor cut the eye off the one-and-a-half-inch hook and finished pulling the protruding sharp end out—was the sanitizing of the wound and a pressure bandage. She'd refused the suggested stitches. With no plans to attempt a modeling career, she wasn't bothered by another small scar.

Archer continued to stand there. He was beginning to make her feel more self-conscious than she already did. "You hang around much longer in a place like this, they're going to send you a bill," she said gently.

Although he didn't break eye contact, his face did turn slightly pink. "That wouldn't surprise me. Don't you ever try that—padding your hours—if you work for me."

Campbell wondered if maybe the Percodan was already making her light-headed. She'd definitely missed something.

"I was prepared not to like you," Archer continued. "I guess it's no surprise to say that I remembered your case considering all the news coverage it got."

"It's hard to shut off those video cameras when the subject looks like a redwood in a world full of magnolias and dogwoods, or is being tattooed by her ex-future-sister-in-law's wedding ring."

He smiled. "Are you going to let me finish? What I'm trying to say is that I'd be proud to work with you anytime. If you ever decide your life's too tame and you want to shift into full-time investigative work, I'd butt heads to get you on my team."

After a year of insults, harassment and cold shoulders, Campbell didn't know how to receive such a compliment. Feeling her eyes burn, she pretended to adjust her bandage. "Damn, Detective…you must think scavenging along riverbanks is a job perk."

"Oh, I do. And if you proved yourself a really good apprentice, I'd let you join me at the county landfill."

Laughing, Campbell extended her left hand. "Thanks. I'll give it some thought. And I'll be in touch as soon as I have my new cell phone and pager numbers." Both had gone into the river with her, as did her gun, which would need a thorough cleaning before she could consider passing out.

By the time she reached her place, the one flight to her apartment seemed more like the stairwell in the Statue of Liberty. Her family had visited the site when she was eleven, and she and Yancy had charged to the top, while her mother, an asthmatic, remained down in the park.

The welcome memory made the climb easier, and once inside her apartment, she eagerly stripped out of her filthy, still-damp clothes. Then she wrapped her bandage to keep it dry and stepped into the shower stall.

Afterward, getting back into uniform was out of the question, and so was drying her hair. Dressing in a gray sweat suit, she settled for tying her wet hair in a loose ponytail and went to check her answering machine.

She listened to the messages while nuking a cup of soup. It was almost six o'clock and her father was annoyed with her again for not checking in or responding to her pager.

"Wait until you find out why," she murmured in a singsong voice.

But she wasn't going to call him and explain. He would understand as soon as she got over there. She did, however, return Blade's call.

"I'm glad I caught you," she said when he picked up.

"What did you do, lose your cell phone?"

"Might as well have. It got kind of wet." Returning to her bedroom, she cradled the receiver in the curve of her shoulder as she collected her black duffel bag from the closet and started packing.

Blade's silence stretched to four, five…seven seconds. "How about the rest of you?" he finally asked.

"Pretty much. I'm about to leave for HQ to change out phones and pagers and, umm, to ask Yancy nicely to clean my gun."

"And you can't clean it yourself because…?" A grim note had entered his voice.

"I had a fish hook cut out of my arm?"

"You're not sure?"

Campbell decided the sarcasm was better than a curse. "Blade, I found Maida's sweater. It means they did use the river to dump anything they thought would be incriminating."

"I could appreciate that more if you hadn't been hurt again." After a deep sigh he added, "Archer should get down on his knees and kiss your feet."

His gruff complaint gave her a warm, fuzzy feeling

and made her wish she was over there. "He did one better, he offered me a job."

"Did he now? Remind me to find out if he's married."

"He is."

"Good. I'm still going to keep an eye on him, though."

"Blade!"

"Too honest for you?"

The honesty she liked. Still… "Maybe a little fast…?"

"That sounds like a request to back off?"

All she'd needed was to hear his disappointment. Her response was soft but definite. "No."

"You want to try for two out of two right answers and tell me that you haven't changed your mind about coming over. I know I'm a selfish pig and that you're hurting like hell, and that this place is crappy—"

"Blade?"

"Yeah?"

"Just tell me where you decided to put the key."

34

After speaking with Campbell, Blade was doubly convinced that it was time to try something different. He left the El Camino at the house and hid his hair under a baseball cap and the turned-up collar of a quilted vest. Then he drove his clunker pickup to the strip shopping center that faced the entrance to Ashley Mize's street and waited. He'd already made sure she was home by calling the house from a pay phone, pretending to be a salesman.

It was his meeting with Snow that had started him thinking his idea of following the teens deserved a try. At first Snow had bought the girls' shock and grief over Stacie's death. But after speaking with Archer, Snow could see the connection between the Livingstone murder and his own case. So tonight Snow would work the crowd at Point East, questioning anyone who had seen Stacie and the others there on Tuesday, in the hopes of finding someone willing to say even more. It was a good time for Blade to be absent. Inevitably, someone would point him out as one of the girls' targets for free drinks, and on whom to practice their feminine powers. Also this would give

Blade the opportunity to watch how they behaved
once they discovered that Snow wasn't through with
them after all.

Through the detective he'd learned that Ashley
didn't have a car and relied on her gal pals to chauf-
feur her around. Whether that was a result of her
growing record, her grades or simply strict parenting,
Blade figured it had to piss her off, adding impetus
for her to rebel.

Sure enough, shortly after seven o'clock, he saw
the reed-thin teen running toward the end of her
street. The way she glanced over her shoulder had
him wondering if she'd snuck out. With suspicious
timing, a red VW pulled over to the corner. Blade
recognized Julianne Willis's vehicle. She'd become
the designated driver since Tuesday's tragedy.

As the passenger door opened and Debra got out
of the front seat and switched to the back, Blade
started his truck. He was idling at an exit by the time
Ashley was securing her seat belt.

To his surprise, they didn't head eastward, but to
the west, into a rougher part of town. Now what? he
wondered. They weren't foolish enough to test their
luck at one of the liquor stores—unless Ashley, who
looked the most mature, had managed to buy a quality
ID.

In fact, they passed the booze store, but they did
turn into a strip shopping center that included a pawnshop, tattoo parlor and bail-bond outlet. Following,
Blade saw there was little traffic at any of the three
establishments, and he continued to the vacated end

of the building where the darkened windows of a defunct furniture business advertised "We Beat All Prices!" Parking parallel to the store, he shut off his engine and lights and reached for his binoculars to see what the girls were up to.

The trio sat in the car talking. Ashley lifted something to her mouth and drank, then passed it to Julianne, who did the same, then tried to offer it to Debra in back. But Debra sat with her arms stubbornly folded, not taking it. That had Ashley twisting in her seat and taking what Blade suspected was the flask-like bottle and thrusting the object against Debra. Finally Debra took a hard swig.

Taking back the flask, Ashley finished off the contents and got out of the VW, tossing the object across the parking lot. The others got out, too, but Debra stayed by the car. Noticing she wasn't with them at the door to the tattoo parlor, Ashley yelled to the girl. It was Julianne who went to her and put her arm around her shoulders, very buddy-buddy, and led her inside the tattoo parlor.

Blade knew there was an ordinance that a customer had to be eighteen to get any permanent body art. He'd seen a handwritten sign on the door, but wondered how well the operator would comply if the customer was willing to pay cash?

For the next hour-plus, he did what was the most tedious part of the job—sit. He wondered if Campbell had made it to the house, hoping she hadn't pushed her luck if the medication she'd mentioned made her sleepier than she already was. Strongly tempted to call, he resisted, wanting her to rest if she could.

The strength of his feelings for her surprised him. Admittedly, he was in serious *lust,* but he was in increasing *like,* too. And he wanted more. There was the soul rattler. His last relationship, his only serious relationship aside from one-night stands and high school back-seat love, was Kathy. Campbell had company when it came to having chosen badly the first time around. When he'd made his life-altering decision, she'd been in the lead of those to turn their back on him.

Since then, his résumé had suffered as much as his reputation. He had some money, but otherwise he lived ready to hit the road in an hour's time. Attachments meant complications. So was this type of work if he pursued her the way he wanted. And who was to say Campbell would remain interested in him once she knew his full story?

Ashley came outside and lit a cigarette. Not used to dwelling on himself these days, he was glad to refocus.

She was angry. He read the body language, rigidity, but uncontrolled. The kid couldn't stay still for more than a few seconds at a time.

"Tick-tick-tick," he murmured. He slid lower in his seat, although she hadn't looked his way yet. "How bad is it, Ms. Time Bomb? Think you're over your head, and yet you want to show 'em you can? Can what? Show who?"

As though hearing him, she kicked back against the brick building.

The door reopened again and the other two emerged. Suddenly, Ashley's demeanor changed. Flinging away her cigarette, she opened her arms and enfolded Debra in her arms. Julianne stood watching for several seconds and then joined them.

"Smart move, Control Princess."

They got into the VW. Blade had to decide whether to follow or question the tattoo artist while he or she was still vulnerable.

He watched the VW turn east on Highway 80. That decided him. But first he paused by the flask. It was actually a pint bottle of blackberry brandy. Wondering if she had acquired a bad habit from her mother, or had used the bottle to slowly steal from her father's Scotch supply, Blade carefully retrieved and sacked it.

The sole person in the tattoo shop was a wild-haired throwback to the sixties, with glasses thick enough to have sent any would-be customer running out the front door. Blade walked in, flashed his badge and said, "The kids who just left were underage." He knew that was only partially true, but doubted this guy did.

The middle-aged failed Renaissance man wipea beer suds from his mouth. He'd ditched the can in the trash the moment the gold shield hit the light. "They had ID. I checked."

"Checked the cash, maybe. Who'd you do?"

"We didn't introduce ourselves. I ain't into lasting relationships."

"How about clean needles, you into those?"

Provoked, the guy with the frizzy ponytail pointed with his thumb to his makeshift operating room behind him. "Hey, I know my work. Some of my customers are killers."

"That much I know is true," Blade drawled.

"So? Come on, man. I don't want any trouble."

"Then tell me which of the three? One? All of them?"

"The whiny one. The others were already done." Mr. Renaissance made a face. "Shit, I hope they never bring me another like that again. If they didn't have the bills, I'd have thrown her out in the first five minutes."

Blade knew he'd been right to linger. "You said done. Done how?"

"Their sign, man."

"Sign—like astrological?"

"No, for their club, sorority…oh, fuck it, I don't know. But they all get one as their initiation, and they all have it done in the same place."

"Show me."

35

Point East
9:00 p.m.

"If my parents find out I did this, I'll be grounded for life."

Up in the passenger seat Ashley Mize rolled her eyes at Debra's childish remark, but she left the explaining to Jules.

"You make sure they don't, Deb. It's not big. If you're wearing clothes that expose it, one of those square Band-Aids will cover it. You can say you're covering a pimple."

"I don't even like dogs," Debra said, hugging herself. "I like cats."

"Will you please shut your trap before I beg Jules to let me out so I can get myself run over!" Massaging her temples, Ashley wished she'd never let Stacie befriend this crybaby. Nothing had gone right since she entered the picture. Nothing. "The tattoo isn't about you, it's about us, the group," she said, striving to get through to the girl. "I've explained it to you before." And before...and before. "We only have one another to rely on. We're together because we can't make it by ourselves. Our families have failed us, school is a joke, and the kids single us out because we refuse to act like the idiots they are.''

"Remember how Rachel Sinclair would make mooing sounds whenever I walked by because of my boobs?'' Though traffic was heavy as she crossed town, Jules glanced in the rearview mirror. "You know what Ash and Stace did for me, Deb? They helped me corner her in the bathroom one day and threatened to stick her too-perfect blond curls into the nastiest backed-up commode if she ever so much as looked at me again. That girl has respect now.''

Ashley squeezed Jules's shoulder. "Exactly. No one messes with a wolf pack.''

Jules turned into Point East's parking lot. Ashley checked out the vehicles already there. She didn't see Fuentes's sweet ivory Beemer, but it was early yet. The El Camino wasn't here, either, and that had her pouting. She felt she was cracking through Blake's icy veneer. While she was only interested in Fuentes to get set up business-wise, she had targeted Blade to teach her about life. He hadn't always been a truck driver, she'd put money on that. He'd been places, done things, it was written all over him. She wanted that information. She wanted him. Who cared that he was almost as old as her father? Her old man was a fraud, a bully in a uniform who had no respect for the opposite sex. Blake was simply indifferent, like he didn't have to prove anything to anyone. There was something ultra sexy about that.

"Looks kinda empty," Jules said, shutting down the VW. "I don't see Charlie's car. Damn. He's good for a few sips of his rum and Coke if I let him look down my sweater."

Ashley watched her friend unzip her top another two inches until her lush breasts tested the strength of the zipper. "If he does show, don't let that old pervert talk you into the dark hallway by the rest rooms," Ashley ordered. Jules was a good kid, but pretty gullible. Like mother, like daughter. All Ms. Nancy Willis got for her sex drive and naiveté was Jules and a life of cleaning houses by day and offices by night. "Advertising is good, but we don't give anything away for free, got it?"

"Can't I have a little fun once in a while?"

Shaking her head at the younger girl's wistful look, Ashley replied, "See if you can convince the debutante to lose her bra and put on more lip gloss. And let's move it, for crying out loud, I'm hungry."

The girls were halfway to the door when a regular named Ted came out.

"I would make myself scarce if I was y'all," he told them. "There's a cop in there asking about Stacie and you girls."

The trio stopped. "Asking what?" Ashley demanded.

"Everything. How often you come in, how long do you stay, who do you talk to? Tru's likely to throw you out now 'cuz he's already lost a half dozen customers who don't want to be hassled."

"Thanks, Ted."

Ashley did a sharp about-face. The others quickly caught up and they all hurried to get into the car.

"What do you think he's up to?" Jules asked, keying the engine again. Her hazel eyes were doubly large with anxiety.

"Fishing, that's all. It was bound to happen. We told the police about this place ourselves. It's their job to check things out. No sweat." But Ashley was worried, at least a little. She twisted in her seat to see Debra stuffing her bra into her purse. "What about when those guys from the Sheriff's Department came to your house, did you say something you shouldn't have?"

"They never talked to me."

"Don't lie." Ashley spoke quietly and stared hard the way Blake did when someone didn't want to pay up on a game. "You're wearing our mark now, you're family. I just need to know so I can take care of us."

"I swear, Ashley."

The kid was close to crying again. "Good. Good girl. Let's get out of here, Jules."

"I wish Stacie was here," Debra whispered.

Ashley did, too. Then things would be only half as bad as they were. God, she thought, she had to make some serious money and get out of this place.

36

The tender caress of lips on her wrist lifted Campbell from the cocoon of a deep sleep. She stretched her fingers, grazing a jawbone and whiskers, and smiled. Although her eyelids seemed glued shut, she forced them open to find Blade sitting on the edge of the bed.

"Hey." Something was different about him...no man-in-black outfit. "Are you okay?"

"I think that's my question." He frowned at the bandage that covered most of her forearm. "Must have been some fishing hook."

"Haven't you ever fished for catfish? Some of them get as big as small sharks."

"Where did it go in?"

"What difference does it make?" At his demanding look, she sighed and indicated the angle. She had no intention of telling him that the doctor called her lucky, that another few centimeters and she could have bled to death. She didn't have to; the knowledge was in the grim twist of his mouth and the shadow in his eyes.

"How bad is it throbbing?"

"Not too much." It felt really good when she was asleep. "Is Trunk okay out there?"

"You mean has he given up his prime rib bone? No, he's sleeping with it as though it was a favorite toy."

"Yancy had prime rib dinners delivered. We're having work done in the office. I couldn't resist claiming the bones for him. The rest are in the fridge."

"I may fight him for them. Was your father curious about where you were going with the scraps?"

"Writhing with it." As quickly as it appeared, Campbell's irreverent grin faltered. "I'll have to tell him about you soon."

"I think he's a safe-enough bet security-wise." Blade looked down at her arm again. "But he won't be any more pleased than he was seeing this."

She couldn't deny that herself, because she didn't know the full story about his past and why he'd left New York. But she didn't have the surplus energy to worry about it. She glanced at the clock on the night table, only to do a double take. "Is that the right time? Something *has* happened."

Blade eased her arm down to the covers and started unbuttoning his shirt. "Nothing as eventful as your day. Snow was doing some interviewing, so I had to alter my schedule somewhat."

"New developments?"

"Debra's an official member of the group."

"Are we talking initiation?"

"It would hardly compete with *The Godfather*."
Slipping out of the shirt, Blade circled the bed to hang
it on the doorknob of the closet. "A swig of bad
brandy and a tattoo."

Ignoring her protesting muscles, Campbell sat up
and drew her knees to her chin. She was as intrigued
with the news as she was with watching him undress.
"What kind?"

"A wolf's paw. On the right shoulder."

His response had her raising her eyebrows. Did he
remember what she'd said about night wolves?
Maybe the girls had heard the song, too. But were
they sophisticated enough to draw the deeper paral-
lels? If they'd been involved with Maida's death, they
had to be.

"I guess it could be worse," she replied. "Strategic
body piercing for example?"

With a grunt of agreement, Blade hung his jeans
over the top edge of the door. "Nothing seems off-
limits or too bizarre these days for those wanting to
make a statement—if only to their underwear."

"Considering their age, I suppose they went to
some dump that cared more about compensation than
infection and ID?"

"And it still wasn't cheap, which demands the
question, where did they get the money? Stacie was
the one who'd managed to keep some kind of job."
Stripped down to his briefs, he resumed his seat on
the edge of the bed and brushed her hair back over

her bare shoulder. Then he caressed her cheek and forehead. "Crazy woman, you're feverish. Get under those covers."

"After I take another pill."

She pushed aside the bedding to access a clear path to the bathroom, but when Blade saw she was naked, he sucked in his breath and drew her between his legs. "Thank you," he said, pressing a kiss to her flat abdomen.

Bemused, she stroked his tousled hair. "For what?"

Raising his head, he slid his hands over every curve and hollow he could reach. "Being here. Looking like you do."

The erotic combination of cool air and his talented hands on her heated skin was just as potent as her medication. But the instant he felt her wavering, Blade turned her around and directed her toward the bathroom.

"Go...before I have the bad manners to ignore your need to rest."

When she returned, he was in bed. The cold water she'd drunk to wash down a new dosage had succeeded in waking her up and her mind was churning out new questions. But Blade tucked her into the curve of his arm, determined she go back to sleep.

Twisting around to face him, she asked, "Did the girls seem different to you? I can't imagine them carousing around town when they've lost someone as close as family—in a way closer. If that happened to me, I'd either be a zombie or in a padded cell."

"No, you wouldn't. You'd be doing exactly what you've been doing. But you're right." Blade considered the question for a moment. "Debra does seem to be lagging wherever they go."

"That could be a good sign—and useful to us." As ancient as it was, the divide-and-conquer strategy paid optimum dividends.

"Unless it's just because she was the one under the needle tonight."

Campbell played with the hair matting his chest. "I'm guessing from your attire and the El Camino sitting in the driveway that you didn't go to Point East?"

"Uh-uh. That's where Snow was, ostensibly to ask about Stacie, but he also wanted to learn what people thought about the whole group. He may want me to appear sympathetic, if not an outright ally to Ashley, so we agreed it was wiser for me to watch from a safe distance. It was the right move, otherwise I'd have missed the trip to the tattoo parlor."

Campbell wasn't thrilled with the ally idea. "Did you get to speak with him afterward? Did he learn anything?"

"Oh, he got an earful. I don't know how useful it's going to be, though. Basically, the women think the girls are baby trash. As for the men…well, you can use your imagination about what they had to say."

"Debra doesn't strike me as being that sexually interested yet—at least not to the degree Ashley might be."

"If Ashley flirts, she has an ulterior motive."

Campbell knew it was unfair to dislike the girl on hearsay, but in this case she was able to accept her prejudice. "Is Snow going to bring them in for formal questioning on Stacie's case?"

"He's been warned off by the D.A.," Blade said, his disappointment unmistakable. "Vickery comes up for reelection next year, and having two trials this politically explosive makes him nervous, especially when two of the three girls are under eighteen. Their defense attorneys would scrub their faces, dress them in cotton and lace, and crucify him in front of the press."

It was nothing new but everything Campbell despised about politics affecting the law. How much more did the D.A. need? How could Snow do anything with his hands tied? About to say as much to Blade, she saw that he was staring up at the ceiling to avoid looking at her.

"What haven't you told me?"

"Stacie's body has been released to her family. The funeral is Monday."

Campbell's heart sank. "They're going to cremate her?"

"No, but you know how the court resists exhuming the dead unless the facts force them."

"If the defense challenges what's in a photograph or what the DNA says—and they will—that certainly won't happen."

"And to make matters worse, Snow got a call from Archer. The hair in Maida's trunk doesn't match Ashley's DNA."

"That can't be."

Hearing her panic, Campbell took a moment to collect herself. They were on the right track, she knew it. What else did they have to do to prove that? She wanted to call Archer and demand they redo the test. Then something Blade had said earlier filtered into her consciousness. "That's why you're going to make yourself available to Ashley."

"Not that available."

Unwilling to say what she felt, afraid to feel what she did, Campbell rolled over and turned out the light.

Before she could find a comfortable position, Blade was looming over her. "What are you doing?"

"What you told me to do—cover up and go to sleep."

"You think I can't control myself."

"I was a cop, remember? Things happen in undercover work. Look at us."

"Yeah, look at us."

His gruff response had her turning back to him and she kissed him. She kissed him for the promise she'd made to herself after surviving today, and again for keeping her sane this week. Then she kissed him because it felt so damned good.

"Now you've done it," he said into her mouth.

If he clutched her any closer, she could be his tattoo, but she wanted him just as much. Not for foreplay or any play, but with the raw honesty that kept breaking down the walls they'd been trying to put between each other.

"Come here."

He drew her on top of him and, gripping her bottom, rubbed her over and over him, all the while coaxing her with his mouth. When she took up the rhythm, he shifted his hands to the outer swells of her breasts…to her already hard nipples.

Aching for him, she sat up and smoothly sheathed him, not only stopping his breath but stealing it. Their gazes met and held. This time she saw the secrets, his doubt. Slowly, Blade turned his head and again kissed her injured arm.

Campbell pressed a kiss to his damp chest and the thundering pounding within. Encouraged by the arms that enfolded her and the whispers that entreated her, she gave him her body and her heart.

Maybe she dreamed it, but the whisper "I won't fail you" let her slip into a peaceful sleep.

37

The south side of Longview
Midnight

"There he is! Pull in."

Julianne turned into the convenience store as Ashley directed, but said, "I need to get home before my mother does. How long is this going to take?"

"Fuentes never stays in one place for more than a few minutes. Here, get some gas and I'll be right back." Tossing a five-dollar bill onto the girl's lap, she got out. Then as the VW eased over to the pumps, she went to the passenger's side of the ivory BMW and leaned over to look in at the driver. After a second the power lock opened and she got in.

"Pretty Ashley bird." Vincent Fuentes paused to exhale a blue-white cloud of cigar smoke. "What are you doing out and about at this hour? You want to reconsider my offer?"

Ashley didn't know what made her want to gag more, the question or his hideous cigars. She wanted to join his harem of hookers about as much as she wanted to stay in Longview the rest of her life. "Not exactly, Vince."

"Well, I know you're not a customer, which is a good thing since I don't have so much as this nail of sweets for you, sugar," he said, holding up the overlong pinky nail that was common with those in the drug business. "No tempting the law when I'm in this beauty."

The plush white leather seats were, indeed, as gorgeous as the rest of the car. Someday, Ashley thought, I'll have one just like this. "That's okay," she said. "I don't want to buy anything for anyone today." She'd done a little of that, but it was too risky when total strangers knew what you did, and more than a few guys had tried to cheat her out of money. "I do want to talk business, though."

In his designer suit, with his black hair slicked back like a forties movie star and a pencil-thin mustache, Vincent Fuentes looked the successful businessman he was. But his business was deadly, and Ashley didn't let herself forget that somewhere within reaching distance was a sleek silver .9 mm.

"That's why I'm here. You've got my attention until I finish my latte."

"I need to make some serious money, Vince."

Fuentes nodded, although he split his attention, checking the rearview mirror as well as the street. "'Need' is good. I like that word. It tells me you would be committed. How can I help you with this need?"

"I want to be one of your drivers."

"You said yourself, you don't even have a car, Ashley bird."

"My friends do."

"What, that tiny red pimple over there? That won't carry ten bills of product."

"What if I said I can get you an eighteen-wheeler?"

Fuentes looked unimpressed. "Baby, I got them, but I don't use them or the interstates for this anymore. That's where your daddy and the other state police are. It's small trucks and vans and driving back roads that get the job done today."

"Fine. I've got the right guy. He knows all of that."

"You finally spreading those long thighs for someone?" He shot her a brief but thorough look. "No, I think not. It's not men that heat your blood, it's money and power. So who is this poor sucker?"

Ashley was relatively new to this side of the business, but she wasn't stupid. "A contact I've been developing." She'd heard that phrase on TV and thought it made her sound savvy.

"How do I know you haven't been duped by a cop? One thing you need to understand—if I go down, it doesn't matter where they send me, I'll have someone find you and you won't be my pretty bird any longer."

He spoke as though discussing what he'd had for dinner tonight, but Ashley had to fight not to shiver. There had been a brutal execution-style killing in town a few months ago and she suspected he'd had a hand in that.

"He's no cop," she said with conviction. "I've had my eye on him for a while. He's an outsider and a loner who lives on his own terms and doesn't take crap off of anyone." A real cool dude, she thought to herself. "What would you pay us?"

"Us? You mean him."

"No, I would ride with him. It would look less suspicious that way."

"What about your girlfriends? I don't think they're cut out for the business. First sign of trouble, they'd spill their guts."

It impressed her that while he never acknowledged most people's presence, he did notice things. "I'd want them to be our backup, at least the first time or two, but then I'd cut them out. I'd set them up in something else."

"Uh-huh…a businesswoman. I like the way you think."

"So? Do we have a deal?"

He sipped his coffee. "You'd have to be available to drop everything and be ready to roll within an hour's time, to be waiting at a location, where you must make the transfer quickly and without attracting attention. At the other end it's the same thing, people will be waiting, you must be on time. Always. You would accept payment and return it to me. All of it."

"How much would you pay?"

"This time? Fifteen hundred."

"Not for that kind of risk."

"I'm the one taking the risk. They'd give you probation. They'd put me away for good."

"I heard you lost another driver this week." The young man, all of twenty, had fallen asleep behind the wheel and driven off the highway, flipped his van and drowned in a creek. "That means less product is moving."

"Two thousand."

"Three thousand," she countered.

Fuentes dropped the cigar butt into the remains of the drink. "Time for me to move." He keyed the engine.

Disappointed, Ashley reached for the door handle.

"For three thousand a run, I expect you to be available twice a week. Both Dallas runs."

She had to work at not squealing like the cheerleaders at those stupid ball games. Six thousand a week! She did the math—John would have to get a third, and she would keep a third for herself. The rest could be divided between the girls. They might bitch, but if they didn't like it, they could go to work flipping hamburgers or sacking groceries.

"When would you want us to start?" she asked coolly.

A minute later she returned to the VW and filled in the girls. As usual, they were impressed with her, but also doubtful.

"You're talking as though John's a sure thing." Jules sped toward Ashley's neighborhood to drop her off. "He's barely said a dozen words to you."

"Which is more than he's said to most people. I'm

taking that as a sign. The point is, he's an independent contractor, so what if I'm the one doing the contracting?'' Ashley's gaze followed a van turning off the road into an all-night eatery. "I just have to figure out how to get a van."

"Rent one at the airport." It was the first time Debra had spoken since they'd fled from Point East. "My father has done that a couple of times when he needed to haul junk."

Ashley glanced over the seat at her. "Well done, Debutante. That's the thing to do." And John's name would be on the paperwork, not hers.

They were in business.

38

Oakmont Cemetery
10:30 a.m.

Whatever her sins, angels from above should have been sent to weep at Stacie Holms's funeral. Only a fraction of the people who had attended her memorial came to her graveside service. Few of them were students, and fewer were friends.

Despite Blade asking her to stay away, Campbell decided to attend. It wasn't that she wanted to challenge him, but between Saturday night and this morning, he'd been directed to take his focus off of Stacie's murder and to put all his attention into nabbing one of the most successful drug traffickers in the area. It didn't matter that, if all went well, Ashley and her friends would be swept up in the same net. They weren't going to confess to anything and their attorneys would scream "coercion" and "sting." In the meantime, any link that existed between the girls and Maida would grow thinner.

The funeral was her huge opportunity to work on

Debra's conscience. Just her presence would have to be a reminder of Maida.

She arrived, pulling in only a few cars after Blade's El Camino. The difference was that when Ashley spotted him, she wasted no time in abandoning her friends and hurrying over to him. Campbell hated seeing the dark beauty play the moment for all it was worth. Pressing her face against his leather jacket, she made it impossible for Blade not to put his arms around her. Then taking his hand, she led him to the others.

Waiting until they were under the tent canopy, Campbell left the Blazer and crossed the lawn, stopping at a stately black oak near the rest of the mourners. It was interesting to see that Stacie's family did not acknowledge the girls, nor did the funeral home personnel invite the teenagers to be seated.

The overcast skies took any promise of spring from the air, and even though her black wool pantsuit and cashmere turtleneck was warm, Campbell felt chilled to the bone the moment Blade lowered his sunglasses slightly to stare at her. She could feel his disapproval, but she hadn't given him her word that she wouldn't attend. He had his priorities and so did she.

Ashley noticed his stare and leaned closer into him to whisper something, then shot her a lethal look. Since they'd never met, Campbell thought that interesting. She might have spotted the Cody Security vehicle, though.

The service was over in less than fifteen minutes; long enough for Campbell to endure watching Ashley press her breasts into Blade's arm and rest her head on his shoulder. Finally, as the minister ended the prayer and Stacie's family began laying flowers on the casket, she was given a reprieve. Debra parted from the group and approached her.

"Go away," she whispered, keeping her back to the others.

The girl had lost weight in the last few days and there were dark shadows under her eyes that makeup wasn't able to camouflage. Her black dress and wool shawl only accentuated her wan appearance. As she reached up to brush her windswept brown hair from her eyes, her fingers were trembling.

"I have as much a right to be here as anyone, Debra," Campbell said quietly. "This is my hometown. Stacie was a local. She was your friend. In the last week, you've lost your grandmother and your classmate. It's the right place to be."

But Debra wasn't buying any of that. "You're no friend, you're stalking me."

"Why would I do that?"

"Because the newspaper and TV said that the police continue to question family and friends and, like them, you seem to think that means we're guilty of something."

Campbell searched the girl's heart-shaped face. "I know you loved your grandmother and would have never intentionally hurt her."

"That's right, I wouldn't and *I* didn't."

Any doubts Campbell had about coming vanished. "On the other hand, I do think you know about something that went terribly wrong and you're having to stay quiet about it. But look in the mirror when you get home, Debra. It's eating at you, and it's going to get worse because these people you're involved with—"

"They're my friends and we want you to leave all of us alone," Debra said shakily.

"All for one and one for all, huh? One fatal flaw with that concept, kiddo. If they go down, you go down."

"Screw you."

Debra walked away. What interested Campbell was that she did not return to her group; she went to Julianne's red VW and got in.

Having seen and heard enough herself, Campbell left.

Returning to the office, she saw that Beth was holding her first interview with a studious-looking young woman Beth's age or slightly younger. She was showing the applicant around the office.

"Ms. Cody," Beth said formally, "this is Cynthia Russell, one of our applicants. Cynthia attends night school over at TJC."

"Nice to meet you, Cynthia." Campbell shook her hand willingly enough since she put a good deal of stock in first impressions. To her relief, the young woman didn't have one of those butterfly-flutter grasps. "What's your major?"

"Business. I haven't decided specifically what,

though. I'd started out thinking accounting, but I realized it's a little tedious for me.''

Hearing Yancy swear in his office, Campbell cleared her throat. ''Well, one thing it isn't here is tedious, right, Beth? Good luck.''

Waving, she went to see what had riled her father. He was on the phone and, upon seeing her, motioned her in.

''Bryce, Campbell's arrived,'' he said. ''I'm putting you on the speaker phone. Why don't you run that argument by her to see if it gets you a better response.''

''*Thanks,*'' she mouthed to Yancy.

''You're the senior partner of the firm,'' Bryce Tyndell replied. ''Can't you make an executive decision? I've been informed that Maida's body is being released to the family this morning.''

Campbell gave her father a here-we-go-again look. The Saunderses must have called Bryce seconds after getting the word from Archer. Chuck had told her when she'd been en route to the service and she hadn't had time to inform anyone.

''The Trails account is Campbell's and she's been in dialogue with the Sheriff's Department, not me,'' Yancy replied.

''Bryce, Campbell here. Tell the Saunderses that as soon as I speak with Detective Archer and get his approval to enter the house without him being present, I can meet them there and they can pick up whatever clothing they need.''

''Under the circumstances, I feel we should give

them a permanent pass,'' Bryce replied. ''They want to start preparing to put the place on the market, and they don't need to be inconvenienced with constant sign-ins.''

Campbell sat on the edge of Yancy's desk and winked at her father. She could always tell when Tyndell had committed to something before making certain it was feasible. ''That's premature. I'm certain Archer will approve this brief access, but no way is he ready to release the house. Since you're obviously in such intimate dialogue with the family, you might also recommend some restraint. You know, property sales often come from resident recommendations to friends. The Saunderses don't want to appear greedy.''

''I have not gotten that impression at all,'' Bryce replied, still maintaining that senior-statesman tone. ''It's clearly an extremely painful episode in their lives that they want resolved.''

Campbell pinched the bridge of her nose and struggled not to tell him he was full of it. ''I'm sorry, Bryce, but there's no way Archer will approve any clean-up or renovations when he knows the first thing that would be done is ripping out the bedroom carpet. Not when it's entirely possible for a jury to be brought to the house and walked through the D.A.'s theory of the crime.''

''Oh, we could never allow that,'' Bryce replied, horrified. ''Do you realize what that kind of circus would do to property values?''

''We don't get a vote on this. Just pray we can

keep the media from appealing for access to take photos of the outside of the house." Campbell could almost hear Tyndell beginning to sweat. "By the way, since you're the man with his fingers on the pulse of the bereaved, what's the latest on Dean McFarland?"

At the sound of the sharp click, Campbell gave her father an innocent look. "Gee…it sounds like he hung up on me."

Yancy stretched to shut off the speakerphone. "You do enjoy riling that man."

"Not really, not anymore. There's no challenge in it."

"How did the service go?"

"Heartbreaking, depressing, infuriating…take your pick."

"I thought you looked like someone had pushed a few of your buttons. Are you ready to tell me about it?"

Campbell considered closing his door, but glancing down the hall, she saw that Beth had shut hers. "Remember the question you asked me the other day?"

"I'm always wanting to interrogate you, give me a hint."

"The personal variety."

"Ah. I finally get a clue as to where my Cadillac spends nights these days?"

In his garage last night, because Campbell had stayed in her apartment. "He's an undercover cop," she said, deciding to go to the heart of the matter.

Not surprisingly, Yancy covered his face with his hands.

"Go ahead and say it," she muttered. "I'm a glutton for punishment."

"Why can't you hook up with a doctor? You've been meeting plenty of them lately." At her warning look, he grimaced. "Okay, okay, go on. He was at the service?"

"Yes. And he didn't want me there."

"Why not?"

"Because I'm a reminder that Maida's killer is still free and he's been directed to focus elsewhere."

Yancy rested his hand in his chin. "Do I have to remind you that it's common in small departments, already in a budget crunch, to reduce the manpower on difficult cases sooner than larger ones would?"

"Of course not, but does that mean I have to stand by and do nothing?"

"Has he asked you to?"

He knew better than that, but he might as well have. Campbell rose and slipped out of her jacket. It was too warm to wear inside. Besides, she needed to keep this short and get changed before the Saunderses tried jumping the gun, anyway.

"Belle…" Yancy said with gruff tenderness, "this is serious, this thing between you two?"

She tried to keep her gaze on the blue-and-black tight-weave carpet, then on the textured ceiling. "I didn't go looking for it. Neither of us did. I'm not the only one with a past."

"What's his story?" While Yancy hadn't exploded, he didn't sound thrilled.

"I don't know yet. It's his call when to tell me."

If her father seemed stunned before, he was openly flummoxed by that reply. "Is this you talking? The same daughter who swallowed a damned big and bitter pill thanks to Gerrard—and who has avoided any and all overtures ever since?"

Campbell sighed. "I don't blame you for wanting to chew my ear off, but right now could I have a hug instead?"

Without hesitation, Yancy rose and extended his arms. Campbell crossed to him.

"It's reassuring to know you're not steel through and through," he said as they stood cheek to cheek.

"It doesn't feel all that great to me." It had been months since they'd been simply father and daughter—since his diagnosis, to be exact. He hadn't been all that thrilled with his vulnerability, either. "So tell me…am I wrong to keep wanting to work Maida's case?"

"But that's not what you're doing, exactly. You're pushing the Saunders girl, and while that might be right on target, it compromises your man's safety. Is that what you want to do? For the interim, while he's going after people, why can't you go after evidence?"

Campbell nodded at her right arm, although her sleeve hid the bandage. "I have to stay out of rivers for a while."

"Now who's telling the bad jokes? Besides, that can't be the only place where there's evidence."

"It would help to know what I was looking for."

Patting her back, Yancy released her and picked up the paper-clip chain he'd been making during phone conversations. It had become his habit since his doctor recommended he take up some kind of stress reliever—a habit that drove both Campbell and Beth crazy.

"You'll think of something," he said. "In the meantime, you were right about the need to check on Dean McFarland. Wasn't he supposed to get out of the hospital today? His family would appreciate—"

Campbell leaned over and covered his hand to stop him from taking apart the chain. "You've got it!"

"Got what?"

"The bracelet. The one Dean gave to Maida. We haven't found it. And the other night Debra got a tattoo, but none of the girls have jobs to pay for something like that. What if they hocked the bracelet to get the tattoo?"

"Then there's a strong piece of evidence out there, and a witness who can testify who brought it in."

"Where's the phone book?"

39

An abandoned campground
11:55 a.m.

"Sorry about the spook tactics," Ashley told Blade after she directed him on a circuitous path that led them to a small lake about seven miles east of Longview. Opening the passenger window of the El Camino, she signaled the VW behind them to stay put. Then she said, "Drive up to that old boat ramp so they can see you."

"Why? So they can shoot me if I don't give you the right answer to whatever this is about?"

"No, so the girls can get me out of here if I have to shoot you for getting the wrong idea."

Blade wasn't wild about this scenario at all, but felt confident enough to play it through. He was glad, though, that he'd left his real ID and gun behind at the house, risky as it was.

"Have you been OD'ing on James Bond movies recently? I'm not a rapist, and I don't make passes at teenage girls."

''Well, I'm not a virgin in any sense and I believe in being careful.''

'''Careful' is not bringing a relative stranger out here in the first place.''

''Maybe, but I had questions and we needed privacy. Why did you come to the funeral? Don't get me wrong, I'm glad you did, even so, it's a change from your previous behavior toward us. Toward me.''

''If this is an example of how pleased you are, I think it's time for me to start accepting longer, cross-country hauls.'' Blade shifted into Park. While he was relieved Ashley hadn't pulled out something Bondish and deadly, he also hoped she meant what she said and stayed on her side of the El Camino.

''Just answer the question, please.''

He shrugged. ''I don't know that I have a clear-cut explanation. It seems a waste. She was a nice kid. Feisty at times, you all are, but she had a good head on her shoulders. She should have had the opportunity to use it.''

Ashley sat scrunched in the corner between the seat and the door, her arms crossed. Her royal-purple sweater over an ankle-length black skirt highlighted the blue sheen in her layered, gypsy-style hair and made her skin seem almost translucent. But there was nothing ethereal or vulnerable in her near-black eyes.

''You've never struck me as the get-in-touch-with-the-inner-child type, John.''

''True.''

''So where is this coming from?''

"She reminded me of someone I used to know. Someone I cared about deeply."

That answer seemed to satisfy Ashley. Blade saw that while it was something she hadn't experienced herself, she believed she could use the energy, like revenge, like ambition.

"Your first love?"

Blade had only to think of Campbell to find the hint of pain he wanted Ashley to see. Just as quickly he shuttered his eyes and reverted to being the mystery man she was first attracted to. "Why don't you get to the point of this?"

Confident again, Ashley nodded. "Okay. I want to make you a business proposition."

"If it has anything to do with Fuentes, count me out."

"How did you know?" she asked, immediately suspicious.

"Honey, you keep closer tabs on him than you do me." Risky as his statement was, Ashley didn't go teenager shrill on him. He saw she was reviewing her past behavior. "Exactly," he said when he knew she'd caught on. "You're an ambitious kid, Ashley, but you could be dangerous because of your lack of subtlety."

"I like being direct," she said, somewhat defensive.

"We have that in common. But you don't see me going up to some yahoo at Point East and saying, 'Want to lose twenty bucks?'"

She digested that, too, then asked, "If you already

know what I'm going to say, why did you ask what this was about?''

"It's your play. I'm letting you show your stuff," he said with a shrug.

"Are you interested?"

"I don't need trouble."

"A minimum of it. We drive at night. Back roads. Two-and-a-half hours to Dallas, then back, and by morning you have more cash in your pocket than you probably make after taxes in a month—and that's just to start."

It was apparent that she had been practicing her speech and Blade pretended to consider the offer. "What kind of rig would I be driving?"

"There's the beauty of it. No big rigs. No interstate where you're hounded by cops. We'll use a van. Low profile."

"That's not a lot of space to hide what you're hiding."

"I agree. But we're in at the entry level, John. I think we should work with Fuentes and make ourselves indispensable."

"No one is indispensable. The guy who gets it right after you fuck up is, maybe. Until he fucks up. And when it comes to the kind of transportation business you're talking about, someone always fucks up. If I agree to participate—and that's a big if—it would be short term only. A few weeks, a couple months at best. The trouble with success is it makes people careless and sloppy. I can live without that much success."

She looked momentarily hamstrung, then slid across the seat. "You tell me what I need to do, John. Tell me the holes in my plan. I learn fast, and I don't repeat my mistakes."

"What's Fuentes offering for your virgin run?"

"Your cut would be two thou a week—that's for two trips. Do the math, that's two hundred an hour just for driving."

"You hope. You don't know the characters on the other end of the road. As for the money, you've been had. Do you realize Fuentes's take will easily be over a half million or better? That's per trip."

Once again Ashley went silent. "Okay…yes," she said slowly, "but how many games of pool do you need to play to make two grand?"

This budding Dragon Lady needed to be taken out of the mainstream, Blade thought grimly. Because in a few years, with a little more experience and confidence, she would make Fuentes look like a missionary. He suspected she was already corrupted beyond the reach of the juvenile detention centers where they saturated young people like her with character-building instruction, something her parents and teachers either hadn't had the time or interest to do. Besides, she was eighteen. Where she would be sent there was far more corruption than opportunities.

He had to force himself to continue playing the game. "Thanks, but no thanks," he told her.

It wasn't the answer she'd expected. "Why not?"

"Because while I believe you might be able to handle the work, your gal pals back there? Forget about it. And I've never done more than an overnight stay in a lockup cell for being drunk and disorderly. I'm not about to start now."

Ashley placed her hand on his thigh. "What if I told you that Jules and Deb are temporary in this?"

Jesus Christ. Sick to his stomach, Blade had to concentrate not to recoil from her. Is that what Stacie had been? Temporary?

"I'm listening." He pretended boredom and glanced out the front of the car and then his side window. But that was mostly to keep from having to look at her one more second than he had to.

"Diversity. My business teacher reads to us from the *Wall Street Journal* every day. You know, don't have all of your eggs in one basket investment-wise? Actually, it was Stace's class, I dropped out, but she would tell us all about it. I'm going to set up the younger kids in some kind of business and they can pay me a percentage." Her enthusiasm growing, she rubbed his thigh. "I'm an idea person, John. The day-to-day grind isn't for me."

It was all Blade could do not to knock her hand away. "Well, Ms. Idea Person, where do we get the van?"

"Would you be willing to go rent one at the airport? I can't, I'm underage."

"I guess." He could already hear the lieutenant cussing up a storm over that expense. "But the cost sure as hell isn't coming out of my cut."

"Fair enough."

Blade doubted it would come out of hers, either.

Ready to get out of there, he wanted to accept, but he knew John Blake was no pushover. "I'll think about it."

"Um…the thing is, if Fuentes decides to use me, I have to be ready to roll in an hour."

"That's doable."

40

12:20 p.m.

When Campbell finished changing into her uniform, she called Archer and returned to her father's office. "Okay, I've got clearance to get into the house for a while, so I'm going to go deal with that. With luck, Patsy or Dwayne won't want to spend any more time with me than I want to spend with them."

"What if they both show up and one tries to keep you busy while the other ransacks the house?"

"I'll throw them out and have Archer arrest them." It was an appealing thought, considering that both appeared to be clueless as to their daughter's condition. "Anyway, that should give me some opportunity to check out a few pawnshops before my shift starts."

"And you'll stop by McFarland's?"

Campbell sighed as she checked the battery on her phone and pager. The rest of the day would go by in a blur. "Yes, thanks for the reminder. I'll check in on him."

Yancy pushed her two-way radio at her. Unlike the rest of the staff, they kept their radios with them at all times, except when they needed charging. "Did you tell Archer about your plan?"

"What plan?"

The deep male voice had both Codys turning. A voice Campbell recognized immediately.

Blade stood in the doorway. She didn't have to guess how he'd gotten in. Since the media had given up their twenty-four-hour stakeout out front, they were leaving the front door unlocked so that Beth's cousin—now making some improvements in the new file and storage room—could have easier access as he moved between his pickup and inside.

"What are you doing here?" Campbell couldn't deny the leap in her chest, or the concern for his safety. It was damned hard to stay annoyed with a man when you were beginning to care so much.

"We need to talk. Maybe you'd like to introduce me first."

"Yancy Cody, Jackson Blade."

"Do I shake his hand or cuff him?" Yancy asked, sizing up Blade.

Campbell shot him a dry look. "Can we borrow your office for a few minutes?"

"I miss out on all the fun," Yancy muttered. But as he approached Blade, he extended his hand. "Just to let you know that I give people the benefit of the doubt. Once."

Campbell watched them. Although her father stood inches taller than Blade's solid six feet, he seemed smaller because of Blade's broader shoulders and sinewy build.

Yancy glanced back at Campbell. "You're right. He doesn't say enough."

When the door was closed, Blade said, "He's obviously not referring to our conversations in bed."

Campbell wasn't ready to be teased. "Aren't you taking a big risk being here? What if someone followed you?"

"The El Camino is well hidden behind the other vehicles out there." His voice dropped a half octave. "I missed you last night."

She missed him, too, but she wouldn't say it. "You didn't look happy to see me this morning at the cemetery."

"I couldn't believe you'd come. Not after what we'd agreed."

Just as she thought, he'd come to give her a dressing-down. "You demanded, and you had no right to."

"Stubbornness in the face of something beyond our control is reckless and places us both in danger. I was given orders, Campbell. It doesn't happen often. Pretty much I can follow my own game plan, and the hierarchy is happy with the results. But hearing we can get into Fuentes's operation just about had everyone upstairs wetting their pants in excitement. It's not that anyone is giving up on Maida or Stacie. In fact, arresting the girls on drug trafficking charges would do more than keep them on ice until we're sure of the role they played in those other cases. We could use the environment to work one against the other and get someone to talk."

"Why didn't you say that yesterday instead of taking that my-way-or-no-way stance?"

Looking thoroughly disgusted with himself, he rubbed his forehead. "I had a flashback. It's nuts, but it was suddenly too much like New York, where people whom I deserved respect from, showed none. I was wrong about the comparison, and I'm here to tell you about my past if you'd care to hear it."

Campbell understood how deeply personal and painful this was for him and knew that maybe only a handful of people had ever heard what he was about to say. "I want to hear whatever you want to share with me," she told him.

"It's been almost three years now," Blade began. "I was a decorated cop, I'd made detective and life was good. I told you, I come from a family of cops, but my father had passed away, and with my record even my uncle looked upon me as the head of the family. Then came this big case, a multifamily racketeering-and-theft operation that half of our department helped crack. We arrested all of the major players and everything looked good until it was discovered that some crucial evidence was missing. It was obvious someone had gotten to one of us. It's bad enough to look at your fellow cops with suspicion, imagine how I felt when I discovered it was my kid brother?"

"Oh, Blade…" Campbell could see the pain still cut deep.

"It turned out that his girlfriend had a heroin habit and certain people arranged for her to build up a hefty bill. When it was high enough, my brother was given the choice to make the evidence disappear or his girl-friend was going to end up pushed in front of a sub-way or something equally gruesome and final. Instead of coming to me or going to his superiors, he took the evidence.''

''Good heavens, why?''

Blade shrugged. ''Because he knew I would tell him exactly what he didn't want to hear—that he had to admit what he'd done and turn in his badge. But he'd developed a little habit himself and he wasn't looking forward to the consequences of having to go through that withdrawal *and* the public and profes-sional scorn. What was worse was that the rest of the family sided with him. 'There would be another day to get the scum,' they argued. 'Ricky had a perfect record otherwise.' But I challenged, how did they know that? I understood I would never be able to trust him again, and I had no right to expect others to. So when he continued to resist, I gave him an ultimatum. Confess, or I'd take the rap.''

''He didn't...and you did,'' Campbell whispered. Campbell couldn't believe his courage—and that his family would never understand he'd ended up paying for all of them. ''Even your mother let you do this?''

''She said she would rather have seen me shot dead than watch me rub my brother's face in his mistake. Mistake,'' he said bitterly. ''That viewpoint said it all to me. I realized I never knew these people at all.''

''Surely there were others on the force who refused to believe you were guilty?''

"A few. That's why in the end it was agreed not to press charges. Those who were against me took comfort in the fact that I'd be totally ostracized by the city. I didn't hang around long enough to find out. The day after I was cut loose, I left New York and began my own odyssey to find a new reason to live."

"I don't think I could ever show the strength of character you did."

"Yes, you could. You have. I realize that's part of the reason I was attracted to you, why I couldn't stay away from you. It's been so long since I've met anyone like you, I reacted like a starving man."

Campbell couldn't stand it any longer, she needed to hold him and launched herself across the short space between them. He crushed her tight.

"I don't know what to say. I want to raise hellfire for you."

"This is better." Blade sought and found her mouth.

Yes, it was much better. Words could only do so much. Touch transmitted to the heart, and soul. She loved that he held her as though he feared he might never again. And when the first rush of desperation was past, she loved that his urgency for her remained at that heady pitch.

"I was afraid to hope you'd understand," he said when she buried her face against his shoulder to catch her breath.

"You're the strongest man I've ever met—and the most noble."

"I know it's a lot to ask, but can you be patient with me as I work through this?"

"I can now."

That had him seeking her mouth again, and for the next breathless minute they sought to make up for the drought of last night.

"Damn," Blade said at last, his arousal undeniable. "I guess there's no way we're going to lock that door?"

"Not unless you want to learn a new punishment for blackmail Yancy-style," Campbell replied.

"Will you come to me after your shift is over?"

"Yes."

"Thank you—and not just for me. Last night your four-legged friend howled loud and long enough to bring in the animal control people."

Eventually, Campbell had to yield to commitments. "Let me go. I have to get to work. People are waiting for me."

"Not near water, I hope?"

"You and Yancy."

"He seems a good man."

"He'll do. Just remember I'm the one you're supposed to butter up."

"I'm game. We haven't tried that yet."

After he left, Campbell stood there realizing her life had just been transformed. She had no clue as to exactly how—she'd barely the time to breathe let alone analyze it.

"Hoo-rah," she whispered, hurrying out the door herself.

41

Maple Trails

It didn't take long for Campbell's mood to change—
only as long as it took to drive up to the entrance gate
and see Kelsey's expression. "What?"

The guard gestured into the park. "It happened
again. I tried to make her wait here for you, but this
time it was Tyndell who came and escorted her up to
the house."

Not at all surprised, Campbell asked, "Has Mr.
McFarland brought his father home yet?"

"About five minutes before Mrs. Saunders arrived."

Signaling her thanks, Campbell set off for Maida's.
She'd about had it with those two. If Bryce had over-
stepped himself this time, she would call in Archer
and leave them to a full taste of his wrath.

It began to rain as she approached the driveway,
and although she saw both vehicles, she couldn't tell
if anyone was inside them. But as she drove up the
drive, she saw two people sitting close together in
Patsy's vehicle. Kelsey hadn't said anything about

Dwayne being here, too. And yet as she came up behind them, she saw the two kissing. Then, abruptly, they parted and both doors opened.

Patsy placed her flat handbag over her head and ran up toward the front door, and Bryce approached, wiping his mouth and smoothing his hair.

"Mrs. Saunders is extremely upset at having to do this," Bryce said as they followed up the sidewalk. "Your keeping her waiting hasn't helped things."

One look at Patsy's smeared lipstick and she knew her eyes hadn't deceived her. Good grief, how long had this been going on? she wondered.

Without comment, she held out her hand to Bryce for the key.

Ducking under the yellow tape, Campbell opened the storm door. When she had the front door unlocked and the alarm deactivated, she glanced back at their guilty faces.

"Stay on the plastic runner, Mrs. Saunders. This is still a crime scene. Try to touch only the clothing you intend to take."

"Bry—I've asked Mr. Tyndell to come with me."

Campbell didn't so much as blink. "Because you're feeling faint again, ma'am?"

"No…"

"I'm glad to hear it. Be assured, though, all of the staff is as capable as Mr. Tyndell in administering CPR and other first aid should you need it."

His face rigid and suffused with blood, Bryce backed from the door and grabbed his pager. Scowling at the screen only he could see, he said, "Bad luck. I have to get back to the office. Mrs. Saunders, please take care. We'll work on getting everything cleared for you.''

As he hurried away, Campbell handed a stunned Patsy a pair of rubber gloves and began pulling on her own. ''You might want to take off those rings, at least the ones with the stones.''

Not at all happy at being left alone with her, Patsy replied, ''Why can't I just point and you get the things?''

''Whatever you say, but you still need the gloves in case you inadvertently trip and touch something to balance yourself.''

The house was beginning to have a stale smell from not having been lived in for almost a week. ''Unloved'' as Maida would have put it.

''Ugh,'' Patsy said softy upon entering. ''Tacky old furniture. We'll probably have to pay to get it hauled off to the county dump.''

In the bedroom, Campbell flipped on the light switch, which turned on the chandelier Maida had loved. Trying to avoid looking at the stain, she continued on the plastic to open the door to the walk-in closet. Turning on that light, she stepped back.

''She loved pink,'' Campbell said, indicating the back of the closet. ''There's a suit in the rose bag at the back she would want you to choose. She's had it prepared for some time. Everything else is in there.''

''How morbid.'' Patsy flicked her hand at it. ''Well, check to be sure, will you?''

Campbell did and saw Maida had even purchased

new lingerie for the occasion. The price tags had Campbell smiling inwardly. Zipping up the bag, she said, "I suppose Dolly would be right for that outfit."

"Excuse me?"

Handing over the bag, she reached up for the first box, knowing it was the correct one, since she and Archer had checked it last week. "She named her wigs. "Dolly is all that's left."

"All right, then." Patsy pretended to need two hands to hold the garment bag and let her deal with the wig box. "Now I'd like to get the papers my husband asked me to look for."

Campbell accepted she had a right to them if Dwayne was named in the will—but Archer hadn't authorized anything else to be taken from the house. "I'm sorry. Everything stays until we're directed otherwise."

"Oh, for heaven's sake." Patsy indicated the jewelry box on the dresser. "What about what's in there? Why can't my daughter have something of her grandmother's for the service? Or do we have to wait for that stuff, too, while you people conveniently lose her most precious things?"

"I take exception to that, Mrs. Saunders. Nothing has been removed from here except trace evidence or items with her blood on it. If you're referring to the bracelet, we didn't know it existed until Mr. McFarland mentioned it. That's why Detective Archer asked you to make a list. Have you done so?"

"How are we supposed to know what she had? She never told us anything. A single strand of pearls that my husband bought for her birthday some years back and she never wore because she said he couldn't afford it. How ridiculous is that? And wasteful.''

"Well, maybe you can put them to good use soon," Campbell said, although the idea left a bad taste in her mouth. "Speaking of Debra, how is she?"

"Upset. What do you expect?"

"I saw her yesterday at her friend's funeral."

"What were you doing there?" Patsy asked, frowning.

Rather than answer the question, she observed, "She doesn't look well. Aside from appearing extremely stressed and nervous, she's lost weight she doesn't have to lose."

"Considering everything we've all been through, it's a miracle we're holding up as well as we are."

Campbell couldn't believe the woman. Was she truly so narcissistic? "Have you considered getting her counseling?" From what little she had seen so far, the whole family had needed it years ago.

Patsy lifted her chin. "We do not believe in wasting money on quacks."

"Your daughter is in trouble, Mrs. Saunders."

"Are you referring to her makeup and sexy clothes? All the kids look like that these days. You go to the junior department at any store and you'll see for yourself. Now if you'll excuse me—" Patsy turned on her heel and strode out of the room "—if you're going to be difficult about the rest of the things, I'd like to get out of this creepy place."

But at the front door, she hesitated. "Listen…about

what you saw earlier. You're not going to say anything, are you? It was one of those crazy things that
happen when you're not yourself. I've been aware
he's been attracted to me since he spoke to my ladies
group, but I am a happily married woman.''

Good grief, Campbell thought, they were having an
affair. No wonder she hadn't seen that Debra was in
a psychological nosedive. She handed her the wig
box. "It's none of my business, Mrs. Saunders."

Whether reassured or embarrassed, the woman
murmured a vague "thank-you" and ran off into the
rain. Campbell turned on the security system and
locked up.

All the way to the McFarland residence, she tried
to get her mind around the idea of Patsy and Bryce.
Approximately five years his senior, Patsy was attractive, but she didn't seem the type for vain Bryce, a
man who never passed a mirror or window without
checking his appearance. Was it really chemistry, or
did one or both of them have ulterior motives? If it
was the latter, could that have a bearing on Maida's
case? Should she tell Archer? As soon as she checked
on Dean, she would call Blade and ask for his input.

It was Dean's son who answered the door. He informed Campbell that his father was resting per the
doctor's instructions. Campbell asked that he tell his
father she had stopped by and wished him the best.

"Have there been any arrests in the case?" the
younger McFarland asked.

"No, I'm sorry. But they're making progress."

"This has changed my father. I'm considering asking him to move down by us,'' his son said. "Do you think he'll consider it?''

Although she knew he would be missed, Campbell smiled warmly. "Yes, I do. And, to be honest, it might be a relief for him. I'll do what I can to encourage him if he asks.''

Once she was out of the Trails, she dialed Blade's number.

Since he had caller ID, he picked up, saying, "I hope this means you're coming over to take a nap with me.''

She could hear the grogginess in his voice. "I woke you—I'm sorry.''

"You should get more rest yourself.''

"No time. I'm on my way to check pawnshops and look for that bracelet.''

"Damn. I should have thought of that—but maybe I can save you time. You know there's a place right next to the tattoo shop.'' He gave her the address.

Grateful for the information, she said, "Now help me with this latest revelation. I just caught Patsy Saunders and Bryce Tyndell making out in Maida's driveway.''

"Tyndell…your nemesis from Administration?''

"That's the one.''

"Interesting. Just when the puzzle seems to be coming together. How do you see that piece fitting?''

"I don't. She begged me to keep this to myself, but how can I not tell Archer?''

"He needs to know. It may end up meaning nothing more than what it is—another ingredient that keeps a dysfunctional family in destruction mode. Stick with the bracelet.''

Campbell could barely hide her excitement as she entered the pawnshop. The owner, a short, slender man of Eastern descent greeted her with a wary nod and waited behind a glass counter as she eyed the rows of watches, rings and coins.

''I'm looking for something specific pawned by a girl or girls,'' she told him. ''A bracelet, gold with garnets.''

''You are police? This is stolen?''

''From a woman killed last week, yes.''

''Maybe I can help.''

He motioned for her to move down to the next case, where he unlocked the sliding doors and from the second shelf brought out the bracelet that was exactly what Dean had described.

''Who brought this in?''

With perfect timing he went into his ''innocent bystander'' routine. ''I do not know. Maybe I'm not here that day.''

Maybe she should ask Blade to sic Lefevre on him. He was in the business to make money and no doubt he was thinking she was going to confiscate it and he would be out a few hundred dollars. ''Take your time. And while you're trying to remember, I'll go out to my vehicle and get my credit card to reimburse you for your loss.''

He brightened immediately. ''Maybe I make mistake. I remember now…a beautiful young girl. Dark,'' he said, motioning over his head.

''Black hair.''

''Very pretty, but so tall, your American young woman.''

Ashley. Campbell wanted to cheer, but tapped the countertop with her finger instead. ''I'll get my credit card. In the meantime, please look for your copy of the receipt you gave her.''

''Privacy guaranteed.''

''Then that all but guarantees you will be subpoenaed to appear in court to physically identify the bracelet and the very tall young woman.''

He produced the receipt with a signature that had Campbell wanting to drive over to the high school and drag the girl out of class by her very dark hair. If this wasn't proof that they were dealing with one of the budding sociopaths criminal psychologists were warning educators and parents about, she didn't know a 747 from a dragonfly.

42

Oakmont Cemetery
2:00 p.m.

On the opposite side of the cemetery in the mausoleum where her second husband rested, Maida was put to rest. The rains had passed and a western front was blowing in. Campbell liked the idea that it was Maida's spirit urging her on to protest her unfair end.

The attendance was comforting for this service. At least three hundred people attended. Maida would have been pleased to see so many of her neighbors and friends at Maple Trails weeping openly. Sadly, Dean McFarland didn't show, but that was under the direct order of his doctor. His spray of pink roses, however, was placed with honor at the doorway to the building by the funeral director.

Campbell was the sole attendee from Cody's and law enforcement. She'd conferred with Archer and Yancy and they'd decided that for what she had planned, a low-key presence was desirable...if Debra's friends showed.

They did, and yet Ashley and Jules stayed away

from Debra and the rest of the Saunderses, standing several rows back. It was when the family led the processional to place flowers on the casket that they moved forward.

Campbell situated herself near the front of the building beside the minister, whom she'd spoken to earlier to vaguely explain her need to observe the crowd. She waited to place the pink rose she was holding onto the casket until Ashley and Julianne were directly across from her.

As she moved, the sleeve of her wool jacket exposed her wrist. The garnet bracelet caught the cold winter sunshine.

Jules continued on, placed her red carnation and was lost in the crowd. In stark contrast, Ashley froze. Campbell would have sworn she heard the stem of her carnation snap between her fingers.

The teenager didn't lift her gaze from the growing mound of blossoms, nor did she speak. But when she followed those exiting the park, she and Jules situated themselves on either side of Debra. Each took hold of an arm and escorted the disconcerted girl to the VW.

43

9:45 p.m.

That night Ashley made Julianne drop off Debra first. "You're emotionally wiped out," she told the newest member of the group. "Go to bed and chill. In a few days everything will look different."

As soon as the door slammed behind Debra, Ashley snapped, "Get me downtown. Quick."

She located Fuentes in the parking lot of an all-night eatery.

Julianne hesitated when she saw the BMW. "What are you doing now? I'm beat, too, you know."

"Stop sniveling. I need to talk to him. After you let me out, go drive up and down the rows of that parking lot over there and I'll flag you down when I'm ready to be picked up."

"I thought you said we were supposed to wait for him to call us."

"So I need help, okay?"

Angry at being questioned and angrier yet at being in this predicament, Ashley slammed the VW's door with enough force to have shattered the window. That wouldn't do in front of Fuentes, though, and she took several deep breaths of the cold night air before she reached for the door handle of the Beemer.

"Ashley bird, this is not good," he said as she settled beside him. "You've disobeyed my directives and we haven't begun doing business."

"I'm sorry, Vince. But I need your help."

"Already?"

"I know. I'll owe you."

"Oh, no doubt. Speak, Ashley bird."

That nickname was beginning to get on her nerves. At first, she'd told herself it was a term of mild affection, but she could hear the condescension now. "There's a woman, a security guard who's making trouble for us. She needs to be removed."

"What kind of trouble?"

She'd be damned before telling him everything. "She found something she shouldn't have, okay?"

"Why was that allowed?"

What kind of question was that? "Shit happens."

Fuentes moved with a viper's speed and slapped Ashley. So strong was the blow that it sent her head cracking against the glass. She didn't see stars, she saw galaxies. Terrified that he would repeat the abuse, she first covered her face with her hands and then wrapped her arms over her head. "No! Stop!"

"You stupid bitch. What have you done?"

"It can be easily fixed." Tasting blood, Ashley wiped her mouth as she tried to talk. "She's an open target where she works. You have the people."

''Who are not wasted on amateurs. Get the fuck out of my car.''

''But—''

Fuentes reached over and shoved open the passenger door, then pushed, punched and kicked at Ashley until she fell out onto the asphalt. Sobbing, she rolled under the extended cab pickup parked beside them. It saved her life.

Fuentes burned rubber as he backed the BMW out of the slot. Then gears protested and tires squealed as he raced away.

Shaking with humiliation and fear, Ashley crept out from under the truck. ''Prick,'' she screamed after him. ''Who needs you!''

She did. And the realization that she'd blown a golden opportunity by misjudging him left her scared and desperate. How was she going to explain? Jules and Debra didn't worry her, but John was a different story.

Nothing was going right and all because of that bitch. Campbell Cody.

44

Maple Trails
3:33 a.m.

"Fuentes has left the area."

"What does that mean?" Campbell asked Blade, gripping her phone tighter. "Moved to another location?"

"No, something must have happened to spook him. We heard about fifteen minutes ago that he's heading back to Houston."

Standing in the gatehouse, Campbell bent at the waist in misery for Blade. This bust had been so important to him. To the city. "Can anything be done?"

"Not by us. Not here. I think our girls really panicked after you showed them the bracelet. It looks like they screwed up."

Campbell had been proud to share her discovery with him as well as Archer. They were supposed to meet in the morning, along with Snow, to review and plan.

"I never liked the idea of you being a trafficker, anyway," she said.

"It would have been a short career."

Things could go wrong on an initial run just as easily as after the tenth or hundredth. "Are you saying I was wrong to have showed them I had the bracelet?"

"Not for that side of things. And you couldn't know they would run to Fuentes. In that respect, I'm glad he's hit the road. God knows what he had in mind for them."

"Wait a minute, I'm losing your signal." Campbell stepped outside of the gatehouse. "What do you—"

Gunfire exploded around her. Campbell hit the ground and keyed her radio. "Ike—shots fired. Secure! Secure!" Then she yelled into the phone, "Blade get us help, fast!"

Disconnecting, she reached for her gun, all the while crawling toward cover. More shots zipped past her head. One struck the edge of the gatehouse spraying stone and concrete over her. Gasping at the needlelike pricks, she turned her head away and scrambled faster.

By the time she got inside, it was over. Or was the shooter changing clips? The sound of a car speeding away gave her the answer.

Her thoughts raced. The shots sounded like they'd come from a handgun—a .9 mm. That was the good news. If it had been a rifle with a scope, she'd have been done for. As reality set in, her hands started shaking and she holstered her gun.

That's how Ike found her. When he burst into the gatehouse, the older man's face filled with increasing dread. He crouched beside her. "Oh, damn. You're bleeding."

45

Security be damned, Blade thought as he raced to Maple Trails. He pushed the El Camino so hard, he expected to hear a piston blow.

Only a deputy sheriff on patrol nearby beat him up the serpentine entryway. As he launched himself out of the vehicle, he heard sirens approaching, but he didn't waste time looking back to see who or how many. The deputy spotted him and reached for his gun.

Blade already had his ID in his hand and flashed his badge. "LPD," he said, passing the man with long strides.

Campbell was leaning against the outside wall of the gatehouse and another Cody guard was dabbing at her face. When she saw him, she grasped the man by the wrist to stop him, then stepped around him and into Blade's arms.

Not caring who watched, Blade crushed her against him. "When I heard those shots, I swear my heart stopped."

"Mine did, too."

"Not from what I heard. That sounded like damned

fast reaction on the radio, lady.'' He leaned back his head to inspect her face. ''You were grazed.''

''Stone fragments when a bullet hit the building as I crawled inside.''

''You've got to stop testing the nine-lives theory.'' Despite their growing audience, he kissed her hard because he was angry and because he'd just had the scare of a lifetime. ''Did you see anything?''

She shook her head, then nodded down the hill. ''I was talking to you when the shooting started from down there. I wish I could say I saw something I could identify, but I hit the ground.''

Thank God. Blade had a good idea who was behind this, anyway.

Campbell looked over his shoulder. ''You need to get out of here before you're seen by too many people.''

''I'm not leaving you. But if it's okay, I'll pull the El Camino inside to get it out of sight.''

''You can't leave your own work.''

''What caliber did those shots sound like to you?'' he asked, ignoring her protest. ''All I could tell over the phone was that it wasn't anything with a lever action.''

''No, .9 mm, I think. A full clip's worth.''

''Well, we've got the help to look for cartridge shells.'' Blade reached for his phone. ''While I move the car, you fill in this trooper who's pulling up. I'm calling in a request that they look for a certain VW.''

''Blade…'' Campbell lowered her voice. ''What if the gun is registered to a state trooper?''

She was thinking that Ashley had stolen her father's gun. It was what he suspected, too. And he knew she was thinking of history repeating itself as ranks closed and cops protected the reputation of cops. "If that's the case, nobody's going to blame him for the shooting," he replied softly. "But he is guilty of failing his kid—and for leaving a deadly weapon accessible. Now let's take back control."

He needed to remind himself as well as her that advantage was psychological as well as physical.

Inevitably, the press appeared and Blade had to stay out of sight inside the gatehouse. By then deputies had recovered several shells and made photographs of the rubber burns on the street.

An LPD officer reported having stopped Julianne Willis's VW a block from her house, but she was in the car alone. The officer said she acted as guilty as hell and scared witless; however, lacking probable cause, he'd been forced to let her go.

The night dragged on. Blade remained, even after the press and the other law enforcement personnel left. Just before 6:00 a.m. Campbell's relief arrived. While the consensus was that she alone faced danger, she took the time to update the fresh team on what had gone down overnight. Ignoring the guards' curious looks, Blade left quietly.

Campbell arrived at his house fifteen minutes after he did. He'd convinced her that it no longer concerned him whether she came in the Cody truck, the Cadillac or an ice cream truck with all the bells and whistles, as long as she came.

The instant he spotted her, Trunk abandoned his rubble—the small bones he toyed with during the day as if they were mementos of treasured times—and launched himself at her. She gave him another gift, a freshly made monster burger from some drive-through, which the dog barely let her unwrap before slurping it out of her hands. She was still laughing when she entered the house.

Blade knew in that moment he was in love. The rain had frizzed the loose tendrils of her hair and had washed off her makeup. She also had a nasty scratch frighteningly close to her left eye. But she was still so damned beautiful and precious to him that his chest ached.

"I should make you shower before you get near me," he said as he reached for her. His voice sounded as raw as his throat felt.

"Yeah? Want to watch?"

"No, I want to join you." Which he did, because he didn't want her out of his sight for a moment and because he needed the physical contact.

Sex at dawn had already become an addiction. Making love, he discovered, was going to be his salvation. Blade recognized the impetus—fear of losing her, the gaping loneliness that only she filled. He strove to show her all that she had become to him as steaming water turned their bodies slick and desire made them slicker. He kissed every wound and caressed every womanly curve, and prayed she would never tire of touching him.

When he finally slid into her, she crested again and he gave her the last essence of himself.

Minutes later as they lay in bed spoon fashion, and about to drift off to sleep, he heard her whisper, "Thank you."

"For what?" he murmured.

"For showing me the difference."

She knew. That's how attuned they were. Blade kissed her shoulder. "*Bella Belle*. Hold that thought."

46

"**S**he's not dead."

"Crap." Jules's news had Ashley pacing around in her bedroom. Would nothing go right for her again? "Are you sure?"

"It was on the TV. Aren't you watching?" Jules squeaked.

Disgusted with her short memory, Ashley snapped, "I'm grounded, remember? No TV privileges. Did they say they have a suspect?"

"No. But they know. A cop stopped me after I dropped you off. It scared the shit out of me, Ash. I want out."

"There isn't anything to get out *of*. We're innocent."

"You know what I mean. I can't keep up with you. I'm just not as angry or ambitious."

"I like you, too."

"I'm sorry. I'm gonna try to keep a low profile

until graduation and then I'll convince my mother to let me visit her baby-factory sister in Utah until I turn eighteen. Then I'm going to Vegas and get a job.''

''Doing what? Stripping?''

''Hey, genius, at least they don't stick you in jail for that.''

At the sound of the abrupt disconnect, Ashley swore. ''The hell with you, then,'' she muttered, tossing her phone onto the bed.

She hadn't gone to school today because along with the split lip and sore hip and knee that she'd received from Fuentes, she was sporting a black eye courtesy of her mother. Previously, it had been her father who'd doled out discipline; at least that son of a bitch knew where to hit so that the marks wouldn't show. But when she'd come home the second time, her mother had roused from her latest drunk to find her in her parents' bedroom closet. Ashley had refilled the gun and put it back in its not-so-secret hiding place; however, her mother thought she was stealing money and went into a rage.

She was tired of being everybody's punching bag, tired of the abuse in general. Earlier, she'd been tempted to go back into the closet, get the gun and blow her mother's booze-soaked head off. But her father's shift was over and he would be home soon after fucking his bimbo girlfriend who nobody was supposed to know about. If she killed them, the cops would definitely know to come looking for her. Staying was out of the question, though. If she did, either or both of her parents would drive her over the edge.

Her decision made, Ashley waited until she heard her mother in the shower. Grabbing her suitcase, she quickly threw in a bunch of things. Next she returned to her parents' closet and stole their emergency cash from the pocket of a winter coat—something else they thought she didn't know about. Finally, she plucked up her mother's car keys, grabbed a few more items in the garage and drove off in the blue Ford Taurus.

For once Jules had it right, but before Ashley skipped town, she had one thing to finish. To do it, though, she needed to find somewhere to hide until nightfall.

47

"**G**et your hands off of her, Lefevre," Blade ground out as he stopped in the doorway to the meeting room, "or so help me, they'll need a mop to pick up what's left of you."

He should have known better than to let Campbell continue on while he'd paused, responding to another call. He could see that Lefevre's grip was only a few inches away from the stitches in Campbell's right arm, and that she was trying her best not to show how much it hurt. That made Blade ready to draw blood.

"What the hell is she doing here?" Lefevre demanded, ignoring the directive.

"Ms. Cody has been of invaluable help in the Livingstone case," Chuck Archer said, easing by Blade. "Actually, in both cases."

At the visiting detective's pointed look, Lefevre released Campbell, but he snorted, "For my part, that sniper should have aimed better last night."

"Thank you." Smiling coldly, Blade sent the loudmouth to the floor with a single punch. "You aren't fit to sit at the same table with her. Get out of my sight."

"Hey, I was called in to this meeting." Lefevre sat up and rubbed his jaw. "Fuentes would be my arrest."

"I'll ask Snow to brief you if there's anything you need to know about that end of things," Blade replied.

"I'll be happy to." A prematurely gray-haired man joined them. "Goodbye, Lefevre…and be assured the lieutenant is going to hear about this."

"Screw y'all." Lefevre stormed out of the room.

Mild in temperament as well as appearance, Detective Gordon Snow placed his files on the conference table and leaned over to offer his hand to Campbell. "Gordon Snow. It's a pleasure to finally meet you."

Campbell shook hands. "Thank you, sir. For the support as well."

His intelligent gray gaze rested on her cheek. "I'm sorry about last night. I hope we have enough to make an arrest today."

The four of them took seats at the end of the table. Without preamble they started brainstorming.

"I think we should go straight to Donald Mize," Blade said. "Ask him if we can have our ballistics expert check his gun. If it's been fired and we can match casings, then we've got our girl—at least for attempted murder."

Archer didn't seem totally convinced. "You think he would give up his own daughter?"

"If he's any kind of cop," Snow replied. "Besides, we now have the bracelet Ms. Cody located for us and a written statement that includes a strong description of Ms. Mize by the pawnshop owner. I say we have enough to impel the father and to lean on her pretty heavily—at least for your case, Chuck." He shook his head, his expression morose as he tapped his pen against his file. "I've got basically zilch on the Holms case, except for the three other girls' DNA in the car, and they all admitted to having been in there within an hour before she died."

Archer turned to Snow. "Could this Fuentes character have something to do with the girl's death?"

Snow signaled in the negative. "We can't totally reject the idea, but from what I've learned from Lefevre, it's not his style. Blade, too, will tell you the location was wrong for him, and that he sure wouldn't have left her still breathing."

"Fuentes prefers an efficient bullet to the head," Blade added.

"I also doubt he uses a .380, am I right?" Having gotten their attention, Campbell continued. "I think we're overlooking something. We're assuming the only weapon in the Mize home aside from Officer Mize's service weapon is a .9 mm backup or something he leaves in the house for his family's security. What if it's neither and he's a collector? He could easily have a .380. My father had several types of guns when he was with the state police. And think about this, a .380 is far more comfortable for a woman to use than a .9 mm."

"Then why do we believe she used the .9 mm last night?" Snow asked.

"To try to throw us off."

The men exchanged glances.

"What idiot let the LPD lose this woman?" Snow asked.

"Whatever you're thinking, forget about it," Archer replied. "She's spoken for."

"She certainly is," Blade replied, pride gleaming in his eyes. He reached under the table and laid a proprietary hand on Campbell's thigh. Then he felt her start and he followed her gaze to the door where a young African-American cop stood.

"Taneeka…is something wrong?" Campbell asked.

"Excuse me for interrupting, but a call has just come in that I know you'd want to know about," the petite cop said. "Officer Donald Mize with the state police has reported that his daughter has stolen his wife's car and almost a thousand dollars and has disappeared."

48

Exiting the police station, Campbell paused with Blade between their vehicles. This is where they split up, she to return to headquarters and her other responsibilities, and he to head over to the Mize residence with Detective Snow. They were taking advantage of Snow's being delayed.

"Are you going to be careful?"

Campbell could tell he had shoved his hands into his vest pockets to keep from reaching for her. "After last night? I'm staying in lock-and-load mode. But you know Ashley would be a fool to hang around. Her friends aren't as strong as she is and she must know they'll spill what they know fast. If I was in as much trouble as she is, I'd get as far away from here as possible. She may be tough to track. As you explained inside, Fuentes taught her to stay off the major freeways."

Blade nodded. "After we finish with Mize, I'm going to check out the park she drove me to. If she was biding her time until dark, she might go there."

"Then you be careful, too."

"Definitely. I'm looking at my incentive." Glanc-

ing toward the front of the building, he muttered,
"Ah, hell," and slid his hand behind her neck and
under her braid. "I wanted to say the actual words at
a better time. Something with candles and wine."

"Just the way you're looking at me is making my
knees pretty weak."

"I hope you can see it. I'm in love with you. Don't
you dare get hurt again. I want a chance at this—at
us."

"Yes, sir. Permission to speak, sir?"

His eyes warmed. "Permission denied. Just kiss
me, dammit."

She did, putting everything she could into it. She
could never tell him how grateful she was to him for
helping her regain her professional integrity—at least
with people who mattered—and much more...for
making her want to feel like a woman again.

At the sound of a discreet cough, Blade broke the
kiss and without a word crossed the parking lot to
join Snow, who was unlocking an unmarked car. She
waited until the vehicle backed out and she and Blade
were face-to-face again. Their gazes locked. Then
Snow shifted and the car pulled away.

Campbell got into the Blazer and eyed the El Camino as she keyed her vehicle's engine. She wondered
if Blade realized which of his trucks he'd chosen this
morning? He'd compromised his ability to work undercover greatly today. But that was a worry for another day.

She drove to Cody headquarters. Last night she'd
called her father to assure him that she was safe and

that the Trails was secure. It was time to do the follow-up reports and to confer on what new precautions they might need for that location.

"It's such a relief to see you," Beth said as she entered the building. She was back at the front desk answering calls and monitoring the radio, since they hadn't chosen a new employee from the applicants yet. "Are you okay? Can I get you anything?"

"Thanks, I'm fine. I'm sorry I haven't been around to help you with the hiring. How are the interviews going?"

"Listen to you. No apologies necessary. I do want your input on one girl, but I can hang on until you have time."

Campbell touched her shoulder, grateful for the understanding. "It won't be long. We're in the final phase of this."

"You damned well better be." Yancy stood in the doorway to his office. "I've a good mind to call Austin and get some state people over here to move things along."

As she crossed to him, he took one look at her face and cupped her cheek. His hand was unsteady.

"You guys have to stop this," Campbell said with an embarrassed laugh. "All in a day's work, okay?"

"I've put an order in for a Kevlar vest, and when it comes, you'll damned well wear it." Drawing her into his room, he shut the door. "Well? Dare I hope some arrests will be made today?"

"As a matter of fact, yes, thanks to one of those state people. Officer Donald Mize himself. He's turned in his daughter for grand larceny. She stole the family car and a considerable handful of cash.''

"She sounds like a piece of work," Yancy drawled.

"The doctors will fill reams of notebooks and recorder tapes trying to figure out what's going on inside her head." If she didn't get herself killed, Campbell thought grimly.

"Let's just hope the lawyers don't screw things up and she walks.''

Campbell sat down and redirected the conversation to their company's immediate concerns. ''There's slight damage to the gatehouse building. One window was shattered, but it should be repaired by now.''

"I hope you ordered bulletpr—''

"Stop. We're using what we always use." Campbell continued ticking items off her fingers. "Several of the stones have bullet holes in them. I expect that as soon as Bryce sees that, he'll demand we pay for a full replacement of the structure.''

"I may chip in for some kind of evergreen bush or ivy. That'll cover the holes fast enough, otherwise I'm tempted to put up steel plate. Considering the thin ice he's put himself on with that Saunders woman, he should be grateful—''

Campbell chuckled. "Don't you dare let it out that you know about that. It's our ammunition for if he gets out of line in the future. By the way, you haven't heard from him, have you?''

"Not a peep." Yancy didn't so much as try to hide his smugness.

It was time to get down to the serious issues. "For the time being, I'd like us to add an additional guard at night. I couldn't have been more pleased with Ike's backup last night, but he could easily have been dealing with something himself. We also need to do more perimeter patrols for a while to reassure the residents. What do you say we call in Munch Robbins? He can alternate with me in the gatehouse and on patrol. His leg has to be well enough for that. Any problems, he can call one of us for backup."

"Good," Yancy replied. "He's phoned here twice to offer, but I didn't want to seem like a cold-blooded bastard and jump at the chance to put him to work."

"All right then." Campbell rose. "I'm going to get something to eat and then return calls and help where I can before my shift starts."

"Everything okay on the personal front?"

"Just dandy."

"How's the man of few words?" Yancy continued probing, clearly wanting more information out of her.

Campbell decided to be generous. "He loosened a few of Lefevre's teeth this morning."

Yancy brightened. "Tell him to stop by sometime. He doesn't have to talk, he just has to listen."

"I'll talk for myself, thank you very much." She headed for the door. "In fact, I think I'm doing quite nicely."

"What does that mean? Campbell? Campbell, you come back here!"

49

South Longview
12:13 p.m.

"Officer Mize, we're Detectives Snow and Blade with the LPD. May we come in?"

Easily six-four in his socks, Donald Mize had traded his uniform for jeans and a T-shirt, but his proud stance and fit body still gave him an air of authority. He curtly nodded and stepped back to allow them entry.

Like the rest of the houses in the modest neighborhood, the Mize residence was a brick ranch about thirty years old with oaks and red maples keeping the houses shaded in summer and the rain gutters cluttered with leaves and acorns the rest of the year. The air in the house smelled of old coffee and unwashed laundry. Constructed from pressed wood and upholstered in crushed velvet, several pieces of furniture had chips or rips, and there was a subtle hint of neglect, giving the impression that the inhabitants had walked away several years ago and had just returned. Blade didn't see any photographs anywhere, and the only plants were of faded silk. He was in no position to judge, but this wasn't exactly his idea of a happy home.

"Did you find my wife's car?" Mize asked, his hands on his hips as he stood in the middle of the den.

Blade and Snow exchanged glances. The guy wasn't interested in his daughter, only his property—and probably the cash.

"No, sir. Not yet," Snow replied. "We need to ask you a few questions."

Mize's strong jaw flexed as he gritted his teeth. "Have a seat. I'd offer you coffee, but the wife burned up the coffeemaker this morning. You can write that one up to the kid, too. She keeps us so stressed it's a relief to go to work."

Since Mize took the blue recliner situated in the center of the room facing the TV, Snow sat on the rose-plush couch. Blade chose to stand. Mize picked up the remote and turned the repeat of last night's basketball game on Mute.

"Is Mrs. Mize here?" Snow said. "It might help if we speak with you together."

"She's at work. She does hair. A place across from the mall, I forget the name."

"That's all right. Maybe it's for the best, anyway." As considerate as a preacher and careful as a mine-sweeper, Snow took no chance of offending and used every opportunity to reassure. "Sir, we know you've had some trouble with your daughter...."

"You don't have to sugarcoat it. I've had more

calls from you people than most fathers with sons have in a lifetime.''

''This might be the ultimate one. We're here to ask if you own any weapons besides your police issue.''

Mize looked from Snow to Blade and back again. ''Shit. What's she done now? Held up a convenience store? My wife told me she'd been in the closet, but once I noticed the money gone, I never thought—''

''We're interested particularly in a .9 mm and a .380.''

Mize closed his eyes. Then, with nostrils flaring as he sucked in a deep breath, he said, ''I got 'em. Both are Berettas.''

''When was the last time you used them?'' Snow asked calmly, his expression impassive.

Mize shrugged. ''A month ago, maybe a little more. I go to the firing range to keep sharp. But I do a full clean after every exercise.''

Blade figured it was the only thing he did tend to in this house.

The trooper rose. ''Well, come on. I guess we'd better go see if they're still there.''

''Would it be all right to check Ashley's room? You know you have the right to wait for us to get you the paperwork.''

''I don't need a search warrant. She's the one who's on the run. Just tell me this—has she killed somebody?''

''Do you think she's capable of it?'' Snow asked.

The man grunted and started down the hall. ''She's her mother's daughter.''

Blade let Snow follow Donald Mize and he brought up the rear, taking his time to check around some more. After the bathroom on the left, Ashley's room was on the right. He nudged the half-closed door open with his shoe—and stared in disbelief. The walls were sprayed with every color available in a can, curses, names, something that was either a graph of a financial catastrophe or a phallic symbol…a knife with blood on it. Had she been trying to ensure her parents would stay out by trying to shock them, or were her drawings a hint of what was going on in her mind?

Blade eyed the mess and deduced she'd left in a hurry. There were clothes on the bed, drawers open. The closet—he glanced around the open door—was a mess, with more clothes tangled on the floor than on hangers. About to go find Snow and Mize, his gaze locked on the wastebasket. It was half full of tissues. She'd either had one helluva head cold or had been crying—and bleeding. Blade leaned over to check the stain on some of the crumpled tissues. No, it wasn't makeup. What had happened here last night?

He couldn't afford to take anything without a search warrant. The defense would rush to have the evidence suppressed and the D.A. would add insult to injury by chewing his ass raw. He went to find Snow.

The detective was bagging the second gun. "Do you have any idea where she would go?" he asked Mize. "Relatives? Friends?"

Standing with his arms crossed over his chest and his legs slightly parted, the father looked ready to disenfranchise himself from the whole experience.

"It's just us, family-wise. I don't know anything about friends, other than the trash who join her at juvenile court whenever she gets herself into trouble."

Snow kept his gaze on the guns. "No boyfriends?"

Mize snorted. "If there is, I pity the guy. She is on birth control, though. It was her mother's idea to at least save us from dealing with the abortion issue. And for the record, I'll say that's the only thing she got right in the last eighteen years."

Snow nodded and started for the door. "Well, thank you very much for your cooperation, Mr. Mize. We'll be on our way, but if we hear anything—"

"You just tell her she sits in that cell this time," Ashley's father snapped. "She's not welcome back under this roof again, and I'm not spending one more dollar on her, either. You tell her."

Nodding again, Snow said, "Please let your wife know not to touch anything in her room. We'll be back with the warrant to do a complete search."

It was good to get outside even though the sky was overcast. Blade had to admit the drying and decomposing leaves smelled pretty good after being in that house.

"Did you catch a glimpse of that kid's inner sanctum?" Blade asked. "I left the door wide open for you."

"Oh, yes. That was a new one for me. You know, it never ceases to surprise me," Snow observed, "that just when I think I've been at this work long enough to where I can't feel any sympathy for a felon, I walk into something like this.''

"Understanding maybe, but not sympathy," Blade replied. "She's not learning disabled, she had educational opportunities. So she had a lousy draw in parents. That's not close to unique. Instead of seeking help, she's chosen to strike back at real and imagined hurts and that makes her responsible for her actions.''

"Easy, Jackson," Snow murmured. "It's showing that this is deeply personal for you.''

"Damned right." And Blade didn't care who knew it.

50

Maple Trails
6:12 p.m.

The first thing Ashley did when she quickly unlocked Maida Livingstone's front door and slipped
inside was to shut off the alarm. So there, Debutante,
she thought, excessively pleased with herself, with the
whole day since she'd left the house. As the final
person to leave the premises last week, Ashley had
asked for the code to secure this place and the trusting
twit had given it to her. That didn't say much for the
old lady's placement of trust, either. What's more, the
kid had never noticed that Ashley had removed the
house keys from the car's key chain.

Quickly peering out the front window, she checked
to make sure no one had noticed her arrival. Satisfied,
she hurried to the bathroom.

She'd been waiting for hours to pee, having refused
to go in the woods. She wasn't interested in being
any Girl Scout and had denied herself food and water
to be able to last in her hiding place behind this estate
while waiting for dark. Unlike last time, she'd parked

the car in a more protected spot than Stacie had found. Cold had added to her discomfort and she'd worked fast but awkwardly to take down the fence the way Stacie had showed her. Stace had been the one with the handyman father. A redneck from the stories she'd heard, but all Ashley cared about was that he'd passed on something useful.

When she returned to the kitchen she went straight to the refrigerator. She was starving and hoped the old biddy had something edible left in the thing. The first whiff was bad, though, and she grimaced. What *was* that stench—fish, cabbage…?

"Yech."

Spotting a potato, she grabbed it, and a package of cheddar cheese. She shoved the potato into the microwave and set the timer, before ripping the cheese open and taking a bite. It actually tasted pretty good, although she knew that had to do with her empty stomach more than the food. She returned to hunt for something else. "Let's see…three eggs…an apple…an onion…cripes, lady, you lived like a monk."

Slamming the door shut, she decided to check the pantry, but the darkness thwarted her. Not wanting to risk the bright light from the refrigerator being seen through the front window, she reached into her pocket and brought out her pen flashlight.

Wine! It was the first thing the tiny beam settled on. Ashley knew little about the stuff except that Chablis was out and chardonnay had been delegated to the boring column, and that it was chic to drink spritzers or sauvignon blanc. This bottle was something called a Riesling.

Shrugging, and too impatient to deal with hunting for a corkscrew, she smacked the neck on the edge of the sink and the top flew off. "Oops," she murmured at the noise. The crack sounded unusually loud in the house, and she paused to listen to make sure the subtle groan she heard was the heater shutting off. She had no fear of the dead—it was the living and breathing that concerned her.

The microwave was still humming, so after pouring herself a glass of wine, she hurried to the front to check outside again, and then she peered out at the back alley. Everything continued to seem to be fine. As she drank more wine, she browsed through the pantry some more. She found a box of chocolates, sugar-free junk, but it was good enough for the moment.

She'd poured a second glass of Riesling when the microwave pinged. Adding butter, she slivered some of the cheese. The wine was giving her a nice little buzz and she hummed as she mashed everything together with a fork. Then she sat on the floor and devoured her food.

When she was done, Ashley felt somewhat revived. Leaving the dirty dishes on the linoleum floor, she headed for the bedroom. "Okay, Debutante, let's see if your greedy folks have cleaned out the place, or if there's something worth hocking," she murmured. She went through the closet, checking pockets and boxes as she often did at home. If Maida had been like her parents, she had some of the silliest, most obvious hiding spots.

To her delight, she found more than three thousand dollars in the bottom of the laundry hamper, and some gold and silver coins in a cigar box behind the soap in the laundry room.

Maybe the wine was helping, but she was laughing with glee. "Ha! Yes-yes-yes! Now I'm set."

51

Campbell was updating Munch on the latest news in the neighborhood when the phone rang. Being closer, she picked up. "Gate—this is Campbell."

"This is Lila Kembrick. I live a few houses down from Maida... I mean where Maida...oh, dear."

"Good evening, Ms. Kembrick, I know who you are," Campbell said gently to the flustered woman. "What can I do for you?"

"Well, maybe it's nothing, but I was walking back from dining up the street with friends. The Smarts. Anyway, I could have sworn I saw a light on in Maida's house."

Campbell frowned. Had they left on a light by accident when she'd helped Patsy get Maida's burial outfit? No one else had mentioned seeing anything unusual. "What kind of light, Ms. Kembrick?" The road lights could play tricks on the eyes.

"Like a flashlight."

A cold hand gripped Campbell's insides. "Thank

you, Ms. Kembrick. We're going to check on that right away. Are you home and safe?''

"Yes, yes. Thank you. I'm fine. I worried you thought I was silly—''

"You did the right thing. Stay put. We'll handle it.''

Campbell hung up and met Munch's questioning gaze. "It may be a false alarm, but there's something suspicious going on at Maida's. I'm going to check it out.''

52

It would be a relief to be rid of the carpet—and the house. Ashley poured the gasoline she'd taken from her parents' garage on the bloodstain. Then she drenched the bed and the curtains. Backing into the hall, she emptied the rest of the one-gallon container in a trail down the carpet. Hindsight had her wishing she'd done this right away. It had been a mistake to think she would have a chance to get back here and finish cleaning the stain. But that's what the golf club had been for—insurance. At least it had seemed a good idea at the time.

Tossing the can into the living room, she went to the back door and removed the stick. Sliding open the door, she sucked in the fresh night air. Maybe they were on to her, but they would get no more evidence from this house. She would have the satisfaction of knowing that.

She went to the stove and turned it on. Then she ripped off a handful of paper towels and held an edge to the electric coils until it lit.

Carrying the burning mass to the hallway, she dropped it on the carpet. In the next instant the room exploded into a ball of orange fury, the force knocking her back into the kitchen. As she slammed against the cabinets, the breath literally knocked out of her, she closed her eyes against the shock and pain.

53

As soon as she saw the strange amber glow, Campbell knew what she was dealing with. She parked on the street and, while running across the grass, she yelled into her radio.

"Fire at the Livingstone residence, call 911! Ike, get over here, but watch your back!"

She knew better than to break open the front door. The flames already glowed in every window. The place would explode with the least bit of oxygen. Was the perpetrator still inside?

She ran around to the back and saw that she'd been wrong—there was air getting at the inferno. The back door was open. Then she heard a bang. Running farther into the yard, she saw the fence in the alley. The same section of fence that had been torn free the night of the storm.

"Ike—where are you?" she called, running across the yard and up the alley. "We have an intruder in the alley, at the fence. Same section. Munch, tell the fire crew we are not in the house. Repeat, we are in pursuit."

When she got to the opening of the fence, she

paused and, with gun ready, checked for an ambush. Instead she heard breaking brush and running in the woods.

She ran into the pitch-black darkness, stumbling and hitting the ground with her knees. But so did the person she was chasing. She heard a feminine voice gasp and curse.

"Ashley!" Campbell called. "It's over, Ashley. Stop!"

She heard a brief rustling sound, then the running resumed.

Campbell scrambled to her feet and ran, too.

She saw the car in the faint moonlight just as the headlights were turned on. Campbell stood in front of the car and aimed her gun. "Turn it off."

The car lurched forward and angled out of the woods and toward the street.

Campbell shot at the front tire. She heard the bullet strike metal and saw a spark, but the car continued its sluggish roll, then came to an abrupt stop.

Running harder, she reached the passenger side and grabbed the door handle with her left hand. The car hung momentarily in the ditch between the woods and pavement. It allowed her to get the door open, but just as she tried to reach inside and grab for the keys, the car broke free of the mud.

It lurched forward and up onto the pavement, throwing Campbell off balance. She lost her gun and had to fight to keep from getting thrown under the rear wheel.

Ashley zigzagged, and at the same time punched

at Campbell's hand, her head, anywhere she could reach.

Sudden bright lights blinded both of them. A second later, Ashley's scream and the huge truck's blasting horn pierced Campbell's eardrums.

Certain they were dead, Campbell yelled, "Turn!" giving a last lunge to reach the steering wheel and yank it to the right. But Ashley beat her to it.

Thrown off balance, Campbell was wrenched from the car. She tumbled out onto the road, her head hitting the pavement with brutal force. Blinded with pain and unable to catch her breath, she waited for death.

54

Oakmont Cemetery

It was difficult to come here, but Blade was fulfilling a promise. He walked across the neatly kept grounds until he came to the mausoleum. There he set the potted pink tulips beneath the carved name of Maida Livingstone. Then he crossed the field and set a single red rose on the grave of Stacie Holms.

He didn't fully understand the second gesture. It had been explained to him, but he still didn't get the rationale—correction, he couldn't agree.

Ready to leave, to get away from the memories of this place, he returned to the El Camino and climbed back behind the steering wheel.

"Satisfied?" he asked his passenger.

Campbell laid her hand on his thigh. "Thank you. I know that was a lot to ask."

"Not too much. Not for you. It's just been—"

"Difficult."

Difficult didn't begin to describe it.

He'd almost lost her. Again. When he'd heard about the 911 call, he'd raced toward Maple Trails as he had before, but had spotted the flashing lights on the farm-to-market road running alongside the estate. Remembering Campbell saying that it was the road the girls had used to access the property, he'd gone to investigate.

There he'd seen the eighteen-wheeler rolled sideways in a ditch, the blue Ford Taurus upside down…and between them Campbell lying so still on the street as EMTs worked to save her. Needless to say, he ignored Ashley screaming to him from the patrol car as it rolled by. *"John…John!"*

Campbell had stayed in a coma for almost two days. If she'd died, Blade knew he would have gone to the county jail and strangled Ashley Mize with his own hands.

And today, Campbell had asked him to put a flower on the grave of one of the females who'd caused her and others so much pain and misery.

"She wasn't like Ashley," she said as though reading his mind. "A bit wild and in need of stronger direction, but she knew what had happened was wrong. What they were doing would take things from bad to worse."

He knew all this. He'd been the one to tell her. He and her father, her friend Taneeka, Archer and Snow—all who had come to the hospital daily to check on her and urge her to fight.

Debra had begun talking almost immediately after learning Ashley had been arrested and Maida's house had been burned. She was afraid of being blamed for that, too. Julianne had picked up where she'd left off.

It was all part of Debra's initiation. Ashley had decided Debra needed to pass a test before being welcomed into the group. They would play a prank on one of her relations. Ashley picked Maida because of the prestige of the Trails and the fact that there was rarely any crime there.

After breaking in to the property, they knocked on Maida's door and Debra introduced her friends. What a coincidence that Ashley's uncle lived on the next block, they told her. Maida bought the story and invited the girls inside, offered them juice and coffee. They declined, but Ashley begged the use of the bathroom. She went down the hall, but not to the bathroom—to Maida's bedroom. The goal was to take something without being caught. Maida was no fool, though. She thought Debra was nervous and noticed the other girls kept exchanging glances. And Ashley was gone too long. She went to investigate and caught Ashley rifling through her jewelry box.

Debra reported that Maida was furious and went for the phone. Debra begged her not to, and Ashley panicked and grabbed the urn, striking Maida. She hit her too hard—or maybe exactly as hard as she'd intended. Debra lost it after that, and Stacie got Debra out of there and back to the car.

"Okay," Blade said, if only to keep Campbell from continuing to obsess. "So maybe Stacie did a good deed for Debra." He just wished she'd gone a step further and called 911. If she had, she would be alive now.

"That's how Liz Junior had been broken," Campbell murmured.

Blade glanced at her as he drove. "You're not going over it all again, are you? No wonder the doctor said you still have a headache."

She gave him a tolerant look. "I'm trying to make sense of it. Debra was closest to Stacie, I think. She would never have become part of the group if it hadn't been for Stacie. Tell me again what Julianne said."

"She and Ashley tried to clean things up. The storm was coming. It gave them an idea—if they could convince people that Maida had left the estate and had an accident, then there would be no search of the house. Ashley fully intended to return there to work on the stain. But she never got the chance. Stacie refused to take her."

"So that was Ashley I saw speed by me that night. She put on a wig and Maida's sweater...and Maida was in the trunk." Although the car was warm from the heater, Campbell shivered.

Blade reached over and covered her clasped hands with his.

"I'm okay," she murmured. "Don't you think it was a little divine intervention for that trucker to break down where he did and spot the car? And then for Maida's sweater to be found?"

"On you," Blade muttered. "There's nothing divine about that."

"I don't regret it. And I'm proud of Stacie for lighting into Ashley as they drove back to the city.

But telling her that she wasn't as smart as she thought and that she wouldn't go to prison for her sealed her fate.''

''Yup, when Ashley told Stacie to drop off Debra and Julianne first, Stacie's intuition should have kicked in.''

''Everyone's. I can't believe those two didn't realize right away that Ashley shot Stacie.''

''I can't understand why Ashley didn't shoot Maida,'' Blade countered. ''She obviously had the .380 on her at the time as a precaution.''

''Noise,'' Campbell replied. ''For all of her flawed thinking, she got a lot right.''

''Well, she lost all of that reasoning when they fought behind that restaurant.''

''I think Ashley must have been a little jealous of Stacie,'' Campbell said. ''How shocking it must have been for Debra when you found Stacie's birthstone necklace in Ashley's locker.''

Blade nodded. ''Especially when we explained to her the history behind Maida's bracelet and where you found it.''

Campbell grimaced. ''It's sick, really. Ashley could never wear either item. Not here. She had to be way deeper into some kind of risk-taking game than the others. Have they gotten her to explain the story behind the golf club yet?''

''No.''

''The more I think about it, the more I've decided it was an accident. Either one of them used it as a lever and forgot to wipe it off, or they accidentally brushed against it with something that had blood on it.'' Campbell sighed. ''It sure sent us down the wrong path for a moment. So many lives ruined.''

''Don't bet on it,'' Blade replied. ''I was waiting to break it to you after you rested more, but the Saunderses' attorney is hopeful of getting Debra probation.''

''Yes, but she'll always have her grandmother's death on her conscience. She's not getting away with anything, just as her mother isn't with that fling with Bryce.''

''Did Yancy tell you—no one has seen Bryce since this all went down, and he's moved out of his apartment.''

Campbell's mouth formed a small O. ''No, he didn't, that rascal.''

''No doubt he was going to let you return to the Trails and find out for yourself.''

''I suppose Bryce was afraid Patsy's tainted family name might rub off on him.''

''Or else he saw all of that inheritance money going for lawyer fees,'' Blade drawled. ''Speaking of that, Julianne's public defender said that considering her age, she would luck out if she'd agree to testify against Ashley. She might serve a few months, maybe a year or two, but she would be free far sooner than she deserves to be.''

''And Ashley? Is the D.A. still planning to go for two murder charges?''

''No, voluntary manslaughter on Maida, but the

murder charge sticks on Stacie's case. There's no doubt it was premeditated."

"I dread the thought of that trial."

"The bitch tried to add you to her list of victims. I'll take the witness stand, and gladly."

They'd arrived at the house, to Blade's relief. He didn't want Campbell dwelling on that part of the future. Fortunately, Trunk took care of that. The beast jumped down from his post and came running to the passenger side of the car and began clawing at the window.

Campbell laughed. "I can't get the door open."

"Come here." He scooped her into his arms and carried her to the front door, much to the dog's dismay. But he had to set her down to unlock the dead bolt, and Trunk got his hugs in after all. "He's going to knock you over," Blade muttered.

"I'm fine. The wall is holding me up."

As soon as the door was open, the dog ran inside.

"What the—hey, pal," Blade said. "No way."

"Oh, give him a minute. He's just happy to see me."

"So am I and I don't feel like sharing."

But the dog refused to leave. In fact, he settled at the foot of the bed, dropped his great head onto his massive paws and stared at Blade as though challenging him to do something about it.

Campbell eased down on the bed. Blade quickly helped her lift her legs up on the mattress and removed her sneakers for her. She looked as white as the pillows he stacked behind her.

"Look at him down there," she mused. "He does dress up the place a bit."

Blade didn't take his gaze off her as he sat down beside her and took her hand within both of his. "You don't like my house?" he asked, faking dismay.

"It sucks." But a twinkle lit her eyes. "The only reason I keep coming back here is for the unrestricted use of your body."

He kissed her poor, scraped, raw knuckles for that. *"Bella Belle."*

Campbell touched his new, shorter haircut. "I've been meaning to ask you, who's Italian in your family?"

"Nobody. I used to live over an Italian restaurant. Ate there practically every day. Compliments sound better in Italian, especially giving them to you." He kissed her hand again. "So what if I found us something less drafty?"

She searched his eyes...and slowly smiled. "With paint on the walls? And more than one stool in the kitchen?"

"Piece of cake with my new salary."

"Your lieutenant is giving you a raise?"

"He offered—and a promotion to Homicide, but I turned him down. I've been offered something better."

"You can miss a lot when you sleep too much," she replied. "What's better?"

"Your job."

She choked. "Excuse me?"

"Yancy and I have been talking a lot. He knows

you came on board at Cody Security for his sake. And he knows how badly Archer wants you over at the Sheriff's Department.''

Campbell frowned. ''Would you be happy with that?''

Blade spread her hair over the pillow. ''After what I've been doing the last few years? Heck, yeah. Provided I can talk your father into a slight name change. How's Cody-Blade sound to you?''

''Very reliable…and permanent.''

Blade lowered his mouth to hers. ''It will be.''

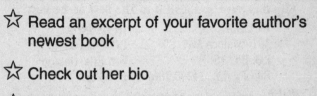

Helen R. Myers

66878   FINAL STAND   __ $6.50 U.S. __ $7.99 CAN.

(limited quantities available)

TOTAL AMOUNT	$_____
POSTAGE & HANDLING	$_____
($1.00 for one book; 50¢ for each additional)	
APPLICABLE TAXES*	$_____
<u>TOTAL PAYABLE</u>	$_____
(check or money order—please do not send cash)	

To order, complete this form and send it, along with a check or money order for the total above, payable to MIRA Books, to: **In the U.S.:** 3010 Walden Avenue, P.O. Box 9077, Buffalo, NY 14269-9077; **In Canada:** P.O. Box 636, Fort Erie, Ontario L2A 5X3.

Name:_____

Address:_____ City:_____

State/Prov.:_____ Zip/Postal Code:_____

Account Number (if applicable):_____

075 CSAS

   *New York residents remit applicable sales taxes.
    Canadian residents remit applicable GST and provincial taxes.

MIRA®

Visit us at www.mirabooks.com   MHRM0404BL